E $_{\text{DE}}$ Q

Jacinto was born abroad to a self-exiled Portuguese Prince of gigantic girth and lavish fortune. He still belonged to the mountains. In *fin-de-siècle* Paris, Zé Fernandes, a fellow scholar at the Sorbonne and a fellow mountaineer, finds the now-grown Jacinto at the center of the social and intellectual life of the city. Jacinto is surrounded by early-devised theatrophones, recently-invented ticker tapes, primitive writing machines, primitive postage meters, manuscript page numerators, far-out critical reviews, books on every subject, ether orange-preservers and all the labor-saving works, as well as servants.

Jacinto had one great obsession: "Man is only greatly happy when he is highly civilized." His theory resolved itself into a formula

Other Eça de Queiroz works
published by the Ohio University Press:

THE MANDARIN
translated from the Portuguese
by Richard Franko Goldman

The City & the Mountains

Eça de Queiroz

Translated from the Portuguese

by Roy Campbell

Ohio University Press

Athens, Ohio

LIBRARY

AUG 2 3 1967

UNIVERSITY OF THE PACIFIC

171635

Copyright © 1967 by Ohio University Press
Library of Congress Catalog Card Number: 67–17895
Manufactured in the United States of America
by the H. Wolff Book Manufacturing Company, New York

Although trained to follow the family profession of law, José Maria de Eça de Queiroz (1843–1900) entered the consular service instead, and underwent tours of duty in the Near East, Cuba, the United States, and England. At the same time, he found opportunities to write the non-fiction and fiction which has earned him recognition as the greatest Portuguese novelist and rank among the nineteenth century's outstanding literary figures. His novel, *The Sin of Father Amaro*, introduced into Portuguese fiction the techniques of naturalism, of which he has been his country's leading exponent.

Frederico de Onis, former head of the Hispanic Institute of Columbia University, has commented that Eça "represents the final flowering of the European novel, and at the same time . . . is uniquely Portuguese, with all the suavity, irony and humor typical of his country." Among his most famous novels are *Cousin Bazilio*, *The Relic*, and *The City and the Mountains*. Soon to be translated into English are two other masterpieces of Eça's irony, *A Illustre Casa de Ramires* and *Cartas de Inglaterra*.

THE CITY & THE MOUNTAINS

1

MY friend Jacinto was born in a palace with an income of a hundred and nine thousand escudos from his estate and the produce of corn, wine, cork and olives.

In the Alentejo province, across that of Estremadura, and in both provinces of Beira, the upper and the lower, dense hedges undulating over hill and dale, river-banks, and road-ways bounded the properties of this ancient land-owning family which was already producing grain and planting vines in the time of King Dom Dinis. His manor-farm and the lordly demesne of Tormes, in the district of the lower Douro river, covered a whole range of mountains. Between Tua and Tinhela, for fully five leagues the whole country paid him rents. His serried pine-forests blackened the land from Orga to the coast of Ancora. But the palace in which Jacinto was really born, and in which he still lived, was in Paris in the Avenue des Champs-Elysées, at Number 202.

His grandfather, the very portly and enormously rich Jacinto, who was nicknamed the " Galleon " in Lisbon, was one day going down the Trabuqueta crossing beside a garden wall shaded over with vines; he slipped on a piece of orange peel, and tumbled down on the paving-stones. From the little doorway in the garden wall, at that very moment, emerged a dark, clean-shaven man in a thick green baize coat, with jack-boots like a picador, who playfully and with easy strength lifted the enormous Jacinto to his feet and even picked up his gold-handled walking-stick which had rolled away into the dirt. After gazing at him for a space with his thickly-lashed black eyes, he said:

" And what are you up to, Jacinto Galleon, skating around here on the stones? " Jacinto was dumbfounded and dazzled to recognize no less a person than the Prince of the Realm, Dom Miguel.

From that afternoon, he loved the good Prince as he had never loved anyone or anything before, in spite of his gluttonous appetite, his belly, and his devout worship of God. In the noble hall of his manor (at Pampulha) he hung the portrait of his " Saviour " enshrined with palm-leaves, as if it were an altar, with the walking-stick beneath it which had been rescued for him by those magnanimous royal hands from the dirt of the gutter. While the adorable, longed-for Prince pined away in his exile at Vienna, the big-bellied landowner rushed about jolting in his yellow gig from the coffee-house of Zé-Maria at Belem to the tavern of the Placido in the Algibebes, uttering groans of longing for the absentee " angel ", and contriving all sorts of plans for his recall. On that day, the most blessed day of all days, when the steamer *Pearl* sailed over the bar with his returning " Messiah ", he festooned the manor of Pampulha with flowers and raised a monument of cardboard and canvas, in which Dom Miguel, represented as his namesake Saint Michael, all in white, complete with aureole and archangel's wings, was seen to pierce with his lance, from the saddle of a rearing horse, the Dragon of Liberalism, which, in its contorted agonies, was vomiting the Constitutional Charter. During the war against " the Other One ", the Free-Mason, he kept sending messengers to Santo Tirso, and to Santo Gens, to bring the King hams, boxes of preserves, bottles of his good wine of Tarrafal, and bags of silk bursting with gold pieces, which he polished in order to brighten the metal. And when he knew that Prince Dom Miguel with two old chests tied on a mule had taken the road to Sines and to his final exile, he, Jacinto the " Galleon ", rushed round his house, shut all the windows as if in mourning, and bellowed furiously, " I shall remain here no longer. I shall remain here no longer! "

He did not wish to remain in the perverse country from which that good King of Portugal, who picked up fallen Jacinto in the street, had been forced to depart. He embarked for France with his wife Dona Angelina (*née* Fafes) of the well-known family and much-spoken-of family of Fafes from Avellan. With his son, Cintinho, a yellow-skinned, soft child covered with warts and phlegmons: and with a nursemaid

6

and a negro boy servant. In the Bay of Biscay the sea was so rough that Dona Angelina, prostrate on her knees, promised the Lord of Calvary, if He saved them, a crown of thorns made of gold with rubies of Pegu for blood-drops. In Bayonne, where they arrived, Cintinho had jaundice. On the Orléans road, on a rough night, the axle of their carriage broke, and the stout gentleman, the exquisite frail lady of the House of Avila, and the little boy, were forced to march, for three hours, in the rain and the mud of a strange land to a village where, after beating at the sullen doors like beggars, they had to sleep on the benches of a tavern. In the Hotel des Saints Pères at Paris, they suffered the terror of a fire which broke out in the stables, beneath Dom Galleon's room; and that worthy nobleman, bounding down the stairs in his shirt to the courtyard, he hurt his foot on a splinter of glass. Then, raising his hairy fist literally to Heaven, he roared out, "Zounds! This is too much!"

Later that week, without seeking farther afield, he bought from a Polish Prince who, since the fall of Warsaw, had become a Carthusian monk, a palatial dwelling at Number 202 in the Avenue des Champs-Elysées. Beneath the heavy gilt of its plaster and the rustling silk curtains, he buried himself to rest from so many troubles, in a life of idleness and good food, with several fellow-exiles (including the Privy Councillor, Nuno Velho, Count Rabacena, and others of less note) until one day he died of indigestion from a pickled lamprey which had been sent by his administrator in Montemor. But the good lady feared the journey home, with its rough seas and broken axles. Besides, she did not wish to separate from her confessor nor her doctor, both of whom understood her fads and her asthma so well.

"As for me," she declared, "I shall remain here even though I miss the good water of Alcolena . . . It will be Cintinho who decides when he grows up."

Cintinho grew. He was a young man, as thin and livid as a wax taper, with long smooth hair, long-nosed, taciturn, and always dressed up in black clothes which were too long and loose for him. At night, sleeplessly, because of his suffocations and his cough, he wandered in his nightshirt with a

7

little lamp through the rooms and halls of Number 202 so that the servants nicknamed him the "Shadow". From this dumbness of indecision, he emerged from wearing mourning for his father, with a lively taste for ornamental carpentry and wood-turning. Then, later, in the mellifluous prime of his twentieth year, another feeling sprang from his bosom, a feeling of desire and wonderment for the daughter of the Privy Councillor, a girl as plump as a pigeon, educated in a convent in Paris, and so skilful that she could enamel, gild and mend clocks and also she could model hats of felt. In October 1851, when the chestnut trees were bursting into leaf in the Champs-Elysées, Cintinho suddenly started to spit blood. The doctor, stroking his chin, advised him, with a deep wrinkle in his brow, either to go to the Golfe de Juan or to the warm sands of Arcachon.

Nevertheless Cintinho in his shadowy obstinacy, did not want to tear himself from the substance of Teresinha Velho, around whom he revolved like a mute, lingering, late shadow across the space of Paris. He married her like a shadow. Like a shadow he made a few more pieces of carpentry; coughed up the rest of his blood : and then faded away, like the shadow he was.

Three months and three days after his funeral, my friend Jacinto was born.

From the cradle which his grandmother had smeared with fennel and amber to drive away evil luck, Jacinto grew with the assurance, the strength and the rich sap of a pine tree on the dunes.

He never caught measles, nor had worms. Latin, the tables, and the alphabet went into him as the sun goes into a glass window. Among his friends, in school-quads, flourishing his wooden sword and giving his bellow of command, he was always the victor, the King, who was flattered and the one to whom was yielded the fruit of the other boys' lunches.

At the age when one reads Balzac and de Musset, he went through none of the tortures of sensibility—none of those warm twilights ever found him at the window suffering with a desire both formless and nameless. All his friends (there were three of us including his old negro page, Cricket)

8

retained for him pure and fixed friendships without ever being tempted by the thought of sharing his wealth, or discouraged by the signs of his egoism. Without enough heart to fall strongly in love, and quite content with this incapacity which freed him from responsibilities, he only experienced the sweetness of love without its bitterness—that honey which is only yielded to those who gather it after the manner of bees, airily, with mobility, and humming as they go. Strong, rich, indifferent to the laws of man, we never saw him with any other ambition than thoroughly to understand general ideas: his intelligence, during the brightest years of the arguments of the philosophical schools, wound itself through the densest philosophies with the ease of a lustrous eel through the clear waters of an aquarium. His personal courage, which was genuine, and of the very finest temper, was never ignored or undervalued by anyone: and any opinion ventured on his part, even when it was thrown out facetiously, always met with an appreciation and sympathy which seemed to raise him and to keep him flattered and shining in the heights. Things always served him with meekness and affection—and I cannot ever remember a button so much as falling off a shirt of his; or a note ever being maliciously hidden from his eyes; or that even a drawer should get jammed and refuse to open to his good-natured vivacity and haste. When, one day, in order to laugh disbelievingly at Fortune and her wheel, he bought a lottery ticket from a Spanish Sacristan, immediately that very same Fortune, lightly smiling upon him from her glittering wheel, churned him out four thousand pesetas. Even the cloudy skies, all cumbered and heavy, when they noticed Jacinto without his umbrella, seemed to withhold their pent-up floods till they saw he had passed by . . . Truly the amber and fennel of his grandmother, Dona Angelina, had triumphantly and forever swivelled aside from him the menaces of evil luck. That lovable grandmother (whom I knew as a fat old woman with a beard) used to recite a birthday sonnet written by the Privy Councillor Nuno Velho which contained a line of good advice.

"Know lady, that this life is like a river."

A river in summer, mild, translucent, harmoniously spreading over smooth white sand, between fragrant groves and happy villages, could not offer to the traveller, borne on its bosom in a boat of cedar, tented above and cushioned within, and full of fruit, ice and champagne, with an angel at the helm, and others pulling the tow-rope—more security, comfort and pleasure than life offered to my friend Jacinto. For that reason we called him the " Prince of Good Fortune ".

Jacinto and I (José Fernandes*) met and made friends in Paris in the schools of the Latin Quarter, to which my good uncle Alfonso Fernandes Lorena de Noronha e Sande had sent me, after those wretches had expelled me from the University for having on the afternoon of a processional ceremony, bashed the sordid face of Dr. Pais Pita.

About this time Jacinto became obsessed with one idea. This " Prince " conceived the idea that " Man is only greatly happy when he is highly civilized ". And by a civilized man my friend meant one who, strengthening the force of his thought with all the notions ever conceived since Aristotle and multiplying the corporal potency of his own organs by every kind of mechanism invented since Tericmenes created the wheel, would become a magnificent Adam, almost omnipotent, almost omniscient, and able to assemble in his own person, within the limits of Progress (as far as it had gone in 1875) all the pleasures and all the advantages which result from Knowledge and Power. At least it was on these lines that Jacinto copiously formulated his Great Idea while we occupied ourselves with the purpose and the destiny of the human race, sipping cloudy beer under the awnings of the philosophical beer-houses of the Boulevard Saint Michel.

This concept of Jacinto's really impressed our comrades of the cenacle, which, having originated in the intellectual life of the period between 1866 and 1875, that is between the battles of Sadowa and Sedan, and constantly hearing during that period from technicians and philosophers that it was the breech-loader with the striking-pin that won Sadowa,

* From now on the narrator will often be addressed as Zé Fernandes, so it is as well to explain that Zé is the colloquial diminutive of José which is accented on the last syllable.

while it was the school teacher that won Sedan, were quite ready to believe that the happiness and success of individuals, or even of nations, could be obtained through the development of mechanics and erudition.

One of these inventive comrades of ours, Jorge Carlande, even reduced the Theory of Jacinto to an algebraic formula in order to circulate it more freely and simply: this is the formula.

$$\left.\begin{array}{c}\text{Absolute Knowledge}\\ \times\\ \text{Absolute Power}\end{array}\right\} = \text{Absolute Happiness}$$

For days afterwards, from the Odéon to the Sorbonne, you could hear the students and young intellectuals praising " The Metaphysical Equation of Jacinto."

However, for Jacinto himself, his concept was not only a matter of metaphysics thrown off to exercise his powers of logical speculation; it constituted a law for him, embracing reality and practice, a law which determined his whole conduct, and governed his life. Just at that time in accordance with his precepts—he began to make use of the *Little Encyclopaedia of Universal Knowledge* in seventy-five volumes, and installed an observatory with a glass dome and a large telescope among the tiles of the roof of Number 202. It was with this telescope that he first palpably illustrated his Idea to me on a soft, warm night in August. The distant skies flickered languidly with summer lightning. Along the Avenue des Champs-Elysées cabs and carriages were already rolling out to the cool shades of the Bois de Boulogne, open, slow, weary, and full of white dresses and frocks.

" Now here, Zé Fernandes, you have my ruling theory well proved to you," said Jacinto leaning at the window of his turret. " With these eyes, which we receive from Mother Nature, at their brightest and healthiest, we can hardly distinguish over there, across the Avenue in that shop, any more than a lighted window. No more than that! But if I take a pair of binoculars, and put them to my eyes, I can even see through the glass—hams, flitches, cheeses, jellies and boxes of dried prunes. Well, I conclude straight away that it is a

Grocer's Shop. I get a *notion* of a grocer's shop. I have the advantage over you with your naked eyes which see only a shining shop-window. Now, if instead of these simple binoculars, I were to make use of my telescope which is of a vastly superior scientific construction, I could see much farther still, even on the very planet of Mars the seas, the snows, the canals, the contours of the bays, and to put it shortly most of the geography of a star which is revolving at many millions of miles from the Champs-Elysées at this very moment. And here is another tremendous Idea. You have here the primitive little eye, that of Nature, raised by the Power of Civilization to its greatest present potency of vision. So therefore, just through the artificial eye, I am as a civilized person, far happier than the uncivilized man just because I discover facts about the universe which he doesn't even suspect and of which he is utterly deprived. If you apply this principle to all the other organs of the body, then you'll see what I'm driving at. As for the intelligence, it draws happiness from the untiring accumulation of notions and ideas—why, I only ask you as a proof to compare Renan with my negro servant Cricket. It must be clear to you that the greater our advance towards civilization and progress the greater will be our enjoyment of the advantages of being alive. Now! Do you agree with me, Zé Fernandes?"

Well, to me it didn't appear undeniable that Renan was any happier than the Negro, nor could I make out what sort of advantage, spiritual or temporal, attached itself to distinguishing across vast distances of space, certain stains on a star through a telescope, or even to discover hams in a shop through a shining window just across the Avenue. Nonetheless, I heartily agreed because I am a good-natured fellow and I would never willingly dislodge from any soul the opinion in which it found refuge, discipline, and a motive for energy. I loosened a button in my waistcoat and with an ecstatic gesture towards the lighted window and the cafés, I exclaimed, "Let us go then, and drink to the Big Idea in the Maximum quantities of brandy and soda!"

For reasons that are natural enough, the Idea of Civilization was, in Jacinto's mind, inseparable from the image of the

City, of an enormous City with all its organs functioning powerfully. In this my super-civilized friend would have included huge stores served by three thousand cashiers, markets which disposed of the orchard-produce and growth of thirty provinces; banks tinkling with the gold of the whole Universe; vast factories eagerly belching smoke and fabricating with frenzy; libraries crammed to bursting with the accumulated documents of centuries; with thousands of streets criss-crossed above and below by millions of electric wires and cables, gas-pipes, drains, water-pipes and sewers. There would be a deafening roar of omnibuses, trams, coaches, velocipedes, bicycles and two-horse carriages *de luxe*. And on top of it all would be millions of the vague mass of humanity panting through the regulating police in search of their daily bread, under the delusion of enjoyment. Thus could the up-to-date man of the Nineteenth Century truly and fully savour the delights of living!

While Jacinto in his room at 202 with his verandah open on the lilac bushes, developed and expounded these ideas, he seemed visibly to grow in stature, and appeared as though illuminated from within. What an august creation was that of the City! "Solely through that superb creation, Zé Fernandes, solely through that, can Man affirm and realize his Soul!"

"Oh, Jacinto! Where then does Religion come in? For surely Religion proves the existence of the Soul, doesn't it?"

Then he would shrug his shoulders. "Religion? Religion is nothing more than a sumptuous display of a surviving instinct common to all brutes—the instinct of terror. A dog licking the hand of its owner, from whom it gets its bone or the lash of the whip, roughly represents the devout Christian, the conscientious Christian prostrated in front of the God who deals out Heaven or Hell! . . . But the telephone, now! Or take the gramophone!

"Just take the gramophone . . . Only the gramophone, just by itself, makes me feel my superiority as a being who thinks and separates me entirely from the mere beast. Believe me there is nothing worth while except the City, Zé Fernandes; nothing save the City!"

13

And afterwards (he would add) it was only the City which gave him the sensation, as necessary as that of warmth to Life, of the solidarity of the human race. And I have to admit that, when in Number 202, one looked out at the dense mass of Parisian housing, with its two million human beings bending to the labour of Civilization (to conserve the lordly dominion of the Jacintos over them) one felt the sort of relief and comfort that a solitary pilgrim must feel on the desert, when he suddenly espies from his dromedary the long file of a friendly caravan glittering with arms . . . And I would murmur, moved to my very heart, " Caramba! How splendid!"

On the other hand in the country, caught between the unconsciousness and the impassivity of Nature, Jacinto would tremble with terror at his fragility and his isolation. It seemed he was lost in an unfraternal world : no copse politely withdrew its thorns to let him pass : even if he was groaning with hunger, no tree, however laden, would offer him its fruit by stretching out a compassionate bough to him. What is more, when confronted by Nature, he suddenly experienced the complete incapacitation of all his faculties of superiority. Among plants and beasts, what on earth would be the good of being a Saint or a Genius? The cornfields couldn't understand the *Georgics* : and a whole miracle on the part of an anxious God, involving the inversion of all natural laws, was necessitated to cause the Wolf of Agobio not to devour Saint Francis, but to stretch out loving paws to him when the latter smiled on him and called him " My dear Brother Wolf ". All intellectuality became sterilized in the country : only bestiality prevailed. In the crass Kingdoms of Animals and Vegetables only two functions prevailed—the coarse functions of feeding and breeding. Isolated, without any occupation, amongst hosts of tubers and roots which never ceased from sucking and nourishing themselves, and suffocating in the breath of universal fecundation, his poor soul (he said) was frozen and reduced to the mere scrap of itself, a tiny trembling twinkle, more dead than alive, on a lump of mere gross matter : and in this matter only two instincts survived, that of devouring and that of begetting. At the end of a week in the country the whole of his noble nature, so generously composed and gifted, was reduced to a mere belly and, beneath that, a phallus! His soul? Sunken beneath the beasts! It was necessary to rush back to town, and whelm himself in the lustral waters of Civilization to wash off the vegetable bark and the animal hide, to be rehumanized once more, and resurrected spiritually as Jacinto himself.

These polished metaphors of my friend expressed very real sentiments—proofs of which I witnessed personally, and which vastly amused me on the only trip we ever made together into the country, to that most sociable and lovable forest of Montmorency. Oh what a delightful farce it was— Jacinto versus Nature! Immediately he was away from polished oak floors and macadamized roads, whatever footing he found beneath him filled him with terror. All grass, the more it was withered, the more it vividly seemed to represent a mortal humanity to him. From every clod, and from the shadow of every stone he appeared to dread the attack of some slimy and disgusting scorpion or viper. In the silence of the woods he seemed to feel the depopulation of the Universe. He could not tolerate the familiarity of branches which grazed his sleeve or his face. To have to climb over a stile or a fence seemed to him a degrading act which sent him back to the original apes. All the flowers which he had not already seen in gardens domesticated through centuries of ornamental servitude seemed to him to be poisonous. And he regarded with the air of a melancholy ropewalker the lively hurry of the brooks, the baldness of the boulders, and all the contortions of the branchy woods with their solemn and idiotic grumblings in the wind.

After an hour in that worthy forest of Montmorency he began to pant with fear and to feel already the slow waning of his soul, which would turn him into a mere brute among brutes. He only recovered when he had passed well into the pavements and gas lights of Paris and when our victoria had nearly collided with an omnibus full of citizens. He insisted that we should walk down the boulevards to dissipate with his stout sociability that *materialization* which made his head feel as vague and heavy as that of a bullock. Then he insisted that I accompany him to the Variety Theatre to rinse out of his brain, with the rousing choruses of *Femme à Papa*, the boring sound of the blackbirds singing in the high poplars which still haunted him. This delightful Jacinto was then twenty-three years old, a superbly-built young man in whom reappeared the strength of generations of ancient rural Jacintos. Only by his sharp nose with its delicate, pale nostrils restlessly mobile as if savouring perfumes, did he appear to belong to the Nineteenth Century at all. His hair was worn in the style of tougher periods, crisp and almost shaggy. His moustache, like that of an ancient Celt, hung in silky threads which he curled upwards. His clothes, his thick cravats of dark satin and his gloves of white doeskin were all ordered from London in boxes of cedar. He always wore in his buttonhole a flower which was of no natural growth but had been synthetically composed by his florist of the petals of different flowers, carnations, azaleas, orchids or tulips, all joined to the same stem amidst a light spray of fennel or wild asparagus.

In 1880, in February, on an ashen and chilly morning of rain, I received a letter from my good old uncle Afonso Fernandes, in which after lamentations about his age (sixty), his piles and the difficulty of managing his property which required a younger man with stronger legs, he ordered me back to our house at Guiães on the River Douro. Leaning against the broken marble of my fireplace whereon the night before my Nini had left a pair of stays wrapped up in the *Journal des Débats*, I severely censured my uncle for thus cutting short in the bud before it could even open, the Flower of my Juridical Knowledge. In a post-script to his letter he had added—" The weather here is fine you could almost call it rosy : and your dear aunt is very pleased with herself because today we have been married thirty-six years; she is fussing around the kitchen because we've got the Abbot and Quintais to supper, and she wants to make them a ' golden broth ' ".

Putting a log on the fire, I thought how good that " golden broth " of my Aunt Vicência would be. It was so many years since I had tasted it, or a roast sucking pig, or the oven-baked rice of our kitchen. With the weather so fine, the mimosa in our courtyard would be bending under great bunches of gold. A piece of blue sky, the sky of Guiães, than which no other is more lustrous or smooth, seemed to enter my room and light up, over the polished sadness of the carpet, lawns, river-banks, marigolds and flowers of clover, over which my eyes strayed, swimming with tears: while through the serge curtains came the fine fragrant wind of the sierras and the pinewoods. Whistling a soft *Fado*, I pulled my old trunk from under my bed and, amongst my socks and trousers, packed my *Treatise on Civil Law* so that I might study, stretched out beneath the poplars, the laws which govern men. Later that afternoon I announced to Jacinto that I was leaving for Guiães. My friend recoiled with a dull groan of horror and pity.

"To Guiães? . . . Oh, Zé Fernandes, how ghastly!"

All that week he kept solicitously reminding me of comforts which would enable me to conserve a little bit of human soul in the barren wilderness so far from the City. "Take an armchair! Take *The General Encyclopaedia*! Take some tins of asparagus! . . ."

For Jacinto, since I had decided to tear myself from the City, I was already doomed, an uprooted shrub that would never revive. The grief with which he accompanied me to the station would have been more suitable for my funeral. And when the door of the compartment closed on me, as if it were the grille of a tomb, I nearly sobbed—but with my own memories and homesickness.

I arrived at Guiães. Mimosas were still flowering in the courtyard: I found the "golden broth" of Aunt Vicência as delicious as ever; with wooden clogs on my feet I took part in the Maize harvest. And so, what with harvesting and ploughing, growing tanned in the sun on the threshing floors, hunting partridges in the frosty woods, slicing fresh melon stems in the dusty fields, messing on chestnuts round open fires, reading by lamplight, heaping huge bonfires on Saint John's Eve, decorating cribs for Christmas . . . seven years passed by so busily that I never once opened my *Treatise on*

17

Civil Law: and so evenly that I can only remember one incident—that was when the Abbot fell off his mare on Saint Nicholas' eve at the gates of Bras das Cortes. From Jacinto I only received rarely a few lines scrawled off amidst the tumult of Civilization. Then one very hot September, in the middle of the wine-harvest, my good uncle Afonso died, peacefully (God be praised for this mercy) as a bird falls silent after a well-sung day. My god-child Joaninha married in the autumn. The roof of the house was being repaired. So I returned to Paris.

2

IT was February again, at the end of an ashen freezing afternoon, when I arrived at the Champs-Elysées on my way to Number 202. Before me walked, slightly stooping, a man who from his glittering boots to the upcurved brim of his hat, fringed with curls of shaggy gold, radiated elegance and a familiarity with fine things. In his hands, clasped behind him in kid gloves, he held a cane with a crystal knob. And when he stopped, at some distance away, in front of 202, I recognized at once the sharp nose and the silken moustache of my friend.

"Oh, Jacinto!"

"O' Zé Fernandes!"

Our embrace was so hearty that my hat rolled in the mud. And both of us began to murmur in a dazed way as we entered the gate.

"It must be seven years . . ."

"It must be seven years . . ."

And yet nothing had changed during those seven years in the garden of Number 202! Still the two well-sanded walks encircled a lawn as smooth and well-swept as a carpet. In the midst of the lawn a Corinthian vase was awaiting April to blaze with tulips, and June to shine with marguerites. And on each side of the steps to the threshold which were roofed and walled with glass, stood two slim Goddesses of marble, dating from the days of Dom "Galleon", and holding dim globes wherein already hissed two jets of gas.

18

But within, in the peristyle, I was surprised to find an elevator installed by Jacinto though Number 202 only had two floors, joined by such a gently shelving stairway that it never even tested the asthma of Dona Angelina. Spacious, richly carpeted, it offered, for the seven-second journey, numerous comforts on the way including a divan, a huge bearskin, a guide-book to the streets of Paris, and shelves with boxes of cigars and books. In the antechamber, where we landed first, I met with the soft warm temperature of an afternoon in May at Guiães. A lackey, more attentive to his thermometer than a pilot to the needle of his compass, was regulating with practiced skill the gilded mouth of a heater. Perfuming-pans between palm-trees, as if on some holy terrace of Benares, steamed a vapour which aromatized and moistened that delicate and superfine atmosphere.

I murmured in the depths of my astonished soul: "This! This is Civilization."

Jacinto opened a door and we entered a hall full of majestic shade, in which I recognized the library by bumping into a monstrous pile of new books. My friend lightly brushed his finger against the wall: and a crown of electric lights, flashing from the roof, suddenly blazed on his monumental bookstands, all of them made of ebony. In these stands were thirty thousand books bound in white, scarlet, and black, with golden markings, as stiff in their pomp and authority as so many doctors in council.

I could not contain my admiration.

"Oh Jacinto! What treasures!"

He murmured with a pallid smile:

"One has to read, you know, one has to read . . ."

I then noticed that my friend had grown much thinner. His nose had got sharper between two well-defined wrinkles, like those on the face of a tired comedian. The curls of his shaggy hair had grown sparser: and he had lost something of his former serenity, like that of polished marble. No longer did he twirl his moustaches upwards: they now hung drooping and somewhat faded. I had noticed already that he stooped. He raised a tapestry and we entered his working-study, which upset me. On the thickness of the carpets our feet lost their sound, and (it seemed) their reality. The damask of the walls, the divans, the woodwork—everything was green, the dark green of laurel leaves. Green silks shrouded the electric lights, dispersed on lampstands so low down that they seemed fallen stars which were on the point of cooling and going out : only one flashed, unshrouded and brilliant, from the top of a square bookstand; and its light seemed that of a towering lonely and melancholy lighthouse over a plain. A screen of green lacquer, the fresh green of grass, stood by a fireplace of green marble, the green of a shadowy sea, in which were dying a few embers of aromatic wood. And amongst these various shades of green glittered, here and there, on various pedestals and stands, the most sumptuous array of mechanisms, apparatuses, model-engines, gadgets, syringes, tubes, platings, cogwheels, tweezers, lancets, along with every possible frigidity or rigidity of glass or metal that modern invention could supply.

But Jacinto sank into the cushions of his divan with an air of weariness which I had never noticed in him before.

"Here, Zé Fernandes, here ! It is necessary to renew the old attachment of our lives, so distantly separated for these last seven years ! . . . Seven years in Guiães ! What on earth did you do? "

"And you . . . what have you been doing, Jacinto? "

My friend shrugged his shoulders. He had lived, he said, fulfilling all the functions that pertain to material and spiritual life . . .

"And by God, you have accumulated Civilization, Jacinto ! Heavens above . . . Number 202 is tremendous !"

He glanced around him but with a look that no longer flashed the old vivacity.

"Yes, a few comforts . . . but how much is lacking ! Humanity is still very, very poorly equipped . . . Life is still full of obstacles."

Suddenly in a corner a telephone bell rang. And while my friend bending over the instrument impatiently exclaimed "Are you there? Are you there? " I examined with curiosity, on his vast working-table, the strange and minute legion of instruments of nickel, steel, copper, and iron, with edges, serrations, rings, pincers, hooks, screws, springs, and teeth—all so expressive of different mysterious uses. I took up one which I tried to manipulate, but I was immediately pricked in the finger as if by a malevolent sting. At that moment was heard in another corner an urgent and hurried tick-ticking. Jacinto broke in with his face still to the telephone, "Go quick to the telegraph. There, by the divan! There is a little ribbon of paper which should be running out of it."

And sure enough, from a glass bell on a column, which covered a busy and skilful little apparatus, running out over the carpet like a tapeworm, I found a long strip of paper covered with indecipherable hieroglyphs, which I seized with wonderment. The line of figures, traced in bright blue, announced to my friend Jacinto, that the Russian warship *Azoff* was entering Marseilles in a damaged condition.

When he left the telephone I enquired of him whether the damage to the *Azoff* was directly prejudicial to him.

"The *Azoff*? . . . Damage? . . . Prejudicial to me? . . . Why, no! . . . It's a news report."

After that, consulting a monumental clock, which, at the end of his library, marked simultaneously the hour of day or night in every capital city in the world, and the course of the planets as well, he said: "I must just write a note: excuse me: only six lines. Here you have the London morning papers, and the Paris evening papers. The *Illustrations* are there in that leather portfolio."

But I preferred to make an inventory of his study, which gave to my countryfied profanity all the sensations of an initiation. By the side of Jacinto's chair, hung thick acoustic tubes through which Jacinto apparently gave his orders to various parts of his household. From the legs of his table soft thick cords, zigzagging over the carpet, ran into the shady corners of his room, like frightened snakes. On a little shelf, reflected in its varnish as if in the water of a well, stood a writing machine or " Typewriter ", and in front of it was a calculating machine with ranks of little cavities from which peeped out expectantly, little rigid numbers made of iron. Then I stopped in front of the four-sided bookshelf on which the bright lamp had reminded me of a lonely lighthouse.

The whole of one side of it was full of Dictionaries: the next side was full of manuals: the next of atlases: and the next of guide-books, amongst which, unfolding a folio, I found a guide to the streets of Samarkand. What a shattering tower of Information! On many shelves I saw machines and apparatuses which I could not understand—one, especially, which comprised slices of some gelatinous material in which were fading, half sucked up, the lines of a letter, perhaps a love letter; another which raised over a paper-bound book, as if to chop it up, a deadly looking cutlass: another which funnelled out the mouth of a tube for the voices of the Invisible. Surrounding the entrance and tied to the cornices were wires which arose across the ceiling and disappeared into space. Everything seemed to merge with universal forces. Everything seemed to transmit Universal Forces. Nature bowed to the discipline of my friend and entered his household with docility.

Jacinto began to swear, "Damn these electric fountain pens! What a nuisance they are!"

In a rage he crumpled the note he had begun, while I escaped to take a breather in the Library. What a majestic product of the Reason and the Imagination! Here were more than thirty thousand volumes, every one of which was more or less necessary to human culture. As soon as I entered, I saw in gold on a green cover the name of Adam Smith. That was in the territory of the Economists. I advanced then in awe through the territory of Political Economy. Then I came in sight of the region of the Philosophers and their commentators, which covered a whole wall from the Pre-Socratic schools to the Neo-Pessimist schools. On these shelves were encastled more than two thousand systems—all of which were contradictory. You could tell their doctrines from the way they were bound and from the positions in which they were placed. Hobbes was heavy, bound in thick black leather on the lowest shelf. Plato on the top shelf shone white and pure. In the centre of the vast hall began the various Universal Histories. But there, an enormous pile of paper-bound books all smelling of new print and new documents, stood against the bookstand as if it were a new layer of alluvial soil covering an old river bank. Turning over this hill of new books I found myself amongst the Natural Sciences, wandering with increasing bewilderment and wonder from Orography to Paleontology, from Morphology to Cristalography. The bookstand bordered on a window which had once opened on the Champs-Elysées. I opened the velvet curtains and discovered another portentous array of books all on Religious History and Religious Exegesis, which climbed mountainously to the highest panes of the window, shutting out, even on the clearest mornings, the air and the light of God.

Beyond that glittered in coats of light morocco the delightful ranks of the poets. As a release from the overstrain of all that positive knowledge, Jacinto had concealed a corner with a divan and a lemon-wood table, more polished than fine enamel, covered with cigars, oriental cigarettes and eighteenth-century snuff-boxes. On a polished wooden chest still lay, forgotten, a plate of dried Japanese apricots. I yielded to the seduction of the cushions, chewed a peach, and opened a volume, when suddenly I heard a noise at my side like the buzzing of an insect with harmonious wings. I smiled at the idea that it might be a swarm of bees making their honey amidst that mass of flowering verses. Then I heard the murmur coming from a little mahogany coffer which had appeared so dumbly discreet. I removed from it a *Gazette de France* and unhooked a cord which emerged from an orifice in the coffer with an ivory funnel at its end. With curiosity I put the funnel to my ear so attuned to the simple sounds of the mountains and the country. And soon a voice, very soft, but very determined, as if profiting by my curiosity to invade and take possession of my soul, whispered captiously in my ear.

"And so by the arrangement of the diabolical hexahedra I have arrived at the verification of Hypermagical space."

I jumped up with a roar: "Oh Jacinto! Here is a man! Here is a man speaking from inside a box."

My comrade, accustomed to prodigies, did not turn a hair.

"It's only the lecturephone . . . which works on the same principle as the theatrephone—or the telephone, for that

matter. It is laid on to all the colleges, lectures and confer-
ences. Very convenient . . . What was he talking about, Zé
Fernandes? "

I was still near the coffer, pale with fright.

" What do I know," I replied, " . . . diabolic hexahedra . . .
magic spaces . . . all sorts of horrors."

Jacinto's superior smile went right to my heart. " Ah,
that's only Dorcas, Colonel Dorcas with his Lessons in Positive
Metaphysics about the Fourth Dimension. Nothing but con-
jectures and a terrible bore! Listen, tonight you dine here
with me and some friends, Zé Fernandes."

" No, Jacinto! I'm still dressed in my country clothes."

And I went back into his study to show him my jacket
of thick flannel and my cravat with scarlet dots in which I
used to go to Church in Guiães. But Jacinto declared that
such highland simplicity would entertain his guests, who were
both artists . . . Who? Why the author of *Triplicate Heart*,
a Feministic Psychologist of transcendent penetration, a very
experienced *savant* much consulted in the Sentimental
Sciences : and Vorcan, a mythological painter who had inter-
preted so ethereally the year before the symbolical rhapsody
of the siege of Troy in his vast composition, *Helen the
Devastator.*

I rubbed my chin.

" No, Jacinto, no," I said. " I've just come from Guiães
in the mountains. It will be necessary for me to enter all this
Civilization slowly and cautiously if I don't want to blow up
and burst. All in the same afternoon to have electricity,
lecturephone, hypermagic spaces, the feminist, the ethereal
and the symbolical devastator—that is too much. I'll return
tomorrow."

Jacinto slowly folded his letter in which he placed two
white violets pulled from the button hole which flowered on
his breast.

" Tomorrow, Zé Fernandes, you'll come here before breakfast with your trunks in a cab to stay here in your own room.
In hotels, one finds embarrassments and privations. Here you
have your telephone, theatrephone, books; everything you
need."

I accepted simply and at once. Then Jacinto, seizing a speaking tube, murmured " Cricket."

From the wall covered with damask that suddenly seemed to split in two, emerged the old servant (the one who had come with Dom " Galleon ") whom I was delighted to find more robust, black and glisteningly venerable than ever with his white tie and golden buttons. He was also delighted to meet " Master Fernandes." And when he knew that I was to occupy the room of Grandfather Jacinto, he smiled his master a flashing smile of pleasure at the idea of Jacinto being re-provided with a family.

" Cricket," said Jacinto, " this note is for Madame Oriol . . . Listen! Telephone to the house of the Trèves and see if the Spiritists are free on Sunday . . . Listen, I shall take a warm shower, 17° Centigrade, before supper. Friction, with geranium juice."

Then heavily falling on to his divan again he said, " And so it's true, Zé Fernandes, that here we are as before, seven years ago, in this same old Paris . . ."

But I did not stray from the table, so keen was I to complete my initiation.

" Oh Jacinto," I asked, " what are all these instruments for? Here is a rogue of a one that pricked my finger. They seem perverse creations—are they any use? "

Jacinto languidly made a comprehensive gesture including them all.

" They are providential, old fellow, absolutely providential, for the simplification of one's work. For instance, this one pulls out old nibs; this one rapidly numbers the pages of a manuscript; this other one scratches out corrections . . . " He enumerated others for printing dates, melting sealing wax, sticking on stamps, and binding documents . . .

" But in the end," he added, " it's all a bore. With springs and nibs one often hurts oneself . . . I've often spoilt letters with bloody fingerprints. It's a bore."

Then, as my friend once more inspected his monumental clock, I didn't wish to keep him waiting for his warm shower and his massage of geranium juice.

" Well Jacinto," I said. " Till tomorrow! Now I've seen

25

you! I'm happy! . . . Till tomorrow morning, with my boxes!"

"What the hell, Zé Fernandes? Wait a minute. Let's go in the dining room and see if you won't be tempted."

Across the library, we entered the dining room, which enchanted me with its cool, serene luxury. White lacquered wood, smoother and more lustrous than satin, covered the walls enclosing, here and there, rosettes of strawberry-coloured cloth. The sideboards were of the same snowy wood, discreetly carved with floral decorations. Strawberry-coloured cloth covered the cushions of the white wooden chairs which were wide and specially constructed for the lentitude of delicate appetites, intellectual appetites.

"Long live my Prince," I cried. "Oh yes, this is a very comprehensible and restful dining room."

"Well, then, stay to supper, man!"

But I began to feel embarrassed when I saw that there were six forks set for each place at table and all of the most cunning workmanship. And I was even more alarmed when Jacinto informed me that one sort was for oysters, one for fish, one for fruit, one for vegetables, one for fruit, one for cheese. At the same time with a thrift that Solomon would have praised there were only two wine glasses laid at each place, for only two wines—one a rosy Bordeaux in crystal pitchers, the other a champagne freezing in silver pails. Nonetheless the whole sideboard verged on a redundant luxury and almost frightening variety of waters—oxygenated, carbonated, sterilized, phosphated, and soda waters, with even more besides, all carrying therapeutic treatises printed on their labels.

"By Heaven, Jacinto!" I cried, "So you are still the same tremendous drinker of water—a sort of *aquatic* (if one may coin such a word on the analogy of *alcoholic*) as the Chilean poet said when he was labouring on a translation of Klopstock."

He gave a disconsolate glance at all this vitreous gallimauffry with its metal clips and stoppers. Then he said, "No . . . this water is because of the city water supply, which is too full of microbes . . . But to this day I can't find any

26

good water which suits me at all, or which satisfies me . . .
I even suffer from thirst."

I was curious as to what the Psychologist and the Symbolist
were going to eat—it was traced in red on little tablets of
marble. It began worthily with the classical oysters of
Marennes. After that was a soup of artichokes and carps'
eggs . . .

" It that good? "

Jacinto slowly shrugged his shoulders and said listlessly,
" Yes . . . but I've had no appetite for a long time . . . for years
in fact."

As to the next dish, I saw that it contained nothing but
chickens and truffles. Afterwards they were going to have a
fillet of venison soaked in sherry, with leichee jelly. And for
dessert there were only oranges frozen in ether.

" In ether, Jacinto? "

My friend hesitated, then described with his fingers the
delicate undulations of a perfume floating away in the air.

" It's a new idea . . . It appears that as the ether evaporates
it makes the inmost very soul of the fruit come to the surface."

I bowed my ignorant head and murmured inwardly,
" There's Civilization for you!"

Going down the Champs-Elysées wrapped in my coat, I
cogitated upon this symbolic dish and reflected upon the
crudeness and backwardness of my beloved Guiães, where the
" inmost very souls " of oranges still remained unknown and
unappreciated in their juicy quarters, throughout the great
orchards which perfume the long valleys from Roqueirinha
to Sandofim. But now, blessed be God, I would be able to
understand these refinements through the agency of that great
initiate, Jacinto.

And better still to aid my affection, I would contemplate
the rarity of a man who having conceived a great idea,
realizes it in action—and through it attains perfect happiness.

How well, in very truth, had Jacinto confirmed his title of
" The Prince of Good Fortune "!

27

3

AT 202, every morning at nine, after my chocolate, still in slippers, I would go into Jacinto's bedroom. There I would find my friend already bathed, shaved and massaged, robed in a dressing gown of Tibetan goat-fleece, sitting before his toilet table of pure crystal (because of the microbes) and covered with all sort of utensils in tortoiseshell, ivory, mother of pearl and steel, which a man of the Nineteenth Century required so as not to disrupt the sumptuous unison of Civilization, and yet retain one's own pattern within it. His brushes, above all, renewed every day my regalement and wonder—they were as broad as the wheels of a Sabine cart : thinner and more curved than the scimitar of an Arab : concave in the form of a village roof-tile : sharp-pointed in the shape of an ivy leaf : stiffer than the bristles of a wild boar : yet smooth as the down of a dove. Like a master who does not scorn even the lowest of his slaves, he used every one of these instruments. And thus, before his mirror enchased in silver foliage, this Prince would pass a whole fourteen minutes rubbing the bristles and hairs of other animals over his own.

In the meantime Cricket and another henchman, behind curtains of Quioto silk manipulated with expert vigour the instruments of the washing room which was merely an epitome of the monumental machines of the Bath Room which was the most marvellous thing in the whole of 202. In these marble vaults were two jets of water, each graded from zero to a hundred degrees : two showers, one of fine and the other of wider jets for the hair : a sterilized fountain for the teeth : a frothy jet for shaving : and still more discreet little buttons, which, if touched, would discharge spouts, squirts, singing cascades, a light summer dew, a cool floating mist, or hot steam, according to one's requirements. From this terrifying retreat, where slim tubes held, in discipline and servitude, so many kinds of boiling, spouting and violent waters or vapours, Jacinto would emerge to dry his hands on a towel of shaggy wool, then on a linen one, then on one made of braided cord to restore his circulation, and lastly on a soft

28

silk one to smooth and polish his skin. After this last rite, which would draw from him sometimes a regretful sigh, sometimes a yawn, Jacinto sprawling on a divan, would turn the leaves of an Agenda, wherein were listed either by Cricket or himself, the different activities of his day, sometimes so numerous as to cover two whole sheets.

All these activities were concerned with his sociability, "his very complex Civilization", and the many new interests which, during the seven years of my absence, my Prince had cultivated in communion with the functions of the City. (As a matter of fact he was president of The Sword and Target Club: a part owner of *The Boulevard* journal: director of the Telephone Company of Constantinople: and associate of the United Markets of Spiritualist Art: and a member of the Committee of Initiation of Esoteric Religions, to mention only a few of his interests and activities). None of these activities satisfied my friend—because in spite of the mildness and harmony of his habits, he often hurled the agenda which enslaved him on to the carpet, with the gesture of a free man.

On one such morning, a windy, snowy morning, I took up this tyrannical book which was bound in leather of a tender, faded rose colour—and I discovered that Jacinto, after breakfast, had to make a visit in the Rue de l'Université, another at the Parc Monceau, and another in the far-away groves of the Muette: then he had to be present at a Club vote: then he had to take Madame Oriol to an exhibition of fans: then to buy a present for the niece of the Trèves: then to be at the funeral of the old Comte de Marville: to preside (*in camera*) at a tribunal of honour on a question of embezzlement between gentlemen . . . And there were even more appointments scrawled in pencil by Jacinto—"The Coachmaker—Five o'clock tea at Ephraim's, that little girl from the Variety Hall—and remember to take that note to the Journal". I then looked at my Prince. Stretched out on the divan, his eyes miserably half-closed, he gave a huge, noiseless yawn.

But the duties of Jacinto at 202 began very early in the morning, as soon as he had had his bath. From eight o'clock the telephone began ringing for him with impatience, almost

29

with rage, as if for a lazy slave. And, hardly yet dried from his bath, in his Tibetan goat-skin dressing-gown or in his thick silk pyjamas the colour of old-gold, he was forever running out into the passage to whisper with visitors who were always in such a hurry that they kept their umbrellas in their hands, dripping on to the carpet. One of these, nearly always there, who must have belonged to the Telephone Company of Constantinople, was a frightful fellow—he seemed to be sucked out, speckled with blackheads, with rotting teeth, always carrying a greasy portfolio, and always darting through the high collar of a shiny hairless fur coat, as if from the opening of a wild beast's cavern, two tiny, cruel, thievish-looking eyes. Inexorably, without ceasing, a footman kept on bringing him cards on a tray . . . These were from contractors of Industry or Art: dealers in horses, always red-faced with white jackets: inventors, with huge rolls of paper: second-hand booksellers bringing in their pockets some " unique " edition of Ulrick Zell or of Lapidanus. Jacinto circulated around the rooms of 202 in a dazed sort of way, scribbling in his pocket book, ringing the telephone, undoing parcels, and shaking with nervousness whenever any ambushed person leapt out of the shade of the anteroom to present him a catalogue, or a memorandum, as if it were a blunderbuss.

At noon a silvery, melancholy gong resounded, calling him to lunch. With *Figaro* or *Novidades* spread on the table, I would sometimes wait half an hour for my Prince to come tearing in, looking at his watch, with a worn-out expression and his eternal complaint: " What a bore! And after such an abominable night too, without sleeping a wink! I took some sulfural. I called Cricket to massage me with terebinth —but it was no good ".

He looked at the table with the eye of a man who has already eaten his fill. And, since throughout his tumultuous morning he smoked innumerable cigarettes, he began by pouring out a huge glass of carbonated, sparkling or gassy water, mixed with a rare, expensive brandy, which he sweetened horribly with some kind of Muscatel from Syracuse. Then, without pleasure, he would pick here and there with his fork, hesitatingly, a slice of ham or a morsel

30

of lobster. Then he would call impatiently for coffee, *the*
coffee of Moka, sent every month by its maker in Djeddah,
boiled in the Turkish manner, very thick, which he stirred
with a stick of cinnamon.

"And you, Zé Fernandes, what are you going to do? "

"I? "

Leaning back, well regaled, with my thumbs in the arm-
holes of my waistcoat I would say, "I am going to loaf,
royally, just like a natural animal."

My solicitous friend, stirring his coffee with cinnamon, tried
to think of an amusement that would suit me amidst the huge
and complex Civilization of the City. But no sooner had he
suggested some exhibition, lecture, monument, or excursion,
than he would disconsolately shrug his shoulders. "It's not
worth it, after all. It's a bore." Then he would light another
Russian cigarette on which his name shone stamped in gold.
Twisting his moustaches in nervous haste, he listened for a
while at the door of the library to his sleek and majestic
secretary Laporte. Then, followed by a servant carrying a
huge pile of journals, to regale him in his brougham, the
"Prince of Good Fortune" would plunge into the City.

When Jacinto's social daily rounds allowed him a little
freedom, and the March sky graciously granted us a little
diluted and watery azure, we sauntered out to lunch, on foot,
through the streets of Paris. These slow and rambling excur-
sions had been a sheer delight to Jacinto in our old days as
Students—because, during such walks, one could take in and
savour the City more minutely, in all its details. But now,
in spite of my company, he only derived an impatience and
fatigue from them, which was the very reverse of his former
illumined ecstasy. With wonder (and even with grief, since
being good-natured, I am always grieved by any disillusionment of ideals) I discovered, on our very first afternoon
together, when we walked down the boulevards, that the
dense swarm of people on the asphalt and the torrent of
traffic on the macadam, afflicted my friend with the brutality
of their haste, egotism, and noise. Clinging to, and almost
taking refuge in my arm, Jacinto began to lament that our
Civilization had not yet covered the streets with soundless

31

india-rubber. Gutta-percha obviously represented to my friend the one discreet substance which deadened the brutality and violence of things! What a wonder! Jacinto wishing for an insulating film of rubber between himself and " the functions of the City ". He would not even let me stop and stare with wonder before some of those be-mirrored and gilded shops which in the old days he was wont to call " priceless museums of Nineteenth Century Civilization ".

" It's not worth it, Zé Fernandes! Everywhere one meets with a terrible dearth of invention. Always those same Louis XV *fleurons*, always the same plush . . . not worth it!"

I was still trying to get my eyes in focus with this transformed Jacinto. What struck me most was his horror of the multitude, due to certain effects produced on him by individuals in the crowd, which only he could feel, and which he called " furrows " or " wakes ".

" You can't feel these furrows, Zé Fernandes. You are fresh from the wilds. They constitute a great impediment to City life, these furrows, wakes, or tracks which people leave behind. It may be the very strong perfume given off by a woman as she passes, which instils itself in your olfactory sense, and spoils the air you breathe for the rest of the day. It might be a saying heard amidst a group of people, which reveals a whole world of knavery, pedantry, or stupidity, and which remains hauntingly stuck to one's soul, like a mud-splash, reminding one of the vast morasses of mud one still has to wade across. Or then, old fellow, you may see a physiognomy which is intolerable for its conceit, bad taste, impertinence, squalor, or cruelty; a repulsive vision which it is impossible to shake off or drive away from one's memory. . . . They are a horror, these furrows, Zé Fernandes. But, what the devil, they are only the petty miseries of an otherwise delightful Civilization."

All this was specious, perhaps puerile—but it revealed to me in this burning devotee of the City, a certain cooling off of devotion. It was this same afternoon, if I remember rightly, that in a soft fine light, we walked through the main centres of Paris, down long streets, through miles of house blocks, bristling with black tin chimneys, with the windows always shut, and the curtains always closed, smothering and hiding the life within. Nothing but bricks, iron, mortar and stucco: rigid lines and sharp angles: all bare, all rigid. And from the floors to the roofs, along each whole façade, hiding the verandahs and eating up the walls, signboards, signboards, and more signboards . . .

" Oh this Paris of yours, Jacinto! What an enormous, what a gross bazaar! . . ."

And rather to sound my Prince than to persuade him, I began to enlarge on the ugliness and sadness of these houses, these cruel shops, whose floors are mere shelves for heaping up humanity! A humanity pitilessly stereotyped, catalogued, and pigeon-holed! The more presentable, *de luxe* humanity arranged on the lower shelves, which are nicely varnished. The shabby and work-worn, shoved away on top, on bare, deal boards, among the dust and cobwebs . . .

Jacinto murmured, shudderingly, " It *is* ugly: very ugly." But he added at once, shaking a kid glove in the air: " But what marvellous organization, Zé Fernandes! What solidity! What productivity!"

Where Jacinto appeared most renegade to his philosophy, was in his lasting and almost religious love for the Bois de Boulogne. As a boy he had woven very complicated and considerable theories about the Bois. He asserted with the flashing eyes of a fanatic, that the City went into the Bois every afternoon to renew its health and strength, receiving through the presence of its Dukes, Courtiers, Financiers, Politicians, Generals, Academicians, Artists, Club Members, and Jews, the consoling certitude that the whole of its personnel was maintaining its level in numbers, vitality, performance and attainments, and that no single element of its greatness had disappeared or would ever disappear. *Aller au Bois*, therefore, constituted for Jacinto an act of conscience and duty. And he returned always to confirm with pride that the City still possessed all its million stars of light, guaranteeing the eternity of its radiance.

Now, however, it was without fervour, dragging himself, as it were, that he would take me out to the Bois, where I, profiting by the clemency of the April weather, tried to appease my longing for trees and woods. While, to the noble trot of his superb mares, we drove up the Avenue des Champs-Elysées and the Avenue du Bois, rejuvenated by the tender lawns and the young shoots, Jacinto, blowing the smoke of his cigarette through the carriage windows, remained the good comrade, with the lovable character, with whom it had been so pleasant to ramble philosophically round Paris. But when we passed the gilded gates of the Bois and came into the Avenue des Acacias, insinuating ourselves into the long files of carriages *de luxe*, in a decorous silence, hardly even broken by the jingle of bits or the rolling of the slow wheels over the sand, my Prince would fall silent, gently fading back into the depths of the cushions from which he only raised his face to give a yawn of boredom. By force of habit, his old habit of reassuring himself as to the continued presence of the full personnel of stars in Paris, he would occasionally look out, and then he would notice some coupé or victoria creaking slowly in the same direction. Then he would murmur a name. Thus I got to know the curly Hebrew beard of the banker Ephraim : the long patrician nose of Madame de Trèves mounting guard over a perennial smile : the flaccid cheeks of the neo-platonic poet, Dornan : the long pre-Raphaelite plaits of Madame Verghane : the smoked monocle of the editor of *The Boulevard* : the conquering moustachios of the Duc de Marizac, reigning over his phaeton of battle : and even other immovable smiles, Renaissance beards, swooning eyelids, flashing eyes, and skins powdered with rice—all of which belonged to illustrious and intimate friends of my Prince. But from the top of the Avenue des Acacias, we began to go down again, with curbed paces, as slowly as before. In the slow file of ascending carriages, coach after landau, victoria after fiacre, what should one behold, all over again, but the smoked monocle of the *Boulevard* man, the furiously black plaits of Madame Verghane, the belly of the neo-platonic, the Talmudic beard, and all those faces, with the immobility of wax, which were so super-well-known to my comrade, and which he had re-passed twice every afternoon during repeated years, with that same waxen immobility, with that same rice-powder, with those same plaits . . . Then

Jacinto would be able to contain himself no longer, but shouted to the coachman, "Back home! Quickly!"

Down the Avenue du Bois and along that of the Champs-Elysées would begin an ardent stampede of those mares, to whom the curbed paces, and the gnawing of their bits (among other horses and mares as super-well-known to them as were Jacinto's friends to him) had already exasperated into a mood comparable to their master's.

To test Jacinto, I began to denigrate the Bois. "It's not so amusing as it was. It has lost its charm." He replied shyly: "No. I still find it agreeable; in fact there is nothing more pleasant: but . . ." Then he would blame the coldness of the afternoon or the despotism of his various duties. We would then return to 202, where, very soon, in his white Tibetan wrap, seated at his crystal table, between a legion of brushes and nail-files, with all the electric lights blazing, my Prince would begin to adorn himself for his social duties for the evening.

And it was precisely on such an evening (a Saturday) that we experienced, in that super-civilized and sheltered room, one of those rebellious and brutal terrors that only the ferocity of the Elements can produce. (We were to dine with the Duc de Marizac at the Club and then go with him afterwards to *Lohengrin* at the opera). Already late and in a great hurry, Jacinto was tying the bow of his white tie—when, in his wash-room, whether because some pipe had burst, or the solder of some tap had melted, a jet of boiling water exploded furiously, whistling like a steam engine, and spraying hot vapour. A thick steam smothered the lights; lost in this mist we heard, between the cries of the footman and Cricket, the sound of this devastating spout spattering on the walls, and filling the air with showers of scalding rain. Under our feet the sopped carpet seemed to be made of steaming mud. And as if all the forces of nature hitherto subjected to Jacinto, had taken courage from the rebellion of the water—we heard dull rumblings from inside the walls, and the wires of the electric lights began to coruscate with menacing sparks. I fled down the passage where the thick mist was spreading. All through 202 ran a tumult of disaster. In front of the door, attracted by the smoke and steam escaping from the windows, the police and a large crowd had collected. I met a reporter on the stairs with his hat on his nape, and his notebook in his hand, crying out to know if there were " any dead ".

Once the water had been dominated by the fire-brigade, and the mist had cleared away, I returned to find Jacinto in the middle of his room in his drawers. He was livid.

" Oh, Zé Fernandes, that's all our Industry is worth! What impotence! What impotence! For the second time, this same disaster. And, this time, with a new system and perfect piping!"

" And I'm soaked through with your damned 'new system', and have no other dinner jacket," I grumbled.

All round, the embroidered silks, the Louis XIII brocades, covered with black stains, were still smoking and steaming. Jacinto, very pale, was trying to dry a portrait of Madame Oriol with bare shoulders, which the brutal jet had covered with blisters. And I, with some rancour, thought of my Guiães, and the stream-water which was heated in safe pots, and was brought up to my washstand by the strong hands of Catarina, in safe pitchers. We did not dine with the Duc de Marizac in the Club. And when we eventually got to the Opera I did not enjoy *Lohengrin*, his white soul, his white swan, and his white arms, or his white armour—pinched, squeezed, and cut in the armpits as I was by the jacket Jacinto lent me, and which smelt, almost to stupefaction, of flowers of Nessari.

On the Sunday, very early, Cricket who had badly scalded his hands the previous evening and had them in bandages, came into my room, pulled the curtains, and with his radiant Negro smile said " It's in *Figaro* ". He unfolded the paper in triumph. It was in the "Echoes" column, twelve lines of news, wherein our tap-waters roared and whistled so magnificently, and with such publicity that I, too, smiled with pleasure.

" And you should have heard the telephone all morning, Master Fernandes," exclaimed the Negro, shining in ebony. "Everybody wants to know . . . 'Are you there? Are you scalded?' All Paris is very sad about it, Master Fernandes!"

It was true that the telephone rang insatiably. And when I went down to breakfast the table cloth was hidden in a mass of telegrams which my Prince was opening with a knife, frowning and grumbling at the boredom of it. He only brightened up while reading one of these little messages, which he threw on to my plate with the same sort of happy smile that Cricket and I had smiled that same morning.

"It's from the Grand Duc Casimiro—the funny old dear! Poor fellow!"

Over my eggs, I enjoyed His Highness's telegram:

"What's this? My Jacinto flooded out! Very chic in the Champs-Elysées! I shall never return to Number 202 without a life-belt! A compassionate embrace. Casimiro."

I also murmured with deference, "How charming! Poor old dear." Afterwards, slowly turning over the pile of telegrams which extended down the table to my cup, I asked: "Jacinto, who is this Diana, who is always telephoning, telegraphing, and writing to you?"

"Diana? . . . Diana de Lorge. She's a cocotte . . . in a big way."

"Yours?"

"No, not mine. I only own a piece of her." And when I lamented that my Prince, a man of such wealth and such pride, to save the expense of a private mistress should wallow with a public one, along with so many others—Jacinto shrugged his shoulders with a shrimp on his fork: "You come from the wilds. . . . A city like Paris needs courtesans of the greatest pomp and splendour. Just to keep a cocotte (in the enormous expense of Parisian life) in her clothes, her diamonds, her horses, her footmen, her theatre boxes, her festivities, her palace, her publicity, and her general insolence, requires several large fortunes, so we have to form a syndicate. . . . There are seven of us, all from the Club. I pay my share . . . but that's purely out of Civic Loyalty, to endow this City with a Monumental Cocotte. But I don't 'wallow': Poor Diana! . . . lower than her shoulders I don't know even the colour of her skin, whether it's snow-coloured or lemon-coloured."

37

I stared : " From the shoulders down? . . . But what about on top? "

" Oh, on top it's rice-powder . . . But she's a bore! Always notes, telephone calls, and telegrams. It comes to 3,000 francs a month, quite apart from the flowers. A real bore!"

And the two wrinkles that furrowed the cheeks of my Prince on each side of the sharp nose curved downward over his salad, were like two very melancholy valleys in the late afternoon.

We finished breakfast when a footman, very discreetly, in a low murmur, announced Madame Oriol. Jacinto quietly laid down his cigar. I nearly choked myself with a flurried gulp of coffee. Between the sumptuous strawberry-coloured curtains she appeared, dressed in black, in the smooth black of Holy Week, giving a graceful gesture to us not to disturb ourselves. Then she said with a sweetly melodious volubility : " It's only for a moment. Don't get up. I was passing on my way to the Madeleine, and I couldn't contain myself. I want to see the damage. A deluge in the Champs-Elysées! It could only happen to Jacinto! Then it came out in *Figaro*. How scared I was when I telephoned. Just imagine! Boiling water, like Vesuvius . . . But it's thrilling. And all the beautiful cloth spoilt, and the carpets . . . I'm dying to admire the ruins."

Jacinto, who seemed not in the least moved, nor grateful for this interest, smilingly took up his cigar, " Why it's all dry now, my dear lady. The beauty of it was yesterday when the water was roaring and spraying. What a pity that not even a wall fell down to show you!"

But she insisted. In all her days in Paris she had never had the pleasure of enjoying the damage of an inundation. *Figaro* had recounted it well . . . " What a delightful adventure, a scalded house in the Champs-Elysées!"

Her whole person from the feathers that curled in her hat to the glittering point of her shoes seemed to vibrate like a delicate branch on which a little bird is singing. Only her smile behind a thick veil continued immobile. And in the air around her spread an aroma, a sweetness which emanated from her mobility and gracefulness.

38

Jacinto in the meantime gaily yielded to her wishes. Down the corridor Madame Oriol continued to praise the friendly *Figaro*, and confessed how frightened she had been . . . I returned to my coffee, mentally felicitating the " Prince of Good Fortune " for this perfect flower of Civilization who perfumed his life for him. I thought also of the elegant harmony with which this flower moved and behaved. And I ran to the mirror in the antechamber to inspect the knot in my tie, and the way I had combed my hair. Then I went back to the dining room and sat near the window, turning over the pages of the *Century Review* in an attitude of elegance and high culture. Almost immediately they reappeared : and Madame Oriol who, still smiling, complained that she had been cheated, having found nothing to remind her of furious torrents, seated herself at the table, where Jacinto found Maltese tangerines for her, frozen chestnuts, and a biscuit soaked in Tokay.

She refused them with her hands kept in her muff. She was neither tall, nor strong, but every fold of her dress, or curve of her cloak, fell and rippled harmoniously, with perfections covering perfections. Under her close veil you could scarcely perceive the whiteness of her powdered skin or the darkness of her large eyes. What with those black silks and velvets and a little, hot reddish-gold hair, strongly twisted, which showed over the black furs on her nape, she gave forth a sensation of smoothness and fineness everywhere. Persistently I considered her as a flower of " Civilization "—and I thought of the centuries of toil, refinement and culture that were required to produce the soil from which such a flower could bud, and then bloom fully, as now, in full perfume, even more beautiful for being a flower of conscious cultivation and the hot house, and for having something in her petals that seemed about to fade and wither.

Meanwhile, with her bird-like vivacity, speaking now to me, now to Jacinto, she showed her pretty wonder at the heaps of telegrams on the table cloth.

" All this morning! And all because of the flood! . . . Jacinto today is the Man, the only Man in Paris! Are many of them from women? "

Languidly puffing his cigar Jacinto pushed the telegram of
the Grand Duc towards her. Then Madame Oriol exclaimed,
" Ah!" gravely and with much feeling. She carefully re-read
the wire which her fingers seemed to caress with an eager
reverence. Still grave and still serious, she said : " He is very
bright."

Oh certainly everything in the disaster had passed off
brightly and brilliantly in a truly Parisian manner! The
delicious creature could wait no longer because she had
booked·a pew in the Church of the Madeleine for the sermon.
Jacinto exclaimed with innocence : " Sermons? . . . Is it now
the season for sermons? "

Madame Oriol gave a little movement of tender scandaliza-
tion and pain. What! Should not the austere House of
Trèves care for the beginning of Lent? But she did not wonder
at Jacinto—he was a Turk! Then immediately she began to
praise a preacher, a Dominican Friar, called Father Granon.
Such eloquence! Such violence! In his last sermon he had
preached about love, and the fragility of worldly love! He
had said things of such inspiration, and such sheer brute-
power! After, he gave such a gesture, such a terrible gesture
of overwhelming and crushing in which he pulled up his
sleeve to show his naked arm, a superb arm, very white and
very powerful.

Her smile remained clear under her glance which deepened
darkly behind her veil. Jacinto began to laugh : " A good
arm for a spiritual director. What! To cane and spank the
backsides of souls!"

She broke in : " No. Father Granon doesn't take confessions
unfortunately." Then she reconsidered suddenly what she
had said, and asked for a glass of Tokay and a biscuit. It was
necessary to take a good cordial before facing up to the
emotions of Father Granon. We both rushed forward, one
with a bottle, and the other with a plate of sweets. She lifted
her veil, and quickly ate a biscuit soaked in Tokay. And
while Jacinto, suddenly noticing the hat she was wearing,
bent over it with curiosity and admiration, Madame Oriol
suddenly stopped smiling, and became serious, on meeting
with a serious subject : " Elegant, isn't it? . . . It's a creation,

40

an entirely new one, of Madame Vial's. Very reverent and very suggestive for Lent."

Her glance, which included me, also invited me to admire it. I approached thrusting forward my rustic muzzle to contemplate this supreme creation of the luxuries of Lent. It was truly marvellous. Over the velvet, in the shade of the curly feathers, in the priceless lace, fixed with a golden pin, and made of the finest jet, nestled a perfect little crown of thorns! We both went into ecstasies. And Madame Oriol, with a movement and a smile that seemed to spread more aroma and light around her, set off for the Madeleine.

My Prince gave a few pensive soft paces on the carpet. Then brusquely rising and heaving his shoulders with a Herculean determination, as if he was displacing the world, he exclaimed: " Zé Fernandes, let us pass this Sunday in a truly simple and natural way."

" How? "

Jacinto revolved his wide eyes as if he was searching through Universal Life for something simple and natural. Then resting his gaze upon me as it returned from infinite space, weary and with little hope, he said, " Let's go to the Jardin des Plantes, to see the giraffe."

4

DURING that productive week, one night we were returning from the Opera when Jacinto yawning announced a party at 202.

" A party? "

" Because of the Grand Duc, poor dear old chap, for whom I'm ordering a very delicious and rare fish which is caught in Dalmatia. I wanted a short breakfast. The Grand Duc insists on a supper. He is a barbarian, besmeared with eighteenth-century literature, and who still believes in having suppers—in Paris, in these days! I am inviting three or four women, and nine or ten typical men, to amuse him. You'll appreciate it too. You will skim through Paris in an epitome. . . . But what a terrible bore."

41

Not feeling any interest in it, Jacinto did not take any pains to prepare this party for an outstanding and brilliant success. He only ordered a band of gipsies. (Even in those remote days the gipsies with their scarlet jackets and their wild melancholy had taken Paris by storm). He ordered the library to be connected by theatrephone to the Opéra, the Comédie Française, the Alcazar and the Comics, thus providing for all tastes from the tragic to the picaresque. Late in the afternoon we visited the dining room, resplendent with the ancient silver-ware of Dom "Galleon". The sumptuous profusion of orchids in long forests along the table cloth with its silken tassels and embroideries, encircling fruit dishes of Saxe, covered with chiselled crystals and filigrane of gold, gave me such a fine sense of luxury that I inwardly exclaimed —"Blessed be the power of money!" For the first time, too, I marvelled at the cupboard with its abundant and minute arrangements—above all, two lifts which rose from and descended on pulleys to the depths of the kitchen, one for fish and meat—heated by hot water pipes, the other for salads, fruit and ices, enclosed in frigorific plates of metal. Oh, that Number 202!

At nine o'clock I went down to Jacinto's study to write a letter to my dear Aunt Vicência, while Jacinto remained at his toilet table, having his nails polished. Then, in this delicious palace, all decked out for gala, we experienced a very common fright. All the electric lights in 202 suddenly went out! In my deep distrust of these universal forces, I jumped clear out of the door, stumbling in the darkness and yelling out for help, in the language of Guiães, a yell which might have been heard from there. Jacinto bellowed from upstairs, with his manicurist clutching his pyjamas. And then once more like a tired servant dragging her slippers, the light slowly flickered back again. But my Prince, panic-stricken, had an engineer sent from the Company of Domestic Electricity. And as a precaution another servant was sent to the grocery for several hundred tallow candles. Cricket unearthed hundreds of old candelabras and candlesticks from the old chests and cupboards, the unwieldy heritage of the unscientific times of Dom "Galleon"! They were ranged like a reserve force of reliable old veterans for the desperate emergency which might be caused if later at supper the raw-recruit forces of Civilization should perfidiously fail in their duty. The electrician who arrived out of breath, swore that the electricity would continue from now on without any more sulks or poutings. Nevertheless I cautiously secreted in my pocket two stout stumps of tallow.

The electricity remained faithful without hitches. And when I descended from my room late (because I had lost my dress-waistcoat which I only found, after a desperate hunt, behind my bed) the whole of 202 was a blaze of light, and the gipsies, shaking their hair, were letting fly the undulations of a waltz so irresistible that even on the walls, the enormous figures on the tapestries, Priam, Nestor, and the ingenious Ulysses all began panting and heaving as they lifted their venerable feet and waved in the wind of the dance.

Timidly, soundlessly, I penetrated into Jacinto's study where I met the permanent smile of the Comtesse de Trèves, who, accompanied by the illustrious historian Danjon (of the Académie Française) was inspecting with amazement the sumptuous array of Instruments and Machinery that belonged to my super-civilized Prince. Never had she appeared so majestic as now in her saffron-coloured silks, with laces crossed on her bosom, in the fashion of Marie Antoinette, with curly red hair raised in a crest over her dominating forehead, with her curved patrician nose, mounting guard over her ever-glittering smile, like the arch of a bridge over a shining and rippling rill. Upright as if on a canopied throne, with her long tortoiseshell lunette close to her small eyes of a troubled azure, she listened, in front of the graphophone, then in front of the microphone, as though she were listening to fine music, to the explanations which Jacinto was stumbling through with laborious affability. Before each wheel, pulley or spring, there was amazement, accompanied with finely-turned compliments, in which all these inventions were attributed, with astute simplicity, to Jacinto. The mysterious gadgets piled up on the ebony table were a discovery which fairly carried her away, " Oh, the numberer of pages!—how extraordinary! Oh, the automatic stamp-licker!"

43

The caress of her fingers warmed the metals. She asked for the address of the manufacturers so as to be able to provide herself with these adorable tools! Equipped with such aids, how easily one's life would glide along! But such talent as Jacinto's was necessary to know what to choose, and what to promote. Yet it was not only on my friend (who received it with resignation) that she lavished her fine honey. Caressing the telegraph with the stem of her lunette, she found an opportunity to praise the eloquence of the historian. And even for myself (of whose very name she was ignorant) she arranged a sweet piece of flattery which I swallowed like a celestial lollipop, when she halted by the gramophone to say something about the voices of one's friends, which it is so charming to record and collect. Like a good old farmer's wife, who went on throwing grain to her hungry chickens, at every step she nourished some personal vanity. Greedy for another lollipop, I followed her rustling saffron-coloured train. She stopped before the counting machine, of whose workings Jacinto was giving her a deeply scientific account. She touched the little cavities and their little peeping numbers: then, with her charming smile, murmured " Yes, it's truly prodigious, this Electric Printing Press! . . ."

Jacinto exclaimed, " No! No! This one is . . ." But she kept on smiling, and drifted on . . . Madame de Trèves hadn't understood a single thing about any of my Prince's wonderful instruments! She hadn't listened to a single word of his erudite dissertations. Amidst sumptuous array of mechanisms she had only been concerned with exercising, with the greatest skill and success, the Art of Charm. The whole of her was a falsehood of towering sublimity. I did not hide from Danjon the wonderment and admiration I felt, since I audibly gasped.

The eloquent Academician rolled his sturgeon-like eyes, " Oh, what taste she has, what intelligence, what charm! Besides, what good dinners she serves at her home. The coffee! . . . I tell you, sir, she is altogether a woman out of the ordinary, out of the ordinary!"

I went off into the Library. Near the entry, just by the bookstand of the Fathers of the Church, where a group of

44

gentlemen were conversing, I stopped to greet the editor of *The Boulevard*, and the Feminine Psychologist, the author of *Triplicate Heart*, whom I had met before at lunch at Number 202. His greeting was paternal: and he retained, greedily and tightly, in his illustrious hand, which sparkled with rings, my hard palm of a mountaineer. All these gentlemen, as a matter of fact, were praising his new Novel, *The Cuirass*, which had just appeared to feminine squeaks of delight and a warm rustle of flurried skirts. From a frock coat with a vast head popping out of it, arranged *à la Van Dyck*, a head which seemed to be entirely artificial, he proclaimed, rising on the toes of his boots, that Experimental Psychology had never penetrated so far into the old Soul of Humanity! Everyone agreed heartily: all pressed themselves around the Psychologist and called him "Master". Even I, myself, who had never even set eyes on the yellow cover of *The Cuirass* but upon whom he turned his beggarly eyes, as if famished, for more honey, murmured emotionally—"It was a sheer delight!"

And the Psychologist, choked by his high collar with its 1830 cravat, became completely radiant, modestly confessing that he had dissected all the human Souls in *The Cuirass* from documentary evidence, from life that was still warm, and could still bleed . . . It was just then that the Duc de Marizac remarked with a smile that was sharper than the edge of a razor, without removing his hands from his pockets: "But in the meantime, my dear chap, there is in this book for which you studied so profoundly, a blunder which is very strange, very curious . . ."

The Psychologist jerked his head back violently . . . "A blunder?"

"Oh yes! A blunder! . . . One which surprises one in a Master so experienced and learned as you. That was to give to the splendidly amorous heroine of *The Cuirass*, a duchess, and one with real good taste, a corset of black satin. This corset, a black one, appears on a good page of analysis and passion, when she is undressing in the room of Ruy de Alize."

And Marizac, with his hands still in his pockets, appealed

to the other gentleman. Wasn't it unreal that a woman like the duchess, aesthetic, pre-Raphaelite, who got her clothes from Doucet and Paquin, who were intellectual dressmakers, should wear a corset of black satin?

The Psychologist was stricken dumb, caught out and pierced through and through. Marizac was by so much the supreme authority on the intimate underwear of duchesses; and he made it quite clear that in the afternoon, in the bedrooms of their boy-friends, they always wore white camisoles and petticoats, purely out of idealistic impulse and the yearnings of their suffering souls!

The Editor of *The Boulevard* next pitilessly condemned, from his own solid experience, this black corset, which would only be worn by some old-fashioned spinster who was still pandering to the effect of naked flesh against black satin. And I, too, that they might not think me without experience in ducal adulteries, added, running my fingers through my hair: " Really, I think it would only be permissible in a duchess who was in heavy mourning for her father."

The poor Master of *The Cuirass* surrendered. His glory as a Doctor of female elegance was destroyed—and Paris would now suspect that he had never seen in his life a Duchess taking off her corsets for him in his psychological alcove. Then passing his handkerchief over his lips which had dried in sheer anguish, he confessed his mistake, attributing it to his spate-like and torrential inspiration.

" It was a false note that escaped me in the heat of creation . . . Of course! It's absurd . . . a black corset!! Even to be in harmony with the state of the soul of the Duchess at that moment, it should have been lilac-coloured, or perhaps the colour of faded mignonette, with a fringe of old Malines lace . . . It's amazing how such a thing escaped me. Because I keep a notebook, well-documented, of all my assignations on the spot! . . . Amazing!"

In his bitterness he begged Marizac to spread it everywhere, in the club, round the salons, at the confessional. It was the error of an artist who works in a fever of haste, sweeping out souls, lost in the dark profundity of souls! He was so engrossed in that, that he did not even notice the corset, he confounded the "tones" . . . Then he shouted out to the Editor of *The Boulevard* with his arms extended, " I am prepared to rectify it in an interview, my dear Sir. Send one of your editors along . . . Tomorrow at ten. Let's have an interview and decide the right colour. Send one of your men, my dear Sir. It would also be a chance for me to praise very emphatically the great services rendered by *The Boulevard* to the psychological and feministic Sciences . . ."

He was thus supplicating, back to back with the Sacred Fathers in the bookshelves, when I scurried off, on seeing Jacinto in a dispute between two men at the far end of the library.

They were both Madame de Trèves's men : her husband, the Comte de Trèves, descendant of the Kings of Candia : and her lover, the terrible banker Ephraim. And so fiercely were they engaged with my Prince that they scarcely perceived me, though each with a soft, vague touch of the hand, mistily treated me to a " my dear Count ". By chance, going to the lemon-tree table for some cigarettes, I overheard that this discussion concerned the *Burma Emerald Company*, a tremendous enterprise, scintillating with billions, for whose support these two inseparable partners (both in bed and in business) were asking for the name, the influence and the money of Jacinto. And now the Comte de Trèves, a dishevelled and weedy man, with a sucked-in face, bristling with a spiny beard beneath a forehead as round and yellow as a melon, was telling my poor Prince that in the prospectus, which was already prepared, the dazzle and grandeur of this enterprise put the *Arabian Nights* in the shade. Above all, this excavation of emeralds would give scope to a spirit so dedicated to the advance of civilization as Jacinto's. It would set up a current of occidental ideas which would invade and educate Burma. He accepted the directorship from motives of patriotism . . . as a European . . .

" And besides," he said, " there will be the exchange of jewels, of art, and of progressive ideas, which ought to take place in the higher circles, between friends . . ."

On the other side, the terrible Ephraim, rubbing a short, fat hand on his beautiful beard, curlier and blacker than that

47

of an Assyrian King, swore to the triumph of the enterprise, by the mighty powers with which it was backed—the Nagayess, the Bolsans, the Saccarts . . ."

Jacinto wrinkled up his nose, anxiously : " But, at least, have they studied the question ? Is it certain that there *are* emeralds there ? "

Such ingenuousness exasperated Ephraim : " Emeralds ! Why of course there are emeralds ! . . . As long as there are shareholders, there are always emeralds ! "

I was wondering at the insolent grandeur of this maxim— when doubled up and breathless, waving a highly-perfumed handkerchief, appeared one of the intimates of 202, de Todelle (Antoine de Todelle) a young man of many gifts, who led Cotillons, imitated singers of the Café-Concerts, arranged rare salads, and knew all the labyrinths of Paris.

" Has he come yet . . . Is the Grand Duc here yet ? "

" No, His Highness has not arrived yet. And where is Madame de Todelle ? "

" She can't come . . . laid up on the sofa . . . skinned her leg."

" Oh."

" Not serious . . . only fell off her velocipede."

Jacinto seemed quite interested, " Ah, so Madame de Todelle already rides a velocipede ? "

" Well, she's learning," de Todelle replied. " But she hasn't even got one. Now, during Lent, she can apply herself to it more fully because it's the velocipede of Father Ernesto, the priest at Saint Joseph's and he doesn't use it so much now. But yesterday in the Bois . . . Crash ! . . . on the ground . . . skinned her leg . . . just here . . ." On his own thigh he indicated the position of the abrasion, vividly, with his thumbnail. Ephraim, brutally but solemnly, muttered, " Damnation ! That's the best place of all ! " But de Todelle didn't even hear him, as he was already rushing up to the Director of *The Boulevard*, who advanced deliberate and big-bellied, with his dark monocle looking like a patch on his eye. Both stood beside a bookstand, eagerly whispering.

Jacinto and I went into the billiard room upholstered in Cordoba-leather, where one could smoke. In one corner, the great Dornan, the neo-platonic and mystical poet, the subtle master of all the rhythms, sprawled on the cushions with one of his feet on his fat thigh, like an Indian god, with the lowest buttons of his waistcoat undone, and his goitrous dewlap falling over his collar, was majestically sucking at the end of a cheroot. Seated next to him, an old man whom I had never before met at Number 202, with white curls brushed back behind his ears, and a very black moustache turned steeply upwards at the tips, was just finishing some story that must have been grossly spicy—because Joban, the supreme critic of the drama who was standing facing him in front of the divan, laughed till his bald head became scarlet with rapture, and a very flaxen-haired youth (a descendant of the Colignys) with the profile of a parrakeet, flapped his short arms like wings, screeching "Delicious! Too divine!" The idealist poet was the only one who remained impassive, keeping his majestic corpulent appearance. But when we drew near, this mystical master of perfect rhythms, after blowing a huge gust of smoke, and saluting me with a flicker of his heavy eyelids, began with a rich and brassy voice: "But better still, an infinitely better one—you all know Madame Noredal. Madame Noredal has tremendous buttocks!" Unfortunately for my regalement, de Todelle rushed into the billiard room making a great outcry for Jacinto. There were some ladies and gentlemen who wanted to hear Patti on the gramophone. My friend shrugged his shoulders in sullen irritation. "An aria of Patti? . . . What do I know of it! All the records are in confusion and there's something wrong with the gramophone. It doesn't work properly. It doesn't work at all . . . I've got three of them . . . all out of order."

"That's all right," cheerfully exclaimed de Todelle, "I'll sing you *La Pauvre Fille* . . . *Oh, la pauv' pauv' pauv'* . . ."

Seizing my arm, he suddenly dragged my bucolic shyness into the rose-coloured room, where like goddesses in the chosen circle of Olympus, resplendently shone Madame Oriol, Madame Verghane, the Princesse de Caraman, and another golden-haired woman with large diamonds in her long locks, with shoulders so bare, arms so bare, and breasts so bare,

49

that her evening gown with pale gold fringes seemed on the point of slithering to the floor like a nightgown. Deeply impressed and still trying to hold de Todelle, I growled in a low whisper, " Who's that? " But already the festive young man had rushed to Madame Oriol with whom, laughing in easy familiarity, were the Duc de Marizac and a youth with a pale maize-coloured beard as flimsy as thistledown, who swayed to and fro on tiptoe like a wheat-stem in the wind. I, stranded against the piano, was slowly rubbing my hands as if to knead my embarrassment, when Madame Verghane rose from the sofa where she had been conversing with an old man, who wore the Grand Cross of Saint Andrew, and advanced, plump and tiny, over the carpet, with a slithering of her full, green-black, velvet train. So narrow was her waist between the fecund rotundity of her hips, and the vastitide of her thorax, half-bare and shimmering, like mother of pearl, that I was afraid she would break in two, in the slow undulation of her gait. Her famous plaits of a furious black colour, entirely hid her ears : and the huge hoop of gold which surrounded her head flashed sparkles from a star made of diamonds, as from the forehead of one of Botticelli's angels. Knowing doubtless of my authority in the household of Number 202, she sent me in passing, like a beneficent sunbeam, a smile which liquified her melting eyes, and murmured, " The Grand Duc—is he coming for certain? "

" Oh yes, Madame, for certain! He's coming for the fish."
" The fish? "

But just at that moment, in the entrance hall, there blared out with rolling drums and triumphal undulations, the march of Rakoczy. It was he! In the library our bellowing major-domo announced : " His Royal Highness the Grand Duc Casimiro!" Madame Verghane, with a short sigh of emotion, inflated her thorax, as if better to expose its ivory magnificence. And the man from *The Boulevard*, the old man with the Cross of Saint Andrew, and Ephraim, nearly crushed me as they rushed towards the door to the irresistible allurement of a Royal Personage.

The Grand Duc appeared, preceded by Jacinto. He was a majestic man with a pointed grey beard, and slightly bald.

He hesitated for a second, balancing himself on his tiny flat shoes which were almost hidden beneath his wide, baggy trousers. Then, portly and smiling, he began to take the hands of the ladies who ducked in their silks and velvets, as they curtseyed before him in true court fashion. Then, slapping Jacinto on the shoulder with cordial jocularity, he exclaimed :

" And how about that fish? Was it prepared according to the recipe I sent you? "

A murmur from Jacinto calmed him at once.

" So much the better! So much the better!" His Highness exclaimed in his commanding bellow, " I haven't even dined yet. I've had absolutely no dinner. You are served deplorably at Joseph's. Why do people still go and dine at Joseph's? Whenever I come to Paris I ask ' Where can one dine? ' And they always say ' At Joseph's ' . . . What? That's not dining! Today for example . . . woodcocks! . . . They were pestilential . . . They haven't got a notion of how to cook woodcocks."

His bluish eyes, of a muddy opaqueness, suddenly flashed fire as they grew round with indignation. " Paris is losing all her pre-eminences and supremacies. Already in Paris, one can no longer dine!"

Thereupon, all the gentlemen around him dolefully agreed. The Comte de Trèves, however, defended the *Bignon* which, he said, kept up its noble traditions. The *Boulevard* man who was all on the side of His Highness, attributed the decadence of French cooking to the Republic, and to the democratic taste for all that is cheap.

" At Paillard's one can still . . . " began Ephraim.

" At Paillard's," roared the Grand Duc, " the Burgundies are so bad! The Burgundies are so bad!" He let his arms and shoulders hang limply in despair. Then, with a slow swaying gait like that of a veteran pilot, holding back the lapels of his jacket, he went to greet Madame Oriol, who was all one flash and glitter in her smile, her glance, her jewels, and the spectrum of her salmon-coloured silks. But scarcely had that sleek and shining creature begun to chatter to him, when His Highness noticed the theatrephone on a flower-covered table nearby, and called to Jacinto: " In communication with the Alcazar? . . . The theatrephone? "

" Certainly, my dear Sir."

" Excellent! Very chic!" His Highness was very sad to miss hearing Gilberte in her new song *Les Casquettes*. It was just half-past eleven. The very moment she was due to sing in the last act of the *Electric Revue*. He clapped the two receivers of the theatrephone to his ears and remained abstracted with a deep furrow in his brow. Then suddenly in a voice of command he shouted . . . " It's she! Hush! Be quiet everyone! . . . Come, all of you. Princesse de Caraman, this way. Here! All of you! Shut up! It's she! Hush! . . ."

Then, as Jacinto had prodigally installed two theatrephones, each one provided with twelve wires apiece, each of those ladies and gentlemen hastened submissively to find a " receiver " and to remain soundlessly immovable so as to enjoy *Les Casquettes* to its full. In the room of faded rose-colour in the nave of the library, where an august silence reigned, I was the only one who remained unattached to the theatrephone, idly standing with my hands in my pockets.

On the monumental clock which marked the hour of day in every one of the world's capitals and registered the motions of all the planets, the fine indicator seemed to be dozing. Over the pensive muteness of those backs and low-necked dresses as they stooped attentively to listen, electricity shone with the sadness of a frozen sun. From each ear, cupped with a hand, hung a black tube like an intestine. Dornan, crumpled over the table, closed his eyes, in the meditation of an obese monk. The historian of the Duc d'Anjou, with the receiver held on the delicate points of his fingers, reared his sharp beaked nose upright, in the grave accomplishment of a ceremonious court-duty. Madame Oriol was languidly smiling, as if the wire were whispering sweet flatteries. To dissipate the numbness I was beginning to feel, I risked taking a timid step. But immediately I was quelled with a severe, " Shshsh!" from the Grand Duc. I recoiled through the curtains of the door to hide my laziness from view. The Psychologist of *The*

Cuirass, a long way from the table, with his long line stretched out, bit his lips in the effort of concentration. The beatitude of His Highness, sunk in an armchair, was complete. At his side the bosom of Madame Verghane swelled and heaved like a sea wave made of whipped cream. And my poor friend Jacinto, in conscientious application, bent sadly over the theatrephone as if it were over a grave.

There, before these people of a superior civilization, who in a religious silence, were sucking in the obscenities screeched to them by Gilberte, under the streets of Paris through wires which were sunk between the sewers and drains—I thought of my slumbering native village. The crescent moon, which, followed by a tiny star was flying through the clouds over the roofs and black chimneys of the Champs-Elysées, was also flying there, more lustrous and more gentle, above the pinewoods. The frogs were chirping in the distance by the rapids of the Dona. The little hermitage of Saint Joaquim, bare and white, glittered on the summit of the mountain. . . . One of the ladies murmured, " But that's not Gilberte . . ." And one of the men said, " It's more like a cornet . . ." " Now they're clapping," said another. " No! It's Paulin!"

The Grand Duc gave vent to the most ferocious "Shshsh-sh! . . ." Dogs barked (it seemed) in the yard of one farm-house and were answered by the dogs of Jao Saranda across the river. Then I seemed to be going down a lane with my cudgel over my shoulder. And then I thought I smelt, between the silk of the curtains, the fragrance of the pine-cones crackling on the farm-house hearth: felt the warmth of the cattle-corrals brought by the breeze over their high fences: and heard the sound of the murmuring, lazy watercourses.

I was awakened from my reverie by a bellow from the Grand Duc who rose furiously shrugging his shoulders— " You can't hear anything . . . only screeches and screams . . . and a buzzing noise . . . what a horrible bore . . . since that song is a real gem . . .

Oh, les casquettes,
Oh, les casque-e-e-e-ttes!"
All now let go their receiving wires and proclaimed that

Gilberte was " too delicious ". Then the major-domo opening wide the two portals, announced loudly :

" Monseigneur est servi!"

At the table, whereon the display of orchids received the stentorian praise of His Highness, I sat between the ethereal poet, Dornan, and the young man with the flaxen thistledown beard who swayed like an ear of corn in the wind. After unfolding his table-napkin and spreading it on his lips, Dornan disentangled from his watch-chain an enormous monocle with which to run through the menu, of which he approved. Leaning towards me with the face of an obese apostle, he said, "This port of 1834, here in the house of Jacinto, may well be authentic . . . eh? "

I assured the Master of Rhythms that that port had grown old in the classical cellars of no less a person than grandfather "Galleon" himself. He drew aside, in methodical preparation, the long dense hairs of the moustache which covered his gross lips. The waiters served a cold *consommé* with truffles . . . The maize-coloured youth who swivelled his blue, bland glance around the table, murmured with laughing regret . . . " What a pity! Only a General and a Bishop are wanting!" Very true! All the Dominant Classes were at that moment eating the truffles of my friend Jacinto. In front of me Madame Oriol rippled forth a laugh as musical as the trill of a bird. The Grand Duc, in a forest of orchids which fringed his cover, noticed one of them, which, horribly sombre, resembled a greenish scorpion, with glittering wings and swollen with deadly venom. With the greatest delicacy he offered this floral monstrosity to Madame Oriol, who, with trills of laughter, ceremoniously hung it at her breast. Against the smooth flesh, in its creamy whiteness, this deadly scorpion seemed to swell and grow greener, with its wings trembling more feverishly. The eyes of the guests lit up, and fixed themselves on that lustrous breast, whose beauty the venomous deformity of the flower seemed perversely to spice and flavour. She triumphed resplendently. The better to arrange the flower her fingers widened her low-bosomed dress, showing off new beauties and guiding the flaming curiosity of all eyes to a single focus. The care-worn face of Jacinto hung disconsolately over an empty plate. The high-minded lyrical poet of *The Mystic Twilight*, passing his hand over his moustaches, grumbled disdainfully.

" A pretty woman . . . but with thin haunches . . . and I bet she has no buttocks."

Meanwhile the youth of the flaxen thistledown reverted to his strange disappointment that we had neither a General with his sword nor a Bishop with his crozier . . .

" My dear sir, what on earth for? " we asked him.

He made a smooth gesture in which all his finger-rings flashed at once: " Why, so that one could throw a dynamite-bomb? . . . We have here a splendid bouquet of the flowers of Civilization with a Grand Duc in the middle. Imagine a dynamite-bomb thrown from that door! What a fine ending of a dinner, for the end of a century!"

And while I considered him in shocked surprise, he, drinking huge gulps of Chateau-Yquem, declared that nowadays the only sensation left which was really a fine one, would be to annihilate Civilization. Neither science, nor art, nor money, nor love could any longer give real and intensive pleasure to our satiated souls. All the pleasure to be got out of *creating* was already outworn. The only pleasure left was the divine pleasure of *destruction*.

He went on retailing other enormities with a bland smile in his clear blue eyes. But I was no longer listening to this gentle pedant, since I was suddenly overwhelmed by another anxiety when I noticed that all round me, of a sudden, the bustle of the table service was suddenly suspended, and had ceased as in the fairy-tale of the petrified palace. The dish that was at this moment due, was the fish of His Royal Highness, the fish that was the inspiration of this whole banquet! Jacinto was nervously crushing a rare orchid between his fingers. And all the waiters stood downcast as if in despair! Fortunately the Grand Duc was telling the story of a hunt in the Parks of Sarvan, in which a lady, the wife of a banker, suddenly leaped from her horse in the middle of an open plain without trees. He and all the other huntsmen drew rein . . . while the lady, livid, with her riding habit raised, rushed behind a rock . . . But we were never to know what preoccupied the banker's wife in that stretch of open plain—because at that very moment the major-domo appeared, glittering with perspiration and stammered a confidence to Jacinto, who bit his lip as though in anguish. The Grand Duc fell silent. We all exchanged glances in light-hearted anxiety. Then my Prince with heroic patience, forcing a pallid smile, began . . .

" My friends, there has been a misfortune."

Dornan leaped upright in his chair : " Fire ? " No it was not a fire. It was the plate-elevator, which suddenly, unexpectedly, on its way up with the fish for His Royal Highness, had suddenly gone out of order, stuck fast, and remained immovable. The Grand Duc flung down his napkin. All his politeness cracked like badly-stuck-on enamel. . . . " This is the limit . . . A fish which has given me so much trouble and work to come all the way here ! . . . What have we come here to eat ? What idiocy ! Couldn't you have brought it simply in your hands ! Stuck fast, is it ? I want to see ! . . . Where is the elevator shaft ? "

Furiously he rushed towards it, conducted by the major-domo who stumbled and bent his shoulders shrugging and bowing, before this shattering fury of the Duc. Jacinto flitted after them like a shadow borne away on the squall of His Highness's wrath. I could contain myself no longer and rushed to the shaft to contemplate the disaster, when Dornan, smiting his thigh, demanded that we should continue the feast without the fish !

There was the Grand Duc, leaning over the dark shaft of the elevator wherein he held a candle which flushed his red face an even deeper shade of crimson. I peeped over the royal shoulder. There, deep down in the shadows, on a large silver tray, a white fish shone stretched out on its plate, and still steaming between slices of lemon. Jacinto, white as his evening tie, was desperately torturing the complicated springs of the elevator. Then it was the Grand Duc who with his hairy wrists gave a tremendous heave at the cables on which the elevator went up and down. In vain ! The whole apparatus stiffened into the inertia of eternal bronze.

Silks rustled round the entry to the elevator shaft. It was

Madame Oriol, and behind her Madame Verghane, with their eyes flashing with inquisitiveness about this outburst in which the Duc had vented so much passion. Marizac, our intimate friend, also came up smiling and proposed a descent into the shaft with ladders. Then it was the Psychologist who approached and attributed sagacity to the fish in refusing to come up. The Grand Duc, scarlet in the face, with a tragic finger seemed to be showing his fish to everybody, in the depth of the recess. All bent their faces over it in turn, and said "There it is!" De Todelle, in his precipitation, nearly fell down the shaft. The parakeet that descended from the Colygnys flapped its wings and screeched: "What a lovely smell! How delicious!" In the crowded shaft the low-necked dresses of the ladies brushed against the uniforms of footmen and lackeys. The grand old man, floury with powder, suddenly placed his foot in a bucket of ice, with the roar of a wild beast. The Historian of the Ducs d'Anjou was cruising around with his melancholy beaked nose held high above everybody else in the room, like a King Penguin.

Suddenly de Todelle had an inspiration. "It is a very simple plan," said de Todelle—"to fish for the fish!"

The Grand Duc slapped his thigh in triumph. Quite right! Fish for the fish! And in his delight at this facetious jest, which he found so rare and original, his fury evaporated, and he became Prince Charming once more, with magnificent courtesy requesting the ladies to be seated, in order to witness this miraculous catch. He himself would be the fisherman. For this amusing feat, he only required a walking-stick, a string, and a hook of some sort. Madame Oriol excitedly offered him one of her golden hairpins. Pressing round her on all sides and breathing her perfume we all praised her amiable dedication. And the Psychologist averred that never had anyone fished with so divine a hook. When two amazed-looking flunkeys returned with a walking-stick and a string the Grand Duc, beaming all over, had already bent the hairpin into a presentable hook. Jacinto with livid patience raised a lamp over the darkness in the well of the lift. And the gravest gentlemen there, the Historian, the editor of *The Boulevard*, the Comte de Trèves, the man with the Van Dyck head, smiled, clustering round the aperture with reverent interest in the fantasy of His Highness. Madame de Trèves examined serenely with her lorgnette the machinery at the shaft head of the elevator. Only Dornan had not risen from the table but sat with his fists clenched on the tablecloth, and his fat neck pulled in, in the sullen boredom of a caged beast from whom his meal has just been snatched away.

Meanwhile, His Highness fished away with enthusiasm. The blunt hairpin dangling and swinging at the end of the soft string could not pierce the fish.

" Jacinto, raise the lamp!" he cried sweating and swollen. "Higher still! . . . Now! Now! . . . In the gills! . . . It is only in the gills that the hairpin can hook him properly . . . Now! . . . What! What the devil! It won't work." He swivelled his face round on his neck, panting and outraged. It was not possible. Only carpenters, with levers, could do it . . . And now we all anxiously implored him to abandon the fish.

The Grand Duc, smiling and shaking his hands, agreed that in the end it was more amusing trying to catch the fish than eating it. The elegant crowd flowed back to the table, to the sound of a waltz of Strauss which the gipsies poured out in swells of ardent languor. Only Madame de Trèves remained behind, delaying my poor Jacinto to tell him how much she admired the arrangement of his elevator . . . So perfect! What an understanding of life, what a fine feeling for modern comfort!

His Highness, quietened by his expenditure of energy, lustily emptied two glasses of Chateau-Lagrange. All applauded the ingenious fisherman. The waiters served out the *Baron de Pauillac*, lamb from the marine marshes of the Landes which, prepared with almost religious rites, had earned this resounding title and been admitted into the nobility of France.

I ate with the appetite of a hero of Homer. Into my glass, and into Dornan's, continuously sparkled and spurted the champagne like a fountain in winter. When the frosted ortolans were served, which melted in the mouth, the divine poet murmured for my delight his sublime sonnet on " Saint Clara ". And since, for his part, on the other side of me, the downy-cheeked youth went on lyrically crooning about the destruction of the world, I sympathized with him also, and sipping champagne curdling into ice-cream, we both cursed the century in which we lived, Civilization, and all the boasted triumphs of Science. Across the flowers and candles, meanwhile, I watched the heavings of the vast bosom of Madame Verghane who was laughing like a Bacchante. I did not even pity Jacinto who, with the meekness of his name-saint on the block, patiently awaited the end of his martyr-dom and of his dinner party.

At last, it ended. I still remember, at three in the morning, the Grand Duc in the entrance hall, very red, unsteady on his tiny feet, making mis-shots at the sleeves of the overcoat that Jacinto and I helped him to put on—inviting my friend with effusive affection to hunt with him in Dalmatia . . .

"I owe my dear Jacinto a good fishing-trip: and I want him to owe me as good a hunting-trip."

Then while we accompanied him, between files of flunkeys, down the vast stairs preceded by the major-domo, with a candelabra of three flares, he continued somewhat glutin-ously:

"A good hunting-trip! What! . . . And we'll also take Zé Fernandes! Good old Fernandes! Zé Fernandes! . . . A splendid dinner, my dear Jacinto. . . . The *Baron de Pauillac* was divine. He should be made a Duc. His Highness the Duc de Pauillac . . . I'll have another slice of the leg of his Grace the Duc de Pauillac! . . . Ah! Ah! Don't come outside! . . . You'll catch cold."

And when he had rolled well back into the seat of his coupé, he went on bellowing still . . .

"That fish, Jacinto, don't forget to recover that fish. It's excellent cold, for lunch, with green sauce!"

Climbing wearily up the steps, overcome with champagne, with sleep overpowering my eyes, I said to my Prince: "It was most amusing, Jacinto. A superb woman—that Verghane. What a pity . . . that lift! . . ."

And Jacinto, in a hollow voice which was half a yawn, half a roar of rage, answered, "A bore! A complete fiasco!"

Three days after this date, my Prince unexpectedly received from Portugal some very disturbing news. Over his ancient family mansion and ranch of Tormes, all along the mountain range, had passed a devastating storm of wind, lightning and floods. Because of the torrential rains, or " for other causes that the experts may find out " (as the manager Silverio exclaimed in his agonized letter) a part of the mountain which stood out over the valley of Carriça had given way, destroying the old church, a little old country church of the sixteenth century, where the ancestors of Jacinto had been ensepulchred since the reign of King Dom Manuel. The venerable bones of these Jacintos were now being buried under a formless mass of earth and rocks. Silverio had just begun, aided by the men of the farm, to try to recover the " precious remains ". But he was anxiously awaiting " His Excellency's further orders."

Jacinto grew pale, and was impressed. That that ancient soil which had remained from since the time of the Goths, could of a sudden roll down in ruin! That those graves of pious peace could be precipitated in thunderous uproar, storm, and darkness down into the depths of the valley! That these bones, each set of which had conserved for centuries its separate name, dates, and history should now be confounded in indistinguishable ruin! . . .

" What a strange thing! What a strange thing! "

All that night he interrogated me about the sierra and the village of Tormes, which I had known since I was a child, because the old mansion with its noble avenues of immemorial birch-trees, rose only two leagues from our own house, on the old road from Guiães to the station and the river. The farm manager at Tormes was the brother-in-law of our steward at Roqueirinha—and many times, since my intimacy with Jacinto, I had entered the huge granite building to value the grain spread through its resounding halls, and to test the new wine in its immense cellars. . . . "And what about the church, Zé Fernandes? Did you ever enter the church? "

" Never : but it was very picturesque with a square tower, quite black, where for many years lived a family of storks . . . What a terrible shock for the storks! "

" What a strange thing! " my Prince murmured ominously.

He telegraphed to Silverio that he should clear the valley of rubble, recover the bones, and rebuild the church: and that for this pious labour he might spend money like the water of a big river, without counting it.

5

MEANWHILE Jacinto, in desperation at so many humiliating disasters, taps which became unsoldered, elevators which stuck, steam which condensed, electricity which faded off, decided to conquer these final rebellions of matter and energy by means of a more powerful accumulation of mechanisms than ever. During the April weeks when the roses were unclosing everywhere, and all the other houses of the Champs-Elysées were basking idly in the sun, our agitated house alone knew no peace, but trembled and rocked incessantly in a drifting dust of débris and demolished stonework, to the sound of breaking stone or hammered iron. In the silent corridors, where it was once so pleasant to smoke a pensive cigarette before lunch, bands of workmen circulated in white blouses, whistling the tune of *Petit Bleu*, and intimidating my footsteps if I tried to cross over in my shirt and slippers for a bath or any other withdrawal. No sooner was some scaffolding carefully manoeuvred, which obstructed the doors, than one's way was immediately blocked with a pile of planks or a heap of metal or a huge tub of cement. Bits of the floor cut open and lifted out showed, as in an open corpse, all the insides of Number 202, its bonework, its sensitive nerves of wire, and its black intestine-tubes of welded iron. Every day a slow cart stopped before the gate, from which the workmen, in shirt-sleeves, unloaded and unpacked their cargoes in an asphalt-paved shed at the bottom of the garden, over the lilac-hedge. Then I would have to go down at the summons of my Prince to admire some new machine which would make our lives easier by establishing our dominion over matter more thoroughly than before.

In the hot weather that followed Ascension Day, we hopefully tested three freezers for mineral waters, soda-waters, and light Médocs, and all three were successively discredited after being assembled and placed in their respective cupboards. With the new strawberries appeared a machine which delicately removed their stalks. Then we got another machine of silver and glass which frantically stirred and mixed up salads. The first time I tried it, it spattered vinegar into the eyes of my Prince, who fled yelling. In the most elementary actions, Jacinto relied upon dynamics to save effort. And now he was all for a machine to button up drawers.

In obedience to his ruling idea, or merely through the despotism of habit, at the same time as accumulating mechanisms, he was also determined to accumulate erudition at all costs. The invasion of books at Number 202! Singly, in pairs, in packets, in cases, withered and wrinkled, or fat and replete with authority, bound in plain, plebeian, yellow paper jackets, or morocco and gold, perpetually, torrentially, they poured in through all the wide doors of the library, where they spread themselves over the carpet, heaped themselves on the chairs, enthroned themselves on strong tables, climbed up to the windows in eager piles, as if, fearing suffocation by their own multitude, they were desperate for space and air. In this learned vault, where only the very highest of the books remained in view over the hedges and fences of other books, throughout the year there gloomed a pensive twilight, even when June was dazzling outside. The library began to overflow the whole of Number 202. You could not open a cupboard or a wardrobe without piles of books falling down in avalanches. You could not rumple a curtain without coming on a heap of books. And my indignation was immense when one day running urgently with my hands holding up my trousers, I was stopped at the very door of the water-closet by a man-high pile of Social Statutes.

But I remember even more bitterly that historical night when returning exhausted from a trip to Versailles, with dust-smarting eyelids, half asleep, I had to dislodge from my bed a fearful Industrial Dictionary in thirty-nine colossal volumes! As I grumblingly arranged my pillows, I cursed the invention of printing, and human discursiveness in general. I was stretching out and dozing, when I nearly broke the precious cap of my knee against the hard back of a volume that had treacherously got wedged between the wall and the mattress. With a bellow of fury I seized it and threw it from me overturning a jug of water, which flooded the costly carpet from Daghestan. Then I must have gone to sleep at once and dreamed—because my feet began moving as if carried by a gentle wind. They seemed to go on stumbling over books in the darkened corridor outside my room; then over the sanded paths of the garden, where the moon shone whitely; then along the Avenue des Champs-Elysées, which was thronged and noisy as on a civic holiday. The Avenue was literally paved with books, and the houses were all made of books. In the foliage of the old chestnut-trees I heard the leaves of a million books being turned. The men and the fine ladies were all dressed in printed paper with titles on their backs and showed, instead of faces, open books, wherein a soft wind slowly turned the pages. At the end in the Place de la Concorde, I saw a steep mountain of books which I tried to climb, now burying my leg in soft damp layers of verses, now knocking my foot on the hard backs of volumes of Exegesis and Criticism. To such vast heights did I climb in this way that I found myself standing amongst the stars and planets. They rolled serenely around, enormous and silent, and all of them encrusted with layers of books, between which escaped every now and again a tiny ray of anxious, suffocated light. Then I rose to Paradise. I am sure it was Paradise: for there with my eyes of mortal clay I beheld the Ancient of Eternity, he that has no Morning nor Evening. In a radiance which emanated from him more brightly than all other radiances, between deep bookshelves of gold packed with codices and old manuscripts, seated upon ancient folios, with the flakes of his infinite beard trailing over reams of pamphlets, brochures, gazettes and catalogues—the All-Highest sat reading. Leaning His super-divine forehead which conceived the world, on the super-powerful hand which created it—the Creator was reading and smiling. I dared, shivering with sacred horror, to peep over His radiant shoulder. The book was a popular edition, paper-covered. The Eternal was reading Voltaire in the new, three-franc, cheap edition, and smiling. A door lit up, creaking open as if someone was entering Paradise. I thought it must be a new saint arriving from the earth. It was Jacinto with a cigar and a buttonhole of carnations, carrying under his arm three spicy novels which the Princesse de Caraman had lent him to read.

During one of these busy weeks, however, my attention was diverted from my fascinating Jacinto. A guest at Number 202, I still kept my trunk and my linen there. Still camped beneath the banner of my Prince, I occasionally made raids on his sumptuous dinner table. But my soul, my stultified soul, and my body, my stultified body, had gone to live at Number 16 Rue Helder on the fourth floor, the left-hand door.

One day I was walking down the Boulevard de la Madeleine, pleasantly at peace in my ideas and feelings, when I espied in front of the omnibus station, prowling to and fro with a slow feline gait, a strange, lean creature, very dark, almost tanned brown, with two deep, sad, taciturn eyes, a huge bush of shaggy, crisp, yellowish hair, under an old hat with black feathers. I stopped as if I had received a blow in the stomach. The creature passed by with a slow prowl, like that of a black cat on the eaves of an overhanging roof in the January moonlight. Two deep wells could not glitter more blackly or secretively than did those taciturn, black eyes. I scarcely remember how I grazed her silken dress, shining and greasy in folds; nor how I muttered a request through gritted teeth; nor how, morosely and silently as two condemned people, we went up to a partition of the dreary and mournful Café Durand. In front of the mirror, this strange creature took off her hat, and her cape spangled with glass beads. The polished, worn silk was cracked at her sharp elbows. Her shock of hair was immense and of two different tones, half of it golden, half of it of more brown, like the crust of a pastry that is being taken hot from the oven.

With a nervous laugh I seized her long, cold fingers.

"What is your name?" I asked.

Seriously and solemnly she said: "Madame Colombe, 16 Rue Helder, fourth floor, left-hand door."

I (unhappy Zé Fernandes) also began to feel very serious, possessed with a solemn emotion as if in that cheap café apartment we had become involved in the majesty of a sacrament.

From the door which was lightly pushed open, a fat-faced waiter advanced. I ordered a lobster, duck with pimientos, and a bottle of Burgundy. It was only when we had finished the duck that, convulsively crumpling the tablecloth, I tremblingly kissed her on the mouth, with a deep and terrible kiss, in which were mingled saliva and the taste of chillies. After that, in an open cab in the cool soft breath of a thunderstorm, we went up the Avenue des Champs-Elysées. When we came in front of 202 I murmured : " I live here all the year round." On seeing the palatial building, she immediately began to rub her crisp yellow hair against my beard with great affection —so that I yelled desperately to the cabman : " Number 16 Rue Helder, fourth floor, left-hand door."

I loved that creature. I loved her with Love, with every kind of Love that is composed in the word Love, divine Love, human Love, bestial Love. I loved her as Saint Anthony loved the Virgin, as Romeo loved Juliet, and as the billy-goat loves the she-goat. She was stupid, she was unhappy. Deliciously I quenched my gaiety in the ashes of her sorrow : with ineffable delight I sunk my intellect into the density of her stupidity. For seven furious weeks I lost entirely the consciousness of myself as Zé Fernandes—Fernandes de Noronha e Sande, of Guiães. Now I was merely a piece of wax that was melting, with delicious horror, in a red and roaring furnace : now I was a hungry bonfire in which crackled, flared and crumbled to ashes a heap of dry faggots. From those days of sordid sublimity, I still preserve the memory of a bedroom draped with grimy cretonne, a lilac-coloured dressing-gown, vague bottles of beer standing on the marble of a washstand, and of a swarthy body with creaking joints and hair on its chest. There also survives in my memory the sensation of incessant and perceptible despoilment, of throwing into a lap which was hollowed between a sunken belly and two thin knees, my gold watch with its trinkets and chain, my rings, my saphire studs and cufflinks, and ninety-five golden guineas which I had brought in a deerskin moneybelt from Guiães. Of the solid, decorous, well-furnished Zé Fernandes, there only remained a plundered corpse wandering through a dream with weak legs and frothing lips.

Then, one afternoon, climbing with accustomed eagerness the stairs of Number 16 Rue Helder, I found the door locked : the little card with "Madame Colombe" which had been pinned to the door, which I always read with such devotion and which was her signboard, had been taken from its place . . . The whole of my being shook as if Paris itself were suffering an earthquake! It was as if the gates of the World were shut in my face! On the other side of it were nations, cities, life, God, and Herself. I was left alone, stranded on the stairway-landing of non-existence. I seemed to roll down those stairs with the incoherent crashes of a toppling stone till I came to the cubicle of the concierge and her man, who were playing cards in blissful indolence, as if no such disaster had dismantled the Universe.

The bearded gossip slowly arranged her cards :

"She doesn't live here now," she said. "She went off this morning to another country . . . and another pig along with her! "

For another country! With another pig! . . . Empty, darkly empty of all thought, feeling . . . I seemed to float upside down like an empty cask, in the urgent current of the Boulevard, till I stranded myself on a seat and covered my eyes with my hands. Late, very late, when the iron shutters of the shops were being pulled down with thunderous din, there rose up from the ruins and rubble of my devastated being, that eternal survivor of all ruin and disaster—the idea of supper! I went into the Café Durand with the numbed steps of a resuscitated corpse. And, in remembrance, though it excruciated my very soul, I ordered lobster, duck with pimientos, and Burgundy. But in undoing my collar, which was damp with the sweaty heat of a July afternoon in the dust of the Madeleine, I thought disconsolately, "By God! What a terrible thirst this misfortune has given me," and I beckoned the waiter meekly: "Before you bring the Burgundy, I'll have a bottle of champagne, with ice, and a large

66

glass." I think that champagne must have been bottled in Heaven where flows forever the fresh fount of consolation: and that in the blessed bottle that I had, before it was corked, a considerable dose of that ineffable fountain must have been poured. Lord, what a transcendent treat was that noble glass, so blurred, so frosted, so foam-tufted, so piercing, in its aura of golden fire! And after that—the Burgundy! And after that—the bottle of brandy! And after that the breathless desire to thrash the pig that ran away with the other pig. In a closed cab which took me at a gallop to Number 202, I did not repress this righteous impulse, but with my farm-hand fists struck out thunderous blows at the cushions around me, where it seemed I saw, in fury, the huge bush of yellow hair wherein my soul was lost one evening, fluttered and struggled for two months, and soiled itself for ever.

When the cab arrived at 202 I was still so desperately thumping the ungrateful little beast, that the coachman called out for the servants who ran to support me and on whose servile shoulders I expended the last exhausted and feeble blows of my fury.

Once upstairs I repelled with indignation the solicitude of Cricket, who offered me the insult of a cup of camomile tea. Stretched out on the ancestral bed of Dom "Galleon", with my boots on my pillow and my hat over my eyes, I laughed a sad laugh at this burlesque world of Jacintos and Colombes. Suddenly I felt a horrible anguish. It was She. It was Madame Colombe who appeared out the flame of the candle, jumped on my bed, undid my waistcoat, sunk herself into my breast, put her mouth to my heart, and began to suck my blood from it in long, slow gulps. Certain of death now, I began to scream for my aunt Vicência; I hung from the bed to try to sink into my sepulchre which I dimly discerned beneath me on the carpet, through the final fog of death—a little round sepulchre, glazed, made of porcelain, with a handle. And over my own sepulchre, which so irreverently chose to resemble a chamber-pot, I vomited the lobster, the duck with pimientos and the Burgundy. Then after a superhuman effort, with the roar of a lion, feeling that not only my innards but my very soul were emptying themselves in the process, I

67

vomited up Madame Colombe herself . . . I put my hat back over my eyes so as not to feel the rays of the sun. It was a new Sun, a spiritual Sun which was rising over my life. I slept like a child softly rocked in a cradle of wicker by my Guardian Angel.

That morning I scrubbed my skin in a deep hot bath perfumed with all the aromatics of Number 202 from the fresh leaves of Indian verbena to the concentrated essence of French jasmin. I then washed my soul in a long letter, which had just arrived that day from Aunt Vicência recounting the affairs of our home, the promise of a rich vintage that year, of the cherry jam which had never been better, of the gay bonfire they had had in the courtyard on Saint John's Eve, and of the beautiful, fat, long-haired baby which Heaven had sent to my god-child Joaninha. After that, I sat at the window, feeling fresh and clean in mind and body, in a white silken jacket, drinking tea from Nai-Po, and breathing the roses from the garden, which had been revived by the rain of that morning. I reflected in amused surprise that I had been making a beast of myself with a thin, bronzed scarecrow for seven whole weeks. And I concluded that I must have been suffering from a long fever, a fever of the soul, a fever of the flesh, a fever of the imagination, caught in a dirty puddle of Paris—one of those puddles which are formed round about Paris by the stagnant waters, slime, dirt, fungi, and worms of a civilization which is rotting away.

My spirit, cured completely of its ill, then turned immediately as a magnetised needle turns to the north, towards my complicated Prince, of whom I had glimpses during the latter weeks of my sentimental infection, drooping wearily on sofas or wandering aimlessly across the library amongst his thirty thousand volumes, with long-drawn yawns of inertia and vacuity. In my unworthy preoccupation, I had spared him no more attention than to ask carelessly : " What's up? " And he in his morose dejection had only replied drily, " It's the heat."

On that morning of my liberation, on going into his room before lunch, I found him with *Figaro* open on his stomach, the agenda lying on the floor, all his features sunk in gloom, and his feet abandoned in supreme melancholy to the pedicurist who was polishing his toenails. Certainly my glance, reanimated and purified, together with the coolness and whiteness of my suit, which reflected the serenity of my feelings, and the harmony and sureness which visibly moved throughout my entire being at that moment—made an impression on my Prince, the sharpness of whose perceptions was never impaired by his melancholy. He softly raised his arm:

" And what about this caprice of yours? "

I released at him the full brightness of a laugh of victory.

" Dead! As dead as the Duke of Marlborough! Dead and buried. Rest in peace or rather roll in peace—for by now it must be gaily rolling down some underground sewer! "

Jacinto yawned and murmured:

" Oh, that Zé Fernandes de Noronha e Sande! . . . "

And in my name, my noble name, thus smothered in a yawn with indifferent irony, could be summed up the whole of the interest of sympathy which my Prince had felt for the sordid tortures with which my heart had struggled during all these weeks. I perceived clearly that Jacinto was passing through a dense fog of boredom, so dense a fog, and one which enveloped him so completely in its soft density, that the triumphs or sufferings of a comrade could not move him, but remained remote, intangible and unreal, separated from his sensibility with deep layers of cotton-wool. Poor Prince of Good Fortune, prostrate on the sofa of inertia, with his feet in the lap of a pedicurist! What a muddy state of dejection to fall into after all his valiant refortification of the abundant mechanisms of 202, in his war against Energy and Matter. He took no further trouble to hide this dejection from his old friend Zé Fernandes, after we had re-established that community of life, which I had so foolishly interrupted that afternoon, in front of the omnibus station, in the Madeleine, that sink of immorality.

He did not make an open confession of his dejection. The elegant and reserved Jacinto did not wring his hands crying " Oh life accursed! " There were expressions indicating surfeit. There were the gestures he made, as if to repel the importunity of things in general. Sometimes a sullen and

69

determined immobility in the depths of a divan, from which, it seemed, he would never disinter himself except for the eternal sleep he so much desired. Then there were those great hollow yawns with which he underlined every step he took. Above all, there was that perpetual grumbling reply to everything which had become a part of his nature . . . " What a bore! " . . . " What for? " . . . " It's not worth the trouble."

One night while taking off my boots in my bedroom I consulted Cricket.

" Jacinto is so depressed, so dejected . . . What can it be, Cricket? "

The venerable negro said with immense conviction :

" His Excellency suffers from Surfeit! "

It was surfeit. My Prince was secretly suffering from a surfeit of Paris : and in the City, that symbolical City, outside of which (as he had so often cried, in his moments of illumination) a man of the nineteenth century could never fully savour the delights of living—in this same City, he could no longer find any form of life, spiritual or social, that could interest him enough to be worth the trouble of a short ride in a carriage. Poor Jacinto! An old newspaper, seventy times re-read from the news to the advertisements, with its print fading and its folds frayed and torn, could not disgust a recluse whose only intellectual aliment it had been for years in his solitude, so much as Paris disgusted and bored my dear friend. If, during that summer, I captiously dragged him to a Café-Concert or to the festive Pavillon d'Armenonville, Jacinto, stuck to his chair, with a wonderful buttonhole of orchids in his jacket and his fine hands wearily clutching his gold-handled stick, would remain so solemnly dismal, that, in the end, out of sheer compassion, I would rise from my seat and liberate him, relieved by his haste in making off, like that of a caged bird which has suddenly been set free. Rarely (but then with the violent effort of a dead man jumping from a grave) did he ever descend on the various Clubs to which he belonged, at the end of the Champs-Elysées. He took no more interest in his Societies or Companies, nor in the *Telephones of Constantinople*, nor in *Esoteric Religions* nor in the *Bazaar of Spiritualism,* whose unopened letters piled themselves on the ebony table where they were dusted by Cricket as if they were the dregs left over from a life that was already finished. He was also slowly severing all his friendships. The pages of the rose-coloured agenda remained spotless and white. And if sometimes he yielded to a ride in the mail coach, or an invitation to some friendly castle on the outskirts of Paris, it was so unwillingly, and with such an effort in even putting on his light overcoat, that I was reminded of a man I once knew who, after a huge country meal which filled him to bursting, had still (in obedience to some digestive dogma of his own) to eat a huge sweet shaped like a lamprey. Lying about the house, behind the security of closed doors and well-defended against all intrusions from the outside world, would have been a pleasure to my Prince if his own Number 202, with all its superfluity of civilization, had not oppressed him, *from inside its own walls,* with a sense of suffocation and congestion. That July was boiling hot, and all the brocades, all his round and puffy pieces of furniture, all his metal gadgets and all his books, palled on him so heavily that he kept staring out of the windows to try to prolong the space, light and fresh air around him. But it was the dust, peppery and dirty, that, blown around in dreary gusts, infuriated him the most.

" Oh, this City dust!" he cried in his anger.

" But why don't we go to Fontainebleau, or Montmorency, or . . ."

" What! The Country? The Country? " he roared.

And his furrowed face flashed such indignation after his bellow of rage, that I cowered humbly in penitence for the outrageous insult which I had just offered to the Prince of whom I was so fond. Unhappy Prince! Smoking his gilded Yaka cigarette, he wandered through the rooms, slowly and wearily, like someone in a foreign land without any occupation or attachment. These purposeless, indifferent paces of his monotonously brought him back again and again to his centre, to the green cabinet, to the ebony-panelled library, where " Civilization had been accumulated in its maximum proportions " to enable him " to extract the maximum proportion of delight in living ". He looked around him with a surfeited gaze. No interest or curiosity tempted his hands which lay buried in the pockets of his coat, in the inertia of defeat. Nothing could be more sadly instructive than the sight of this supremely gifted man of the nineteenth century in the midst of all the instruments that strengthened his organs, sharpened his perceptions, and reinforced his senses, all these wires which disciplined the Universal Forces to his service, and the fifty thousand volumes filled with the knowledge of centuries—standing there defeated, with his hands in his pockets, and reflecting visibly in his facial expression and the flabby indecision of his yawns, the boredom and trouble he experienced in merely keeping alive.

6

EVERY afternoon, cultivating one of those intimacies which, amongst all things that weary us, never grow wearisome, Jacinto with devoted regularity, called on Madame Oriol at four o'clock—because this flower of Parisianism remained in Paris, even after the Grand Prix, so as to fade quietly into the calm of the swept-out city. But one of these afternoons, the telephone rang to tell Jacinto that his sweet friend was going that evening to Enghien with the Trèves. (These noble people enjoyed their summers in a beautiful white lakeside house belonging to Ephraim, and surrounded by white roses).

It was a silent Sunday, misty and mild, inviting one to the pleasures of melancholy, and I suggested to Jacinto that we should go up to the Basilica of the Sacré Coeur then in construction on the heights of Montmartre.

" It would be a bore, Zé Fernandes . . . "

" Come on ! I've never seen the Basilica ! "

" All right ! All right ! Let's go to the Basilica, you man of Fate, Zé Fernandes Noronha e Sande."

As last we came to the steep, narrow-streeted quarters beyond the church of Saint Vincent de Paul, where there was a countrified quietude, with old walls enclosing almost rural back-yards, uncombed women sewing on their doorsteps, unharnessed carts outside wine-shops, stray hens picking in the dust, wet swaddling clothes drying on reed fences. My friend smiled at the easy-going freedom and simplicity of such things.

The victoria stopped in front of a huge flight of steps which had to be climbed cutting through many narrow alleys and lanes up to the esplanade, where, surrounded with scaffolding, rose the immense Basilica. On every ramp of the steps were stalls as for some religious fair, crowded with images, scupulars, Hearts of Jesus embroidered with silk, and bright clusters of Rosaries. In the corners, stooping old women mumbled their *Aves*. Two Fathers came down the steps, laughing and taking snuff. A bell tinkled in the grey mildness of the afternoon. And Jacinto murmured with a certain pleasure: "It's curious." But the Basilica above did not interest us; white and stern, hidden in scaffoldings and built with new stone that was, as yet, without a soul. So Jacinto, moved by a truly Jacintian impulse, began to walk eagerly to the edge of the terrace in order to contemplate the view of Paris. Under the ashen sky, on the ash-coloured plain, the ash-grey city lay like a layer of cement, and tiles, and slates. In its immense immobility and silence, here and there, a flimsy wisp of smoke finer than that which trails from a half-dead cinder, was the only visible trace of all its magnificent life and energy.

Then I began to tease my Prince. That, then, was the City, the august Creation of Humanity! Behold it there, my fine Jacinto! A few moments before we had left it prodigiously alive, full of strong people, with all its powerful organs functioning, filled with wealth, resplendent with wisdom, in the triumphal fulness of its pride, like the Queen of the World crowned with grace. And now Jacinto and I had merely climbed a hill, and looked around, and listened: and of the whole of that strident and radiant Civilization, we could not perceive a single murmur or sparkle! And Number 202, the superb Number 202, with its wires, its gadgets, its machines and its fifty thousand books? Sunk and lost in a confusion of roofs and ashes. From the height of a hundred metres how little to contemplate was there in all this immense work of mankind, to raise which the human worker had panted and gasped with such agonizing effort. What about it, Jacinto? Where is your vast store served by three thousand assistants? Or your bank where clinks the gold of the whole world? Or your libraries stuffed with the knowledge of centuries? All is melted in a dark stain which seems to soil the face of the earth. To the weak eyes of a mere Zé Fernandes, once he has climbed, smoking his cigarette, to the top of an outlying hill —the whole sublime edifice of all the ages is nothing more than a dunghill of the consistency and colour of the final dust . . . What it will be then in the eyes of God?

After these taunts which I launched at my Prince with affable malice, he muttered pensively: "Yes. Perhaps it is all an illusion . . . And perhaps the City is the greatest illusion of all!"

To find myself so easily victorious, I redoubled my eloquence. Yes, my Prince, an illusion! And the most bitter of all illusions, because man thinks that in the City he founds the base of all his grandeur, but in the City he has only the source of all his misery. Look, Jacinto! It was in the City that man lost his strength and the harmonious beauty of his body: he became withered and lean, or obese and drowned in his own grease, with bones as soft as rags, with eyeglasses, wigs, and dentures of lead, bloodless, without brawn, twisted and hunchbacked—a being in whom a horrified God would find great difficulty in recognizing the slim, sturdy, noble Adam of His creation. In the City the moral liberty of man came to an end. Every morning the City imposes a necessity on him: and every necessity throws him upon a dependency: if he is poor and subordinate, his life is one endless round of soliciting, flattering, bowing, cringing, and enduring: if he is rich and powerful, like you, Jacinto, Society immediately enmeshes him in a web of tradition, precepts, conventions, ceremonies, customs, rites, and a servitude of far greater discipline than that of a prison or barracks. His peace of mind (such a valuable treasure that it is God's most precious gift to His Saints) where is it, my dear Jacinto? Submerged forever in this desperate battle for bread, for fame, for power, for pleasure, or for the slippery discs of gold! How can you ever have happiness in the City for these millions of beings who are forever rioting in the breathless occupation of *wanting*, *needing*, and *desiring*, and who, never satisfying the need or desire, incessantly feel the disappointment, despair and defeat of it? The most genuinely human feelings become dehumanized in the City. See, Jacinto! They are like lanterns which the rough wind of social life never allows to burn with serenity or clearness: here one is shaken and made to tremble: there one is brutally extinguished: and there one flares up with unnatural violence. Friendships are never more deep than alliances of common interest, in the anxious hour of defence or in the eager hour of attack; it binds them with a momentary hasty tie, which will snap at the first sign of rivalry or pride. And what is Love in the City, my dear Jacinto? Just consider those vast shops with mirrors wherein the noble flesh of Eve is sold on tariff by the pound, as if it were mutton or beef. Consider this old God of Hymen who goes around, not with the ardent and waving torch of passion, but the tight-clasped purse of the dowry! See that group which slinks away from the open roads down which the fauns chase the nymphs according to the sane laws of nature, and sorrowfully seeks the dismal recesses of Sodom and Lesbos! But what the City most destroys in Man is his intelligence, because it either imprisons him within the pale of banality or else forces him out into the wastes of eccentricity and extravagance. In the dense and restless layer of Ideas and Formulas which constitute the mental atmosphere of the City, the man who breathes it and is completely surrounded with it, can only express what has already been expressed: or else, to distinguish himself from the flat and dull-grey boredom of routine and climb the crazy scaffold of renown, he must invent, at the cost of much groaning effort, some novel deformity which will shock and arrest the crowd like some freakish monster at a fair. Most are like sheep, trampling the same track, bleating the same bleat, with their muzzles hanging in the same dust, where they tread, in single file, the same footprints of these who have gone before them. Some are monkeys, jumping about on the tops of gaily-

75

coloured poles with strange antics and somersaults. And so in the City a creation so anti-natural that you have nought but pitch, wood, felt or linoleum for your soil, and nothing but coal smoke for a sky, the people live in layers like the cloth stored in the shops, and the light comes through tubes, and lies are whispered along the wires—and man himself appears an anti-human creature without beauty, without strength, without freedom, without true feeling, like a slave or an imprudent mime . . . And there, my fine Jacinto, you have the long and the short of a fine City!

Before these hoary and antiquated invectives let fly by every bucolic moralist for centuries, since the time of Hesiod —my Prince meekly bowed his neck, as if they had been original, unexpected sayings, which had burst out of some divine revelation on the Mount of Montmartre.

"Yes," he said, with a sigh, "The City! It may well be a perverse illusion after all."

I insisted, with redundancy, pushing out my fists and thoroughly enjoying my shallow and trite philosophizings:

"If this illusion of the City were to bring any happiness to those who believe in it, well and good. . . . But no! Only a very small and brilliant caste enjoy in the City any of the pleasures which derive from City life. The rest, the obscure, immense *plebs*, can only suffer and they can only suffer those especial sufferings that are derived from city life. From this terrace beside this sumptuous Basilica consecrated to the Heart that loved and bled for the Poor, we can see well the dismal rows of houses where the common people cower beneath that immemorial opprobrium from which neither religions, nor philosophies, nor morals, nor their own brutal violence can ever liberate them. There they lie scattered about the city like vile manure which fertilizes the City. Centuries roll by. The same dirty rags cover their bodies, and always beneath those rags, all through the long day, their men will drudge and their women will weep and whimper for ever. How this labour of theirs edifies and enriches the City! Look at it, covered with beautiful dwellings in which they can never take shelter: stacked with stuffs in which they can never clothe themselves: crammed with food that

76

will never satisfy their hunger. For them there is only the snow . . . the snow falls, numbs, and buries the children nestling under the seats in the squares, or sheltering under the arches of bridges. The snow falls, dumb and white in the darkness. The children freeze in their rags. The police go round—attentive that nobody shall disturb those who love the snow and the ice because it makes them feel so snug indoors, and above all because they can go skating on the ponds of the Bois de Boulogne with fur coats worth three thousand francs. But what of that, Jacinto? Your Civilization incessantly demands fêtes and pomps which it can only obtain in this bitter social discord if Capital gives to Labour, for every panting effort it makes, a much-haggled-for, grudging crumb of bread. It is therefore irremediable that the people should slave and suffer. Its overworked misery is the very condition on which depends the serene splendour of the City. In their bowls steam their precise rations of soup—otherwise rich helpings of truffles and *foie gras* would never be able to appear on silver dishes to the pride and glory of Civilization. There are tatters on the ragpickers—so that the Madame Oriols can undulate sweetly up the stairs of the Opera in silks and laces. There are frozen hands that stretch out and sunken lips that thank you for the magnanimous gift of a ha'penny—so that the Ephraims can have ten million pounds in the Bank of France, warm themselves at the rich flames of aromatic woods, and give their concubines (grand-daughters of the Dukes of Athens) collars of pearls and sapphires. A whole people and its little ones weep with hunger—that the Jacintos, in January, may toy, yawningly, on plates of Dresden china, with strawberries frozen in champagne and reanimated by the evaporation of a film of ether!

"And I have eaten your strawberries too, Jacinto. Oh, miserable me and you!"

He also muttered with a desolated air: "It's horrible! We ate those strawberries . . . and perhaps through mistaken ideas!"

Pensively he left the edge of the terrace as if the presence of the City, extended over the plain, was scandalous to him. Then we began to walk slowly away under the ashen grey sky of the evening, philosophizing together and realizing that for the iniquities of which we spoke, there never had been any human remedy produced by human effort.

"Ah, the Ephraims and the Trèves—the shadowy sharks of the human sea, would only cease from their depredations if some celestial influence, by the operation of a new miracle, more wondrous than those of old, could convert their souls. The bourgeois triumphs in his strength, hardened in all sin—and the complaints of Humanitarians, the reasoning of Logicians, and the bombs of Anarchists, are alike impotent against him. Only divine kindness could soften so hard a granite. Now you see the hope of the world pinned on the Messiah! . . . One certainly did descend from the highest heavens : and to prove his mandate, entered the world meekly through the door of a stable. But his passage among men was so brief! A tender sermon on a mountain at the end of a smiling afternoon : a moderate rebuke to the Pharisees who were then editing the *Boulevard* : a few cuts of the switch for the pedlar-Ephraims of the Temple : and then through the terrible gates of Death a radiant flight back to heaven. This adorable Son of God was in too much of a hurry to return to the house of his Father. The men to whom he entrusted the continuation of his work had fallen a prey to the influences of the Ephraims and the Trèves of this world, and had soon forgotten the Sermons on the Mount and at the Lake of Tiberias—and they in turn clothed themselves in purple and became Bishops and Popes, who allied themselves with oppression, and founded the duration of their Kingdom upon the misery of the homeless and the breadless poor. So the whole work of Redemption must begin anew. Jesus, or Guatama, or Krishna, or some other of those sons of God who, conceived in the breasts of virgins, come to life in the flowery orchards of Asia—should descend to this earth anew. Will he come—the so-long-desired? Perhaps already some grave King of the Orient has seen a star, taken the myrrh in his royal hands, and mounted his dromedary. Perhaps even in the precincts of that hard-hearted City where Caraphas sups with the Magdalene nightly *chez* Paillard, an unseen angel glides with low flight looking for a humble stable. And, from

78

far away, without a farm-hand to goad them, come trotting
a cow, an ox and a donkey!"

" Do you know that, Jacinto? "

No. Jacinto did not know it. He wanted to light a cigar.
I lit him a match. We walked round the terrace scattering
other substantial ideas around us, which the wind dispersed
like smoke. Then we were on the point of entering the
Basilica when a fat sacristan with a velvet cap closed the
door and a Father passed us burying his Breviary in his pocket
with a final gesture of weariness as if for ever.

" I'm feeling thirsty, Jacinto—it was that tremendous burst
of philosophy."

We went down the steps, which were furnished like a
religious fair. My pensive friend bought a picture of the
Basilica. We jumped into a victoria when someone called
out loudly, as if in surprise—" Jacinto!"

My Prince opened his arms, himself overcome with surprise: " Maurice!"

In great excitement, Jacinto crossed the road to a café,
where, under a tent of checkered canvas, a robust-looking
man with a pointed beard was stirring a glass of absinthe,
with his straw hat tilted back on his nape, his blazer open
over an open silk shirt, tieless, and looking as if he were
taking a rest on his own garden seat.

Both of them, after shaking hands, wondered at this chance
meeting on a Sunday afternoon in the middle of the Summer
vacation, on the heights of Montmartre.

" Oh, I'm at home here, in my own quarter," gaily
exclaimed Maurice . . . *"en famille,* and in my bedroom
slippers, as you see. It is three months since I ascended these
heights of Truth . . . but to see you here on this Holy Mount,
you profane dweller of the plain and the streets of
Israel!"

My Prince produced me, saying: " Why, I came here to
accompany my friend here on his pilgrimage to the Basilica.
. . . This is my friend, Zé Fernandes . . . Maurice de Mayolle,
an old comrade."

Monsieur de Mayolle (who with his broad face and nobly
large nose resembled Francis de Valois, the King of France)

raised his straw hat. He drew up a chair insisting that we join him in a hock or an absinthe.

" Have a hock, Zé Fernandes," Jacinto reminded me. " You were complaining of thirst "

I ran my tongue over my lips which were drier than parchment and replied : " I'm keeping that thirst for supper time, to punish it with frosted wine."

Maurice greeted, with the silence of admiration, this well-advised shrewdness of my taste. Then he addressed my Prince :

" It is three years since I saw you, Jacinto . . . How can that be possible in such a little village as Paris, and one which you almost overshadow in your single self? "

" Life, Maurice, is so scattered about everywhere . . . Yes, by jove! It must be three years since we met, at the Lamotte-Orcels' house. Do you still visit that sanctuary? "

Maurice made a wide scornful gesture which seemed to shake off the world.

" Oh, it's more than a year since I separated myself from that heretical *canaille* . . . A mob without discipline. No fixity of purpose, horrifying dilettantism, a complete and comical lack of any basis of experience! When you last went to the Lamotte-Orcels, what was the rage with them? "

Jacinto seemed to search for his memory in the hairs of his moustache : then he said : " Now I remember. . . . It was Wagnerian mythology : Ragnarsk, the Edda, and the Nornies. . . . Plenty of Pre-Raphaelitism, too. Mantegna, and Fra Angelico . . . and, in morals, it was Renan . . ."

Maurice shrugged his shoulders : " All that belonged to the dead past almost as far gone as the lake-dwellers and the troglodites Then Madame Lamotte-Orcel draped her drawing room with William Morris velvets, representing enormous artichokes, on a saffron background. . . . As for Renanism it is already as dead as Cartesianism. . . . And were you with us when we were going in for the cult of the Ego? "

My Prince answered laughing : " Oh yes, I did cultivate it for a time."

" Well and good. Soon after Eddic mythology, came Hartmanism, the Unconscious. Then Nietzschism, a sort of spiritual Feudalism. Then Tolstoyism, an immense delirium of neo-cenobite renouncement. I can still remember a scarecrow of a Slav, with a huge scurfy mop of mane, who threw terrifying glances at the decolleté evening dress of the poor Comtesse d'Arche, and who groaned at us, pointing his finger —'Let us humbly seek the light, very low down, in the dust of the earth!' . . . Then at dessert we drank in the delights of humility and servile labour along with that ice-granulated champagne Marceaux, that Matilde used to serve in cups made in the shape of the Holy Grail! Then came Emersonism. But the worst plague of all was Ibsenism! In short, my lad, that place was a veritable Babel of Ethics and Aesthetics! Paris seemed to have gone mad. There were even some eccentrics who took up Diabolism. And some of our pretty young friends degenerated with Phallism, a sort of hotch-potch of mistico-rascality of whom the prophet was that same poor La Carte who afterwards became a White Father and now lives in the Sahara . . . That was a real horror . . . Then one afternoon all of a sudden, the whole mob of them went crazy about Ruskinism."

I, holding on to my walking-stick which was well planted on the ground, felt as if a cyclone was whirling around in my skull. Even Jacinto murmured in wide-eyed amazement: "Ruskinism? What's that?"

"Yes, the old Ruskin . . . John Ruskin!"

"Oh, you mean the *Seven Lamps of Architecture* . . . *The Garland of Wild Olive* . . . and the Cult of Beauty," said Jacinto, understanding him.

"Yes, the Cult of Beauty," Maurice confirmed him. "But by that time I was sick of chasing these vain clouds and shadows . . . I was already treading on solid, more fertile ground."

He slowly sipped his absinthe, closing his eyelids. Jacinto waited with his fine nostrils dilated, as if to smell the Flower of Novelty which was about to burst from the bud.

"What then? What then?" he asked.

But the other murmured somewhat incoherently, through the reticences in which he veiled himself:

"Well, I came here . . . up to Montmarte . . . I have a

friend, you see, who has been all over India. He lived with the Toddas in the monasteries of Garma Khian and Dashi-Lumbo, where he studied under Gegen-Chutu in the sacred retreat of Urga . . . Now this Gegen-Chutu was the sixteenth incarnation of Guatama and is therefore accordingly a Boddi-Sattva . . . We work. We are seekers. Not for visions, but for facts, ancient experiences which come down to us perhaps from the time of Krishna . . ."

After these names which exhaled a faint perfume of anti-quated rites, he set aside his chair. Standing and absently letting fall on the table some silver and copper coins to pay for his absinthes, he continued with his eyes turned to Jacinto, but really lost in remoter visions . . .

"In short, everything is reduced to the supreme develop-ment of the Will within the limits of the supreme purity of life. That is the whole science and power of the Hindu Masters—but the absolute purity of life, that's the obstacle: that's where the struggle comes in. Even the desert does not suffice for that, nor even the woods surrounding the most ancient temple in Tibet. But even so, Jacinto, we have obtained very extraordinary results. You know Tyndall's experiment with sensitive flames. That poor little chemist, in demonstrating the vibrations of sound, almost passed through the very doorway to Esoteric Truth. But what do you expect? The scientist remained on this side of it amongst his retorts and tubes. But we have been beyond that. We have verified the *waves and vibrations of the Will*! In front of us, by means of the energy projected by my comrade's will, and in cadence with his commands, a flame ten feet high undulated rhythmically, crept horizontally along the ground, threw off burning tongues, licked the top of a high wall, went black and roared with fury, turned vertically silent and radiant, and suddenly vanished in a streak of soot!"

Then this strange fellow with his hat on the back of his head and his arms stretched out wide on each side, remained staring wide-eyed, as if in a renewal of the tranced amaze-ment which he had first felt at the sight of this prodigy. After that, he suddenly recovered his serene and easy-going manner, lit a cigarette, and went on:

" One of these mornings I'll come to lunch with you at Number 202, and bring my friend. He only eats rice, and a little salad or fruit. We shall then converse together. You have a copy of the *Sepher-Zerijak* and another of the *Targum d'Onkelas*. We shall need to turn their pages."

He shook the hand of my Prince, cordially saluted this gaping and astounded Zé Fernandes, and serenely went his way along the street, with his straw hat on the back of his head, and his hands in his pockets, just like a natural man in natural surroundings.

" Jacinto! For God's sake! Who on earth is this weird wizard or warlock? . . . Who is he, in the Holy Name of God? "

Leaning back in the cab which we had summoned my Prince told me all about him. He was a noble and loyal fellow, very rich and very intelligent and descended from the Dukes of Septimania. Then he murmured after a customary yawn :

" The supreme development of the will. Theosophy. Esoteric Buddhism. Asperations. Disillusionment. I've tried it . . . and it's a horrible bore."

We crossed the noise of Paris in silence, under the closeness of the summer twilight, to dine in the Bois at the Pavillon d'Armenonville where the gipsies, seeing Jacinto, struck up the *Liberal Anthem* with passionate languor, in a cadence of agonized and harsh *czarda*.

I said, regally unfolding my table-napkin : " Now for that little bottle of frosted wine to quench my rich thirst! I have merited it fully, so splendidly have I philosophized . . . I really believe I have at last really established in the heart of my Prince a sane and healthy horror of the City."

My Prince was running through the wine list and stroking his moustache, while the wine waiter stooped reverently beside him.

" Tell them to ice two bottles of champagne Saint Marceau. But before that, bring an old Barsac, not iced, but just cool . . . with a bottle of Evian water . . . No, Busrang water! . . . Oh well, a bottle of Evian *and* a bottle of Busrang . . . and we'll lead off with a Bock each."

Then yawning and unbuttoning his grey jacket he said:
" I've decided now to build a house on the heights of
Montmartre with a watch-tower on top, made of glass and
iron, where I can rest in the evenings and dominate the City."

7

JULY ended with refreshing and consoling showers of rain. I
was thinking of finally realizing my tour of the cities of
Europe, which I had so often postponed on account of the
ambushes of the world and the flesh. But suddenly Jacinto
began to insist on my accompanying him every afternoon,
when he went to Madame Oriol's. And I understood that my
Prince (following the example of the divine Achilles who,
while sleeping with the insipid white Briseïs in his tent, yet
could never dispense with the comradeship of Patroclus)
wished for the presence, the comfort, and the support of
Friendship during the decline and death of Love. Poor Jacinto!
Early each morning he would compact for this hour of
quietude and tenderness. And so we always encountered this
superfine lady each afternoon, expecting us, all alone, in that
room of the Rue de Lisbonne, in which Jacinto and I could
hardly find room to breathe, suffocated as we were with the
confusion of baskets of flowers, of golden ornaments,
Japanese monsters, mixed with the fragile Saxe porcelain,
the furs and pelts of wild beasts stretched out by slumbrous
sofas, with screens of Aubusson forming favourable and
languid alcoves. Nestling in a bamboo chair, amongst cushions
aromatized with verbena, and a novel in her lap, she would
await her lover with a sort of meek and passive indolence
which reminded me of an Oriental harem. But in her cool
Pompadour silks, she reminded me in another way of a
Marquise at Versailles, who was weary of the Grand Century.
At other times in dark brocades and long, gold-studded sashes
she reminded one of a Venetian lady waiting for a Doge. My
intrusion into the intimacy of those afternoons did not worry
her in the least—it only brought her one more vassal with
two more eyes to contemplate her. At once I became her
" dear Fernandes!"

Scarcely opening her reddened lips like a fresh wound she immediately began to chatter—and soon the hum and the rumour of Paris involved us completely. She only knew how to talk about her own person which was an epitome of her class: and about her own existence which was an epitome of her Paris: and her whole existence (since her marriage) consisted in adorning her pretty body with extreme skill and knowledge: in entering a room in perfect style, and irradiating splendour: in contrasting or matching materials in learned consultation with her dress-designer: rolling through the Bois in the pose of a waxen image: whitening and baring her neck and breast: daintily picking the leg of a woodcock at tables of luxury: threading gracefully through crowded ballrooms: going to sleep with her vanity drained from overwork: taking chocolate in the morning while running through the "Echoes" and "Festive Events" in *Figaro*: and sometimes saying to her husband "Oh, it's you?" . . . Beyond that nothing except, at twilight, with a few short sighs, to fall into the arms of someone to whom she was constant. And all these duties of the City and of her class, she performed with a sweet smile. She had smiled so much and so fixedly, since she had been married, that already two folds were indelibly forming on each side of her lips. But neither her soul nor her skin showed any other signs of fatigue. Her visiting agenda contained thirteen hundred names, all of the nobility. Behind this glittering sociability, however, she had arranged a few General Ideas, which had penetrated her skull along with some of the rice-powder with which, ever since leaving school, she had liberally plastered her brows. In politics she was for the Princes: and all the other "horrors", the Republic, Democracy and Socialism, she shook off with a laugh as if shaking a handkerchief. During Holy Week she put into the lace of her hat a tiny crown of thorns, because those were the days which all well-bred people devoted to penitential grief. She was thirty years old. She had never been embarrassed by the tortures of passion. She always marked down her expenses with rigid regularity in a seal-green Book of Accounts. Her real intimate religion was Order, far more genuine religion than the one which took her every

85

Sunday to Mass at the Church of Saint Phillipe du Roule. In the winter, when under the arches of the bridges shelterless children began to die of cold, she prepared her skating costumes with the greatest of care. Also she prepared her Charity costumes, because she was very good and always attended bazaars, concerts, tombolas and raffles, when they were got up by Duchesses in her "set". Afterwards, in spring, very methodically she sold to an old clothes dealer her dresses and cloaks of the winter. Paris admired in her the supreme flower of Parisianism.

Thus, savouring the perfume of this smooth fine flower, we passed the afternoons of that month while other flowers faded and withered in the dust and heat. But in the intimacy of that perfume Jacinto never seemed to meet with that contentment which amongst all others never grows tired or faint. He showed already that slow patience with which everybody mounts to his Calvary, even the most finely-carpeted Calvary, as he mounted slowly the sumptuous stairway of Madame Oriol, so coolly fringed with delicate ferns and palms on each side of the stair. When that appetising creature devotedly unfolded her vivacity to entertain him as a peacock unfolds its tail, my poor Prince pulled his moustache with the dejected air of one who on a fine May morning, when the blackbirds are singing, has to attend in a black church the funeral liturgy of a dead Prince. And in the kiss which he gave the hand of his beloved when he said good-bye there was always alacrity and alleviation.

But some days, towards evening, after wandering about the library and the cabinet, and giving a listless pull at the tape of his telegraph, then murmuring some soft message through the telephone, he would sweep his dejected gaze round his thirty thousand volumes and the mountain of magazines and reviews, and end up by calling me with that resigned lassitude with which one undertakes an enforced task : " Come, let's go to Madame Oriol's, Zé Fernandes. I've got six appointments marked down for today, but each one is a bore. Let's go to Madame Oriol's; at least we can get a little peace and coolness there."

It was on such an afternoon, when my Prince was thus

86

desperately seeking " a little peace and coolness " that we met, in the very middle of the stairway up to her room, between the ferns and the palms, no less a person than the husband of Madame Oriol himself. I knew him by sight because Jacinto had pointed him out to me one night, in the Grand Café, having supper with some of the girls from the Moulin Rouge. He was a fat, lazy-looking young fellow, of the whiteness of bacon fat, with a shimmer of premature baldness on the top of his head, whose nakedness he kept on caressing with fat fingers covered with rings. But this afternoon, he was crimson and quite beside himself, as he tried to pull on his gloves with his fingers trembling with rage. He halted in front of Jacinto, and without shaking hands, made a gesture up to the landing.

" Going visiting up there, are you? You'll find her in the very worst temper . . . We've just had a tremendous scene!"

He gave another tug at his straw-coloured glove which he had torn already : " We are separated and both of us live as we please. An excellent arrangement. But in all things there's a limit. She still uses my name : and I can't allow her to carry on with her footman with the full knowledge of the whole of Paris Society. Lovers of our set? Why, yes! A bloody flunkey? No! If she wants to go to bed with servants she should do it out in the country far away, say at her house at Corbelle. I wouldn't mind if she did it with the animals away down there. . . . And so I told her! I left her glowering like a wild beast."

Then he shook the hand of Jacinto who was " of his set ", and bundled himself down the ancestral and flowery staircase. My Prince, motionless on the stairway, slowly stroked his moustache. Then looking at me with his being so saturated with boredom that it could admit no more he said with irony : " And now shall we go on up? Yes? "

It was then that I left Paris on my longed-for tour of the cities of Europe. I was going to travel! I travelled. Thirty-four times, in haste, panting, I packed and unpacked my trunk. Eleven times I passed a whole day, in a train coach, smothered in dust and smoke, suffocating, and jumping off at every stop to gulp miserable lemonades which upset my stomach. Fourteen times I made back-breaking ascents up endless stairways in unknown hotels in the wake of a porter or waiter : looked around me in a strange bedroom : and lost my bearings in a strange bed, from which I awoke to ask, in a strange tongue, for coffee and milk which always tasted like broad beans to me; and to take a bath in a tub which always smelt of mud. Eight times I had brawls in the street with coachmen who swindled me of my money. I lost a hat-box, fifteen handkerchiefs, three pairs of drawers, two boots, one brown, one of patent leather, and both belonging to the right foot. At more than thirty little round tables did I wait disconsolately till they brought me boeuf-a-la-mode, cold, with the gravy coagulated; and more than thirty times the wine waiter brought the Bordeaux, which I no sooner tasted than I rejected in disgust. I wandered, in the fresh twilight of granites and marbles with reverent, muffled steps through twenty-nine cathedrals. I softly trod, with a dull pain in my neck, through fourteen museums, covered all over their ceilings even, with Christs, heroes, saints, nymphs, battles, buildings, vegetables, nudities, sombre stains of bitumen, and the infinite sadness of immobile forms! . . . The most pleasing day was when at Venice, where it poured cats and dogs, I met an old Englishman with a flaming red nose, who used to live at Oporto and knew Ricardo, José Duarte, the Viscount of Bom Sucesso and the Limas of Boa Vista. I spent six thousand francs. I had travelled.

At last one blessed morning of October, in the first cold mist of Autumn, I beheld with tender emotion the silk curtains, still drawn, of Number 202. I patted the porter on the shoulder. On the landing, where I found the same warm flowery air I had left in Florence, I hugged the bones of the excellent old Cricket to me.

" And how's Jacinto? " I asked him.

" His Excellency still goes about . . . but he is bored and surfeited. He came in late last night from a ball at the Duchesse de Loches' house to celebrate the engagement of Mademoiselle de Loches. He took a cup of tea before going to bed, and rubbing his head, said 'What a bore! What a bore!' "

After a bath and a cup of cocoa, consoled and warm in my velvet dressing-gown, I burst in upon Jacinto, with open arms:

" Oh Jacinto!"

" Hullo, traveller!"

After embracing him heartily, I stepped back to examine his face—and in his face, the state of his soul. In a cloth jacket, lined with marten-fur, with the ends of his moustache drooping mournfully, with the two wrinkles on his face deeper than ever, and with a certain flabbiness in his broad shoulders, my friend appeared to be cowering beneath the oppression and terror of the coming day.

I smiled, to try to make him smile:

" Valiant Jacinto," I cried, " how have you been living? "

And he replied, with great serenity: " Like a dead man."

I forced a laugh, as if his malady were a slight one.

" You were bored, eh? "

My Prince gave a gesture of such utter defeat and ejaculated an " Oh " of such extreme weariness, that, overcome with sudden compassion, I embraced him again, as if to communicate to him a part of that solid and pure happiness that I received straight from my God.

From that morning onward Jacinto did not hide from me any longer the excruciating boredom with which his existence saturated him. His chief interest now became to try to fathom and to formulate this utter dejection—in the hopes of being able to conquer it when he knew its origin and the extent of its potency. My poor Jacinto began to reproduce the rather uninteresting comedy of the melancholy man who did nothing but analyse and rationalize his melancholy. In this rationalization, he always started from the irrefutable point that his special life as Jacinto comprised all the interests and all the facilities possible, in the Nineteenth Century, for any man to acquire who was neither a Genius nor a Saint. In spite of having had his appetite blunted with twelve years of champagne and exquisite sauces, he still conserved something of the rugged vitality of the mountaineer: in the bright candle of his intelligence no flicker, nor snuff, was perceptible : the good soil of Portugal and some very solid Companies still furnished him his hundred thousand a year : he was surrounded with the sympathies of a City which generally betrayed and mocked its other idols, yet were strangely and actively loyal to him : Number 202 overflowed with comforts : no bitterness gnawed at his heart : yet he was always sad. Why? From this hypothesis he deduced with dazzling certitude that his sadness, this ash-grey wool in which his soul walked shrouded, did not come from his individual self as Jacinto but that it came from life itself; and was, in fact, the result of the disastrous state of being alive. So the wholesome, intellectual, rich and popular Jacinto became wholly converted to Pessimism.

An irritated Pessimism too! Because as he asserted he was born to be as naturally optimistic as a sparrow or a cat. And, till he was twelve years old, with his skin so well clothed, and his plate always full, he had never known a moment of sorrow, melancholy, or contrariety, or pain; and tears were to him so utterly foreign and incomprehensible that even to weep had seemed to him to be vicious and wicked. Only after he had grown up and passed from the animal to the human state, did he come to notice this fermentation of grief which for so long lay hidden behind the excitements of his earlier curiosity and wonder, but at last took hold of him entirely and permeated the blood in every vein. Suffering was inseparable from life; it was life itself. In the mass of humanity it is the agonized struggle for bread, shelter and warmth, and in the higher caste, as desperately struggling for higher necessities, it is the bitterness of disillusion : the shock of one's pride against an obstacle : and in Jacinto who had all his needs supplied and wanted for nothing, it was tedium, boredom. Misery of the body, torment of the will, disgust of the intellect! And now at the age of thirty-three, almost his entire energy was spent in yawning and running his hands over his face as if to feel, to encourage, and to coax the skull from beneath its covering.

It was then that my Prince started reading *Ecclesiastes* and Schopenhauer, and all the lyrists and theoreticians of Pessimism. Through this sort of reading he managed to convince himself that his ailment was not mischievously and perversely his own, Jacinto's, but, more grandiosely, a direct effect of the Universal Law. Already four thousand years ago, in remote Jerusalem, the most triumphant delights had epitomized themselves as a mere illusion. The incomparable all-conquering King, in his divine wisdom, the supreme builder of the ages, himself, had become disgusted and yawned amidst the triumphant spoils of his conquest, the new marbles of his Temple, the beauty of his three thousand concubines, and the Queens who, from as far as Ethiopia, would come to him for the purpose of conceiving a Divinity in their wombs. The more one knows, the more one suffers. Both the just and the unjust, born of the dust, return to the dust alike. Everything tends to the dust whether in ancient Jerusalem or modern Paris. And he, Jacinto, sequestered in Number 202, was suffering from nothing more than from being a man, and from being alive—just as the magnificent son of David suffered as he sat between the four golden lions that flanked his golden throne.

He was never without his copy of *Ecclesiastes* by day or by night. He circulated round Paris in his horse-carriage carrying Solomon in his hand, as the twin brother of his grief, with whom he repeated the desolate cry, as the epitome of all human truth: " Vanity of Vanities! All is Vanity!" At other times one would find him in his silken bath-robe, lying on the sofa absorbed in Schopenhauer—while the pedicurist, kneeling on the carpet, polished his toenails with reverence and professional skill. At his side was a Saxe porcelain cup full of the Moka café which was regularly sent him by the Emirs of the Desert, but which he never found satisfactory either in its aroma or in the exact strength he required. Sometimes he would lay his book on his chest and glance compassionately at the pedicurist to see what kind of grief was torturing him, since it was the lot of every living creature to suffer. Certainly, always to be rummaging about with other people's feet must be a terrible bore—so whenever the pedicurist got up to go, Jacinto always had a deep smile of fraternal sympathy for him, as he said " Good-bye, my friend——" but really meant: " Good-bye, my brother in grief!"

This was during the splendid and superbly diverting period of his weariness and boredom. Jacinto had really found a congenial occupation—that of *cursing Life*. And so as to be able to curse it in all its forms, the most opulent, the most intellectual, the most pure, he widened his experience and surcharged his life with greater luxury, new spiritual interests, humanitarian ardours, and supernatural speculations.

Number 202, all that winter, fairly blazed with magnificence. It was then that he initiated in Paris the Feasts of Colour, following the example of Heliogabalus as recounted in the *Historia Augusta*; and offered to his female friends that sublime rose-coloured dinner at which everything was coloured rose, the walls, the furniture, the plates, the crockery, the glasses, the ices, the champagne and even (by some culinary invention) the fish, the meat and the vegetables; the footman, powdered with rose, wore liveries of rose : while from the roof, covered with rosy veils, fell showers of fresh rose-petals. The whole laiety, dazzled with such splendour, cried out " Bravo, Jacinto! " But my Prince, as this brilliant feast came to an end, with his hands in his armpits, planted himself before me, and cried out in triumph : " Phew! . . . What a bore it was! "

After that, he took up Humanitarianism, and founded in the country, among lovely gardens, a Home for homeless old men. He built another magnificent home for ailing children on the shores of the Mediterranean. Next, with Major Dorchas, Mayolle and the Hindu friend of Mayolle, he explored once more the mysteries of Theosophy : and staged tremendous experiments to prove the mysterious *exteriorisation of motion*. After that he linked Number 202 by means of telephone wires to the head office of *The Times*, so that in his study, as if in a single heart, might pulse the whole of the social life of Europe.

After each one of these prodigious efforts of elegant display, humanitarianism, sociability or intellectual research, he would return to me with open arms and a victorious cry : " You see, Zé Fernandes. It's only a farce and a bore! " Then he would snatch up his *Ecclesiastes* or his Schopenhauer and voluptuously enjoy the exact concordance of his Doctrine with his experience. For now he had a faith in which he believed—Pessimism! He was a rich and valiant apostle: there was nothing he would not attempt in order to prove the truth of his creed. My unhappy Prince fully enjoyed the whole of that year!

At the beginning of winter I noticed, with some alarm, that Jacinto no longer fumbled the pages of *Ecclesiastes*, and that he had deserted Schopenhauer. Neither feasts, homes for the poor, Theosophy, nor wires connected to *The Times*, interested my friend any more, even as illustrations of his Creed. His entire function limited itself once more to the abominable habit of yawning, and searching for the outlines of his skull beneath its covering of skin and bone. He incessantly spoke of death as the only liberation. One afternoon in the melancholy twilight that precedes the lighting of the lamps, he considerably frightened me by speaking of sudden, painless deaths, whether by shock from some huge electric battery, or by the compassionate violence of prussic acid. The Devil! Pessimism, which had first appeared in the intelligence of my friend as an elegant and harmless concept—was now attacking and undermining his will.

From then on, his progress seemed to be that of an unconscious ox, moving under the yoke and the goad. No longer did he expect the slightest contentment: he ceased even to complain of boredom and sadness. " Everything is indifferent, Zé Fernandes." And he would have received the Imperial Crown as a gift from the entire people with the same indifference as that with which he stretched himself on the sofa, to chat, or to lie in glum silence. Since everything was useless, what mattered the most dazzling activity or the most shameful sloth? His habitual gesture, which irritated me, was to shrug his shoulders. Between two ideas, two paths, or two plates of food, all he did was to shrug. What did it matter? And in his slightest action, whether striking a match, or unfolding a newspaper, there was such a morose dejection that he seemed to have been tightly bound, from his fingertips to his very soul, by the endless twists of an invisible cord which held him prisoner.

I remember, with disgust, his birthday on the tenth of January. Early in the morning he received a basket full of camellias, azaleas, and lilies of the valley with a letter from Madame de Trèves. It was this that reminded him that it was his birthday. He blew out the smoke of his cigarette on the flowers and said with a slow, sneering laugh: " And to think that I've been carrying on with this miserable farce for thirty-four years."

Then when I proposed telephoning some friends to come and drink a " birthday champagne " to his health at Number 202, he angrily rejected the suggestion "No! No! What a horrible bore that would be!" And then he yelled to Cricket:

" Today I am not in Paris to anyone who calls or rings up. I've gone to the country . . . I've gone to Marseilles . . . I've died!"

His sardonic remarks did not cease till lunch time, and he opened and read the cards, telegrams, and letters of felicitation, which rose in a great hill, completely covering the ebony table, as if it were the homage of the entire City. Other masses of flowers, that came in beautiful baskets done up in gay ribbons, he sarcastically compared to the funeral wreaths that are laid on a tomb. He was only momentarily interested even in the ingenious present of Ephraim, a table which could be lowered to the level of the carpet, or raised to the height of the roof—but for what reason, God in heaven only knows!

After lunch, as it was lugubriously raining, we huddled up in Number 202 with our feet to the fire in slothful silence. I ended by going beatifically to sleep. Jacinto buried in his armchair with a pair of scissors was cutting out paper like a child! Never did I feel so sorry for my friend, who had worn out his youth in assembling all the ideas formulated since Aristotle, and all the inventions realized since Jeramines —as on that afternoon of his birthday, when surrounded by civilization in its maximum concentration, in order to enjoy the delights of living in their maximum proportion, he was reduced in his own home to cutting out paper patterns with a pair of scissors.

Cricket brought in a present from the Grand Duc; it was a silver box, lined with cedar and full of a precious tea, collected flower by flower from the gardens of Kiang-Sou, by the pure hands of virgins, and brought across Asia by caravan with all the veneration of a holy relic. Then, to dispel our torpor, I suggested that to partake of this divine tea would be an occupation in harmony with this melancholy afternoon, with the heavy rain showering the windows, with the flame dancing on the hearth, and the acquisition of Ephraim's new adjustable tea-table. But my Prince after elevating it, to my consternation, as high as to touch the crystals of the chandelier, could not bring it back to its natural household dimensions, however hard he sweated in his desperate struggle with its levers and springs. The footman had to take it away again, like some tall, chimerical scaffolding which could only be put to its proper use by the giant Adamastor.

Now came the silver box of tea amongst kettles, spirit-burners, filters, strainers, and silver implements which conferred on the operation of tea-making (so simply and pleasantly done at my Aunt Vicência's) the complicated majesty of a rite or ceremony. Prepared by the expatiations of my friend, for the sublimity of this tea of Kiang-Sou, I reverently raised the teaspoon to my lips. It was a muddy-coloured infusion which tasted of marsh-mallows and ants. Jacinto sipped, spat, and blasphemed!

After some minutes of pensive silence I asked him " What news of the reconstructions at Tormes? The Church? Have they rebuilt it? "

" I don't know. I don't seem to have heard from Silverio, or I have not opened his letter. Nor can I imagine what has happened to the bones of my forbears. What a lugubrious business!"

Then came the time for lighting up and supper. I had ordered through Cricket, from our masterly cook, a dish of " sweet rice " cooked in the manner of our peasants at home in Portugal, with Jacinto's initials done in cinnamon on the top of it. My Prince, as he went over the ivory tablet on which the menu was written, praised this patriarchal idea of mine.

" Sweet rice!" he cried. " What an excellent memory! It's written on the menu with a double S instead of a double

E, but there's no doubt. . . . It is years since I tasted it, since before the death of my grandfather!"

But what vexation when the "sweet rice" finally appeared! It was a monumental work of art, no doubt. The rice was moulded into the shape of a pyramid of Egypt. It emerged from a thick sauce of cherry juice and disappeared in layers of dried fruit which coated it on all sides to the summit, on which was balanced the Crown of the Counts of Tormes in chocolate, plugged with frozen quarters of tangerine! And the initials which I had wanted to be traced in simple cinnamon on the rice itself, had been worked round the edge of the dish in candied violets. We rejected it in silent horror.

Jacinto raising his cup of champagne as if at a pagan funeral, drank solemnly, "*Ad Manes*, to the shades of our Dead!"

We came back to the libary to drink our coffee in the comfort and cheerfulness of the fire. Outside the wind roared as if in the solitude of the sierras. The windows rattled, streaming with water, in the sudden furious gusts of rain. What a rough night for the ten thousand poor who nightly roam through Paris without food or shelter! Perhaps in my own village, between the range and the valley, the tempest was roaring in the same manner. But there each poor person under the shelter of his own roof, sure of his pot of meat and cabbage, nestled back in his huge mantle in the warm blaze of the hearth-logs. And for those who had neither pot nor hearth-logs, provision was made by João das Quintas, or Aunt Vicência, or the old Abbot, who knew every one of the poor personally by name, and always took them into account whenever the cart went to the forest for fuel, and whenever the meal entered the oven for cooking. Ah, little Portugal, who are still so good to the little ones, the humble, and the poor!

I sighed. Jacinto sulked and loafed, and we ended the evening by turning over the pile of newspapers which the major-domo brought in on a silver tray—journals of Paris, weeklies, magazines, Reviews and illustrated papers. Jacinto unfolded and threw them away one by one. Of the Reviews he read only the contents, and was already surfeited by that. Of the illustrated papers he turned a few pages with an indifferent finger and yawned over the engravings. Then, lying back in front of the fire, he said : " It's a bore! . . . Nothing to read!"

Then suddenly as if in revolt against this oppressive disgust, which was enslaving him, he would leap up with the fury of one who was breaking his fetters, and stand erect, darting a hard and imperative glare around him, as if insisting that this, his Number 202, which he had so lavishly crammed with Civilization, should at the very least, in return, even if it were only a moment, furnish him with some transitory interest or fugitive pleasure. But Number 202 remained insensible : not even one electric light intensified its even, dumb lustre to encourage him. Only the window-panes trembled and rattled in the squalls of wind and rain.

Then my Prince succumbed to his fate, dragging his slow steps to his study, and began to tinker with his apparatus to complete, improve, and facilitate the process of life—his telegraph, his telephone, his gramophone, his radiometer, his typewriter, his calculating machine, his electric press, his magnetic one, all his tubes, his wires, and his strings. So a supplicant goes from altar to altar in the desperate hope of succour. But all this sumptuous machinery remained unbendingly rigid, and coldly gleaming. Not a wheel turned, not a blade stirred, to entertain its Lord and Master.

Only the monumental clock that marked the hour of day in all the capitals of the world and registered the course of the planets, took pity on him and struck midnight to announce to my friend that one more day had departed with its load of care and boredom . . . For a moment or two he stood in the middle of the library looking at his sixty thousand volumes assembled in the pomp and majesty of Doctors in Council—then at the piles and mountains of new books which awaited, heaped in the corners and all over the carpet, the repose and consecration of new book-cases of ebony. Twisting his moustache, he finally went towards the shelves of the Historians, reconnoitring centuries and smelling out nations; he seemed to be attracted first by the splendours of the Byzantine Empire : then he tried the French Revolution from which he soon recoiled in disappointment : then he handled unpremeditatedly the whole of the vast "glory that was Greece" from the foundation of Athens to the destruction of Corinth. Then abruptly he turned to the poets, who glittered in pale morocco, with their titles in gold lettering, which reflected in its brilliance or faintness, the interior ardour or languor of their souls. Not one of those six thousand souls could interest him in the least. Next he turned disconsolately to the biologists. So massively and closely crammed was the book-case of biology that Jacinto stopped, frightened, as if before an impregnable and inaccessible citadel. He rolled the ladder along on its castors to his artificial heaven in the dome of the library—and fleeing from the other subjects, climbed for refuge into the heights of astronomy: there, he detached stars, and located worlds till a whole solar system fell to pieces with a crash. Half-stunned, he then came down from his artificial Heaven, and started to place in stacks the new books, which were still clothed in their light battle-dress of paper, before being bound. He picked them up, turned the pages, and put them down. Sometimes in search of a single book he would demolish a whole tower of doctrines. He leaped over problems. He trampled religions. Glancing at a line in one book, scratching at an index in another, he seemed to question all books, to find interest in none, rolling about as if completely adrift in the vast waves of books that washed around him, and whelmed in the despair of ever finding a single book that could interest him. He then stopped in the middle of the vast library, contemplating the serried walls, which were crammed, and the wide floors which were heaped and toppled over, by his sixty thousand books without even having tried the matter of a single one of them, entirely surfeited, utterly discouraged, sickened and nauseated by the sheer oppression of their abundance. He ended up by returning to the heap of crumpled newspapers; there, disconsolately selecting a week-old copy of the *Daily News of Lisbon*, he slowly went upstairs to sleep, and to forget.

8

TOWARDS the end of that dark and pessimistic winter, one morning as I was loafing in bed, sensing a timid hint of spring in the still-pallid sunlight that played on the panes—Jacinto, clothed in light flannels of lily-white brilliance, looked into my room. He stopped beside my bed and with the greatest gravity, as if announcing his own marriage, or his own death, let forth this formidable declaration :

" Zé Fernandes, I am leaving for Tormes."

The leap I gave profoundly shook the whole massive wooden fourposter bed of the late Dom Galleon.

" For Tormes? " I cried. " Whom have you assassinated? What murder have you committed? "

Pleased at my emotion, the Prince of Good Fortune pulled from his pocket a letter and began reading these lines, which he had obviously re-read and profoundly studied many times before: " Most illustrious and Excellent Sir, I have the greatest satisfaction in informing you that this week the construction of the new . . . "

" Is it from Silverio? " I enquired.

" From Silverio," he replied, and went on " . . . the construction of the new chapel will be completed. The venerable remains of your noble ancestors can therefore be transferred from the Church of São José where they have been deposited by the kindness of the Abbot who commends himself affectionately to your Excellency. I dutifully await your Excellency's orders concerning this majestic and painful ceremony."

I threw up my arms, understanding his drift.

" Well, don't you think I should, Zé Fernandes? Not for the sake of the other old ancestors whom I never knew— but for the sake of dear old grandfather Galleon. Of course I hardly knew him either. But this 202 here is full of him. You're sleeping on his bed. I still use his watch. I cannot just leave to Silverio and the servants the care of transferring his remains to their new resting place. It's just a scruple of decency, or moral elegance . . . Well, I've made up my mind at last! I pressed my fists against my head and shouted ' I am going to Tormes!' and *I am* . . . And you're coming too!"

I put on my slippers and tied the cord of my dressing-gown.

"But you know, Jacinto, that the house of Tormes is uninhabitable."

He fixed his eyes on me in alarm: "Is it too frightful?" he asked.

"Frightful, no! Not at all! It's a lovely house, of beautiful sound stone. But the farm-hands and cowboys have been in it for thirty years sleeping on hurdles and pallets, eating their broth on the hearth and using the rooms to dry the mealies and store the corn. The only furniture that was left at Tormes, if I remember rightly, was a cupboard and a lacquer spinet without any keys and lame in one leg."

My Prince gave a sigh, but with a gesture of surrender, in which he abandoned himself to destiny, he cried:

"I have said! . . . The die is cast. And as we're not leaving till April there's time to paint, to plank the doors, and to put in the panes. I'll send beds and carpets from Paris . . . An upholsterer from Lisbon will go and cover up and disguise the cracks and holes. We'll take books and a machine to make ice. It's a good chance to go and put my Portuguese houses and properties in a state of order and decency. One of them dates from 1410 . . . when the Byzantine Empire was still in existence!"

I was spreading soap over my face with my shaving brush. My Prince very thoughtfully lit a cigarette and would not leave the washstand but studied my ablutions with a fixity that annoyed and embarrassed me. At length, as if he were chewing over some severe sentence to which I had condemned him, and as if to keep up his morale, he said:

"Well definitely, Zé Fernandes: do you think it's a duty, an absolute duty, to go to Tormes?"

I turned my soapy face from the mirror to meet his gaze with amused astonishment.

"Oh Jacinto! It was in your breast and yours alone that the idea of this *duty* was born: not in mine! The honour is yours! Don't try to pass it off on anyone else!"

He threw away his cigarette and, with his hands in his trouser pockets, walked up and down the room, bumping into chairs, stumbling against the old carved bedposts of Dom Galleon, like some boat which, loosed from its rope moorings, goes drifting over an uncertain sea without a course or destination. Then he wedged himself over the table where I kept portraits of all my family, ranked according to the affection I felt for them, from the daguerrotype of my father to the photograph of my greyhound, Carocho.

Never had my Prince appeared so round-shouldered or so shrunken, as if worn away by a file, which had been at work for a long time, grinding him deeply away. Thus it seemed, was going to end the mighty, mountaineering race of the Jacintos—in this super-refined, over-domesticated spindle-shanks. Those thick-maned Jacintos who when they returned to their highlands at Tormes, after beating the Moor at Salado, or the Castilian at Valverde, did not even doff their rough armour when they returned to plough their fields, or train their vines to the elms, but built the kingdom both with the lance and the hoe at the same time, each as strong and stiff as the other. And now this last of the Jacintos, this Jacintulus, with his smooth skin soaked in perfumes, his narrow soul choked with philosophies, stood fettered in trivial indecision before the mere prospect of going on living.

" Oh, Zé Fernandes, who is this hefty, plump farm-wench?" asked Jacinto.

I stretched my neck to see the photo which he picked up from my little gallery in its scarlet frame.

` "Here! More respect, my fine cavalier, if you please! That's my cousin Joaninha from Sandofim at the Farm of the Geranium."

"Farm of the Geranium," he murmured. "Why that was the House of the Lord High Constable, Nuno Alvares."

"House of the Rose, you silly! In the province of the Trans-Tagus. It just shows your shocking ignorance in all things Portuguese."

My Prince let the photo of my cousin slide from between his soft fingers, which he raised to his face once more in that horrible gesture of trying to trace his skull beneath its covering of flesh. Then suddenly he straightened his back with a superb effort which made him grow visibly.

"Good!" he cried, "*Alea jacta est!* The die is cast, and we leave for the mountains. No more reflection, no more hesitation! To work! On the march!"

He stretched his hand to the gold nob of the door as if it were the black padlock on the hatch of the Destinies: in the corridor he yelled for Cricket in a deep urgent voice which I had never heard him use before, but which reminded me of a general ordering his army to break camp, and to march with banners and baggage . . .

Soon after that same morning (with an alacrity in which I recognized the shuddering nauseous hate with which one forces oneself to swallow down a dose of castor oil) he wrote to Silverio telling him to whitewash, floor, and pane the house. After breakfast, he came into the library and rang violently on the telephone for the Director of the Transport Company so as to get his furniture and comforts packed and sent on to Portugal.

The Director was almost like a poster or hand-bill to advertise his own Company. He appeared in a tight-fitting jacket of a dark, fine chequer-work: with travelling gaiters buttoned over white deerskin boots: a double-pouched wallet of morocco leather, on a sling round his neck, and on his lapel a multi-coloured rosette comprising the exotic decorations he had received for his services from the Queen of Madagascar, the President of Nicaragua and the Shah of Persia, and yet more besides, which testified to the many-sidedness of his world-wide activities. Hardly had Jacinto mentioned "Tormes, by the Douro" when he, with a superior smile, raised his hand to restrain any further explanations and showed us that he was minutely and intimately acquainted with every inch of the whole region.

"Tormes? Exactly! Exactly!" On his lap he made a rapid note in his pocket book, while I computed, with amazement, what must be the vastitude of his whole chorographical knowledge, from his intimate familiarity with such an out-of-the-way corner in the remotest sierras of Portugal. Already he had slipped his pocket book back into his pocket. We, " his dear sirs," had nothing more to do, he said, than to pack our boxes. He would send his carriages for them and mark them in big lettering with our names and destination: "Tormes. Exactly! On the North Spanish Medina-to-Salamanca line . . . Oh! Exactly! . . . Tormes very picturesque . . . besides, ancient, historical . . . Perfectly! . . . Perfectly!"

He unhinged his head in a profound bow and shot out of the library with such long, rapid strides that they seemed to devour leagues, and to symbolize the rapidity and the efficiency of his transport service.

"Do you see that?" murmured Jacinto. "What promptitude, what efficiency! In Portugal, it is a tragedy! You only get that sort of thing in Paris!"

Now began the colossal operation of packing all the comforts that would be necessary for the apostle of civilization during a month in the wild and rugged sierras—feather-beds, nickel baths, *Carcel* acetylene-flares for light, divans, curtains to hide cracks in the walls, carpets to soften rough floors. The cellars where the massive furniture of Dom Galleon had lain locked up for years, were opened and ransacked, because the mediaeval house of 1410 would be well suited by the romantic furniture-style of 1830. From all the big shops of Paris, bundles, packets and formidable-looking packages arrived, which the packers undid, strewing the passages knee-deep in straw and brown paper. The cook, out of breath, organized a consignment of cooking-stoves, freezing-machines, jars of truffles, bottles of mineral water, and tins of jam and pickles. Jacinto, remembering the thunderstorms of the sierra, bought a lightning-conductor. From the peep of dawn, in the passages, the courtyards, and the garden, there was a din of hammering, sawing and nailing up, as if in the construction of a city. The processions of baggage from the front door recalled the page in which Herodotus recounts the march of the Persians.

From the windows, with his arm extended, Jacinto thoroughly enjoyed directing all this activity, and delighted in the efficiency with which it was conducted and disciplined.

"Look, Zé Fernandes! What efficiency! We leave Number

103

202, only to find another Number 202 in the sierras. It's only in Paris that things are done like this!"

My Prince began to love the city again, as soon as he prepared his exodus from it. After having, all the morning, exhorted the packers, discovered more necessities and comforts for the God-forsaken mansion in the mountains, and telephoned huge lists of orders to most of the big shops in Paris—it was with real delight that he perfumed, flowered, dressed and buried himself in his victoria carriage, or else jumped on to the leather cushions of his phaeton, to drive out to the Bois, and salute the Talmudic beard of Ephraim, the furiously black plaits of the Verghane, the Psychologist of the fiacre, or the Comtesse de Trèves in her new calash, with springs, which had been furnished by the joint operations of the Stock Exchange and the bedroom. At the theatre of the Nouveautés, at the Palais Royal, and at the Buffos he laughed, smiting his thigh, at the hoary facetious jokes and out-of-date farces—as he had never laughed since his infancy, before the war, under the second Napoleon.

Once again the pages of his agenda overflowed with appointments. The magnificence of his dress as Frederic II of Swabia at the fancy dress ball of the Princesse de Cravon-Rogan (where I also went as a Portuguese bull-fighter) dazzled society. And at the Association for the Development of Esoteric Religions he made a brave fighting speech for the erection of a Buddhist temple on the heights of Montmartre.

To my amazement, he began once more, exactly as he had done at College, to speak of "Civilization in its maximum proportions." He had his largest telescope packed for use at Tormes. I began to fear that the idea was germinating in his soul, to create a whole city out there on the tops of the mountains! At least Jacinto was not going to let those sylvan weeks at Tormes interfere with his illimitable accumulation of ideas—for he burst one morning into my room, very upset indeed, and crying out that, in spite of all the comforts and necessities of civilization which we had thought of, we had forgotten the most obvious—which were *books*! What a vexation for our intellectuality! But what books were we to choose from the thousands, under whose weight the whole massive house of 202 was bending and creaking? My Prince decided to devote his stay in the mountains to the study of natural history: so we immediately ballasted a large new packing-case with twenty-five volumes of Pliny. Then we threw in armfuls of geology, zoology, botany and mineralogy, and covered the whole with a substantial layer of astronomy. To fix these oscillating sciences from rocking about too much on the journey, we wedged them in, at the sides and corners, with tight wads of metaphysics.

But when the last case, nailed up, and bound with bands of iron, sailed out of the front door to catch the last van of the Company of Transport, all this sudden animation of Jacinto's went out of him like the effervescence goes out of a glass of champagne. It was in the middle of March when the weather was already getting warmer. Once more his disagreeable and shattering yawns bombarded Number 202, and the sofas began to creak with the weight of his recumbent form, overcome with surfeit, boredom and yearning for the last, eternal slumber in solitude, oblivion and silence. I was in despair. I had to suffer all over again the sight of him feeling for his skull under the skin, and, when nightfall saddened the library, the hoarse, hollow sound of his voice expatiating on the sweetness of "rapid, painless death by prussic acid." No! I had had enough! One afternoon when I found him lying with crossed arms on his divan, like a statue on a tomb of granite, I seized him and shook him with fury, as I bellowed in his ear: "Wake up, man! We are off to Tormes . . . The old house will be ready . . . The bones of your forefathers are demanding rest in their own graves! . . . Come on! . . . On the march! . . . Let us bury the dead, and let us try to live, who are still living! . . . Faugh! . . . It's April the fifth . . . Now it's the weather for the mountains."

My Prince came slowly out of his trance of stone.

"Silverio hasn't written to me yet. He never writes . . . But I suppose everything must be ready by now . . . There will be servants there, and a cook from Lisbon . . . I'm only taking Cricket and Anatole, who is good at shining boots and has a knack as a pedicurist . . . Let's see . . . today's Sunday."

I stamped on the carpet and said heroically: "Well, we leave on Saturday . . . Warn Silverio."

Then began a laborious study of railway time-tables, while Jacinto's finger moved backward and forward on the map between Paris and Tormes. To choose the special private coach-saloon and state compartments in which we were to live during the dreaded journey, we twice went through the parking yards of the Gare d'Orléans, covered in mud, in the tracks of the chief of the station, whom we drove half-crazy. My Prince refused one saloon because of the sad colour of the upholstery: another he refused because of the wretched niggardliness of its water-closet. One of his anxieties was his morning bath on the days when we would be rolling along on the rails. I suggested a bath made of rubber. Jacinto sighed, unable to decide. What terrified him most was the thought of changing trains at Medina del Campo in the dark in old Castile. In vain did the Railway Company of Northern Spain reassure him by letters and telegrams that, the moment he arrived on the Spanish frontier at Irun in his state-saloon, there would be another state-saloon ready to receive him, well-lighted, well-heated, and well-furnished, with a special dinner to which one of the Directors of the Company was going to treat him, namely Don Esteban de Castillo, so frequently a noisy and rubicund guest at Number 202.

Jacinto anxiously ran his fingers over his face:

"And the bags, and the furs and the books . . . who will transfer them from the Irun saloon to the Salamanca saloon?"

I bellowed that the porters at Medina were the quickest, the most expert and efficient in the whole of Europe.

But he went on murmuring: "Well, may be . . . but still, in Spain . . . in the middle of the night."

"Night", far from the City, without telephones, electric lights, or police-stations, was peopled, for Jacinto, with strange terrors, surprises and attacks. But he was somewhat tranquillized after verifying at the Astronomical Observatory, on the personal guarantee of no less a person than Professor Bertrand himself, that it would be full moon on the night we passed through Medina.

At last, on the Friday, we terminated all our tremendous preparations for that historic journey. The pre-destined Saturday dawned with a generous sunlight of a caressing mildness. I had just finished putting into my bag, wrapped in brown paper, the many photographs of all the sweet, soft young creatures who for the last twenty-six months had been calling me "*mon petit chou! mon rat cheri!*" etc., etc.— when Jacinto burst into my room with a superb bunch of orchids in his frock coat, looking pale and nervous.

"Shall we take a farewell drive round the Bois de Boulogne?"

We went to take a grand farewell. It was delightful. Even in the cushions and springs of the victoria I felt a more restful and lulling elasticity. When we got to the Bois de Boulogne, I felt a sort of regret that we could not continue the rocking and rolling along forever, to the trot of these perfect mares, in their glitter of furbished metal and leather, along that macadam that was smooth as marble, between the lawns and flower-beds of such voluptuous freshness, among the pick of Humanity, of such exquisite elegance, who had just been sipping their chocolate from porcelains of Sèvres or Minton, and risen from silks and fabrics of three-thousand francs apiece, to take the air of this lovely April in luxurious and light-hearted refinement. The woods were resplendent in harmonies of green, blue and gold. No graveyard or open country interrupted the smooth lanes and flowery walks which Art had traced in mazy convolutions through the thick foliage of the Bois. Not a single untidy branch or shoot disgraced the smooth undulations of greenery which the Government trimmed, swept, watered and washed. The subdued trills of birds lent a faint sense of winged life to the landscape, to which the creaking of the new saddles of the mounted Amazons gave a more authentic expression, as they swayed in slender grace, in stays supplied by Redfern. In front of the Pavillon d'Armenonville, we passed Madame de Trèves who bracketed us in a caressing smile, which was all the more vivacious because her lipstick hadn't had time to dry. Then, just behind, came the Talmudic beard of Ephraim, also not yet dry from its morning unction of brilliantine, in a high phaeton tintinnabulating with bells. Other friends of Jacinto's were circulating the Bois, and the hands that waved to him were gloved in gloves the colour of straw, pearl, or faint lilac. De Todelle suddenly radiated before us in metallic splendour on a huge bicycle. Dornan, spread on an iron seat, under a flowering hawthorn, was sucking an immense cheroot, in whose smoke he seemed to be seeking greasy, sensual rhymes. Further on, the Psychologist, who did not see us, was engaged in some funereal courtship in a cab which looked more like a bedroom, but to which a fat coachman lent dignity and decency. We were rolling along thus, when the Duc de Marizac, on horseback, raising his cane, drew up by our carriage, to ask Jacinto if he was appearing in the " living tableaux " of the Verghanes. My Prince mumbled something like " No . . . leaving for the South," and Marizac said what a pity that was, because it was going to be a stupendous show. Living tableaux from the Holy Gospels and Roman History! Madame Verghane, as the Magdalene, with naked arms washing the feet of Christ! The Christ was a superbly-built, great big fellow, a relative of the Trèves' who was employed in the War Ministry, and it was worth seeing him groaning and breaking his back under the big pasteboard Cross! They were also going to have Lucrece in bed, and Tarquin, with his dagger drawn, trying to pull off the bedclothes. Afterwards they were going to have supper, with everybody still wearing his or her historical costume. He himself was partnered by Madame de Malbe, who was Agrippina, Nero's mother. This was a wonderful *tableau*—Agrippina lies dead, while he, Nero, comes to study the figure and form that bore him, admiring some points, and criticizing others as imperfect. But as a matter of courtesy, it was agreed that Nero, in this case, must praise all the anatomical characteristics of Madame de Malbe—without reserve. It was a colossal programme, and stupendously instructive historically—what?

The gay Marizac waved us a long adieu. We turned back without a word from Jacinto, who, plunged in an abysmal silence, with his arms crossed rigidly, seemed to be ruminating profoundly, and making terrific efforts of will-power. When we were in front of the Arc de Triomphe he turned his head

108

and murmured: "It's a very grave thing to be leaving Europe."

At last we started our journey. In the mildness of an afternoon which was clouding over, we left Number 202. Cricket and Anatole followed us in a cab piled up with books, bags and rolls of rugs. Behind a huge horse-omnibus rumbled with a load of twenty-three trunks. At the station Jacinto still went on buying newspapers, illustrated magazines, time-tables, and a corkscrew which looked both complicated, dangerous and hostile. Guided by the traffic-master of the station and the Secretary of the Railway Company, we copiously occupied our saloon. I put on my silk skull-cap and my slippers. A loud whistle pierced the night. Paris flashed past in a last glitter of lighted windows. To drink in the City to the last, Jacinto was leaning at one of the windows. But now we were already thundering through the darkness of the Provinces. Jacinto fell back on the cushions:

"What an adventure, Zé Fernandes!"

We turned over illustrated magazines till we reached Chartres. At Orléans, an attendant came respectfully to arrange the beds. Exhausted by all these months of Civilization, I slept soundly and did not wake till Bordeaux, where I was awakened by the zealous Cricket, bringing us our morning's chocolate. Outside, a fine rain softly fell from a sky of dirty cotton-wool. Jacinto had not gone to bed, suspecting the dampness and the roughness of the bedclothes. In his flannel dressing-gown with a furrowed and despairing face, he was dunking a bun in his chocolate and grumbling: "What a horror! And rain . . . to crown everything!"

At Biarritz we both observed with lazy certitude: "It's Biarritz." Jacinto, who was peering out of the steamy window, thereupon suddenly recognized the long-legged gait, and the beaky, sad nose of the Historian, Danjon, on the platform. It was he, that most eloquent man, dressed in a check suit, with a plump lady who led a little shaggy dog on a leash. Jacinto violently opened the window, and bellowed to the Historian in a last desperate attempt to communicate, even by proxy, with the City and Number 202 . . . But the train had already merged with the rain and mist.

On the bridge of the Bidassoa, foreseeing the end of his hitherto easy life; and sensing the rocky shores and breakers of " Uncivilization ", he sighed despairingly :

" Farewell to everything now ! Spain has begun !"

In indignation, as I was already savouring the generous air of that blessed land, I jumped upright in front of my Prince, where, clicking my fingers like castanets, and shaking my body in Spanish style, I defiantly launched out into a suitable *petenera* in Spanish :

" A la puerta de mi casa
Ay Soledad. Soleda-á-á-á-á "

He stretched out his arms.

" Ah, Zé Fernandes, have pity on one who is sick and sad."

" *Irun! Irun!* "

At Irun we feasted succulently—for the omnipresent goddess, the Railway Company of Northern Spain, was watching over us. The chief of customs and the station-master then saw us sumptuously installed in our new saloon which was richly draped in olive-green silk, but was so small that our luggage overflowed into the sleeping quarters where Cricket and Anatole, both crowned with fashionable Scotch tam-o-shanters, were puffing away at fat cheroots.

" *Buen viaje! Gracias! Servidores!* " With loud whistles the train entered the Pyrennées.

Under the influence of the misty rain of these evenly monotonous mountains, which sailed into view with wrinkled sides, half-blurred in mist, a mild somnolence prevailed; and when I opened my dozing eyes I noticed Jacinto in a corner, with thin fingers crossed over the book that lay forgotten on his lap, sadly contemplating the mountains and valleys, with the air of a condemned man on the way to exile ! A moment came when, throwing down his book and pulling down his soft hat over his eyes, he rose suddenly upright with such determination, that I feared he was going to stop the train and jump out. I came out of my torpor exclaiming : " Here ! Steady on !" But it was a false alarm. He had made this effort only to continue his tedium, in the opposite corner of the saloon, buried in other cushions, with a different unopened book in his lap.

The alarming way in which the darkness of the afternoon grew more intense, and the gusts and showers increased in volume and force, filled my Prince with anxiety, now that he was lost to Civilization and being rushed away into wild nature whose churlish rudeness was already beginning to appal him. He kept plying me with questions about Tormes.

" The nights there must be horrible, Zé Fernandes—aren't they? Everything black . . . Enormous loneliness . . . and how about a doctor? . . . Is there one? "

Suddenly the train stopped. Heavier and louder than ever, the rain lashed the windows. It was in the middle of a wilderness where a huge loose wind rumbled and rolled around. A lantern flashed and passed down the line at a run. Jacinto stamped his foot. " It's fearful! It's fearful! " In the uncertain light of the train-window heads looked out nervously.

" *Que hay? Que hay?* " (What's the matter?)

At a sudden shower which splashed me, I recoiled from the window and shut it. We waited many long, silent minutes, rubbing the misted glass to try to penetrate the darkness around. Suddenly the train started to roll serenely on its way once more.

Soon appeared the little lights of a station enclosed with huts. A conductor clothed in dripping oilskins climbed into the saloon. From him, as he hurriedly clipped our tickets, we learned that our train was so late that it might miss its connection with the Salamanca train at Medina del Campo.

" ——But what then? "

The oilcloth slid out of the door leaving a smell of oil and dampness, as it melted into the night. Now we had begun to suffer a new torment . . . If the Salamanca train had gone already? Our saloon, booked to Medina, was to be uncoupled there : and there would we be, stranded on the mud with our twenty-three trunks, in a wild scrimmage of Spanish confusion, under a tempest of wind and rain.

" Ah Zé Fernandes! A whole night in Medina! "

To have to spend that night in Medina seemed to my Prince the supreme misadventure of his whole life; to have to stay in some sordid railway inn, reeking of garlic, with armies of bugs marching over the soiled coarse linen of the beds!

I kept anxiously looking at the hands of my watch, while Jacinto stared out of the open window, lashed with wind and rain, in the hope of distinguishing, through the blackness, the lights of Medina and a train patiently smoking as it awaited our arrival. After a while he sat down, wiping the rain from his eyes and moustache, and cursing Spain. The train panted away across the desolate plain. Every whistle was a false alarm. Medina? . . . No! Some wretched siding where the train delayed, panting exhaustedly while sleepy, hooded figures, shrouded in heavy mantles, crowded under the roof of some barrack, which the light of their smoky lanterns only made more sinister. Jacinto smote his thigh:

"What on earth is this infamous train stopping for? There's no traffic. Nobody getting on or off? Oh, this Spain!"

A moribund bell tinkled. Once more we clove through the night and the tempest. Resignedly, I began to read through an old *Jornal do Commercio* which I had brought from Paris. Jacinto paced the thick carpet of the saloon, rancorously grumbling and growling like a wild beast. And so, drop by drop, passed away an hour that was filled with eternity. One whistle! Then another whistle! Stronger lights twinkled far off in the darkness and mist. The wheels ground on the rail-points with stiff jolts. Medina at last! A dirty wall of sheds showed dimly white on one side and suddenly, through the door, which was violently opened, a bearded figure in a Spanish cape appeared shouting for Don Jacinto.

"Hurry Sir! Hurry! The Salamanca train leaves at once. There is not a moment, gentlemen, not a moment."

I grabbed my coat and the *Jornal do Commercio*. We jumped out, feeling anxious. Across platforms, railway tracks, and puddles, tripping over bundles, pushed violently by the wind and also by the man in the Spanish cape, we went through another carriage-door which closed behind us with a terrific bang. We were both panting for breath. The saloon was upholstered in green cloth which seemed to eat up the scanty light. I was already reaching out an arm as if to relieve the hurrying porters of our baggage, when, in complete silence, without a warning whistle, the train began to

112

roll out of the station. We both yelled from the open windows:

"Stop! Our bags! Our bags! This way! Cricket! Oh Cricket!"

A squall of wind and rain drowned our yelling voices. Again it was a wild, savage plain under a torrential rain. Jacinto raised his arms.

"What an infamous service! What incompetent *canaille*! It could only happen in Spain! . . . And now? All our boxes lost . . . Not even a shirt or a brush!"

I tried to calm our friend: "Listen. I saw two porters piling up our luggage . . . Cricket was superintending . . . but in his hurry he had to bundle everything into the first compartment that was handy. It was a mistake not to bring Cricket with us . . . We could have played cards."

For the rest, the solicitude of that ever-present goddess, the Company, was watching over our comfort—for before the door of the lavatory glittered a huge hamper with our supper and a card on the cover in Spanish from Don Esteban:

"To Jacinto and his distinguished friend, hoping they will enjoy it."

"Are you hungry, Jacinto?"

"No, I am furious, horror-stricken and—sleepy!"

It is true that after such disconcerting emotions the only thing we really wanted was sleep and rest in the open, smooth, white beds that awaited us. When I fell on my pillows, collarless, in my underpants, my Prince, without undressing, with his feet wrapped in *my* coat, our unique remaining property, was snoring majestically.

Very long afterwards I noticed by my bunk, in the first light of the dawn which filtered faintly through the green curtain, a uniform and a peaked cap which murmured in infinite sweetness:

"Has your Excellency nothing to declare? Have you no hand baggage?"

It was my native land! I replied with a tender murmur: "We have nothing here. Will your excellency please enquire after our servant, Cricket? . . . Back yonder, in some other compartment. He has all the keys and all the luggage. He goes by the name of Cricket."

The uniform disappeared, like a benevolent shadow. I went to sleep again with my thoughts at Guiães, where Aunt Vicência was surely at work, with her white kerchief crossed on her breast, preparing the sucking-pig in welcome for my arrival.

I woke at last in a deep, long silence. It was a very restful station, well-swept, with small white roses climbing the walls, and other roses beyond clustering, in a garden, round a little weed-choked pond where mimosa trees poured forth the scent of their flowers. A pale youth, in a honey-coloured coat, bending his walking-stick against the ground, pensively contemplated the train. Crouching beside the garden railing, a woman with a basket of eggs was counting coppers into her lap. Pumpkins were drying on the station roof. Over all was spread the silky azure that made my eyes moisten with its beauty.

I shook Jacinto: "Wake up, man, you are in your own country."

He disentangled his feet from my coat, and came to the window, which I opened, to make his acquaintance with his native land.

"So this is Portugal, eh? . . . It smells nice, anyway!"

"Of course it smells good, you great fool!"

A bell tinkled languidly. The train gradually and restfully slid onwards as if it was for its own pleasure that it went out driving on the steel parallels to absorb and to enjoy the beauty of the earth and sky.

My Prince spread out his arms in despair: "Not a shirt, nor a brush, nor a drop of eau-de-Cologne . . . I enter Portugal in a filthy state."

"We stop some time at Regoa, where we can call Cricket and get all the comforts we require . . . But look at the river," I cried.

We were going along the side of a mountain over crags which fell into terraces planted with vines. Far beneath, surrounded with an esplanade, was a noble white mansion, in stately repose, with a little chapel brightly whitewashed in the midst of an orchard of ripe oranges. On the river where the muddy slow water did not break or foam on the rocks, was a boat with its sail fully spread, loaded with wine-barrels. Beyond were other terraces, of a pale, mignonette-green, were olive orchards dwarfed by the magnitude of the mountains; these terraces rose to clusters of huge crags which soaked themselves in the fine abundance of azure sunshine. Jacinto stroked his moustache saying:

"So that's the Douro? . . . It's interesting. It has grandeur. But oh, how hungry I am, Zé Fernandes!"

"So am I!"

We opened Don Esteban's hamper and drew forth a prodigious largesse of ham, lamb, partridges and other cold meats which the gold of two noble bottles of Amontillado and the red of two bottles of Rioja warmed with the heat of an Andalusian sun. During the ham course, Jacinto contritely lamented his grave error in having left such a historic mansion as that of Tormes, unfurnished, abandoned and empty. How delightful it would have been on such a warm and brilliant morning as this to go up to the mountain ranges to a house that was all in readiness with civilized comforts. To cheer him up I reminded him that the labours of Silverio with all the huge cases we had sent from Paris would by now have rendered Tormes a comfortable residence even for Epicurus. Oh, but what Jacinto meant was a perfect palace, a Number 202 in the wilderness. Thus discoursing, we began to attack the partridges. I was uncorking a bottle of Rioja, when the train, very serenely, drew into a station. It was Regoa. My Prince put his head out to call Cricket, and to demand the luggage which contained the necessaries for our toilet.

"Wait, Jacinto! We've lots of time," I said. "The train stops here for an hour. Go on eating in peace. Don't spoil this meal with the bundling about of luggage . . . Cricket won't be long in arriving."

I drew back the curtain, because, from the outside, a very tall priest with the end of a cigarette on his lip, had stopped indiscreetly to spy upon our feast. When we finished the partridges Jacinto unwrapped the Manchego cheese. Still neither Cricket nor Anatole put in an appearance : so I went, somewhat anxiously to the carriage door to hasten these tardy servants . . . and at that very moment the train started sneaking out of the station with the same crafty silence as before. It was a disaster for my Prince.

" Again we're stranded without a comb or a brush . . . And I had to change my shirt. It's all your damned fault, Zé Fernandes!"

" It's frightful. The train usually waits here for an eternity. Today it no sooner arrives, than it's gone! Patience, Jacinto. In two more hours we'll be at the Station of Tormes . . . Also, what need is there to change your shirt to go up into the mountains. You can have a bath before supper. They must have installed a bath by now!"

We both consoled ourselves with little glasses of a divine brandy from Chinchon. Then lying back on the sofas we savoured our two last cigars with the windows open to the adorable fresh air. We spoke of Tormes. Silverio would certainly be at the station with the horses . . .

" How long does it take to ride there? "

" About an hour. After having washed, there will still be time for quite a long excursion round your acres, with the excellent Melchior, your head farmer, so that the Lord of the Manor may solemnly take possession of his land and heritage. And tonight your first feast in the mountains with all the famous tit-bits and delicacies of the real old Portugal."

Jacinto smiled. He was intrigued and charmed. " Well, let's see what sort of *cuisine* this Silverio has arranged for me. I insisted that he should be a superb cook of classical Portuguese dishes. But that he should also know the elements of French cooking—how to truffle a turkey, how to serve beef in a broth of gizzards, and such simple things as that. But the worst of it is you're not staying but going on to Guiães!"

" Yes, old fellow; Aunt Vicência's birthday on Saturday . . . A sacred day. But I'll come back. In two weeks I'll be at Tormes, to have a real bucolic with you. And also to attend the interment of the remains? "

Jacinto stretched out his arm. "What mansion is that away on the hillside there, with a tower?"

I did not know. Some country house belonging to a squire of the Douro . . . Tormes was built in that stout and massive fashion. A house centuries old, and good for many centuries to come—but without a tower.

"And can you see it from the station?"

"No, it's very high, in a fold of the mountains, hidden among trees."

In my Prince's mind a real interest in his ancestral home was beginning to form. He looked impatiently at his watch. Still thirty minutes more. Then, fully savouring the light and the air with the first enchantment of an initiate, he murmured: "What mildness! What peace!"

I kept my old copy of the *Jornal do Commercio* in the coat which hung over my arm. Both of us were standing at the window excitedly waiting for the little station of Tormes to appear, the end of all our trials. It did appear at length, humble and white, on the bank of the river amongst great rocks, with its bright sunflowers filling a narrow garden, two tall fig trees shading its courtyard and, behind, the range clothed in dense woodlands . . .

Soon I recognized, on the platform, the huge paunch and the chubby cheeks of the station-master, the blond Pimenta, once my school-mate in the course of Rhetoric at the Lyceum of Braga. The horses would certainly be waiting in the shade of the trees.

Hardly had the train stopped when we leaped lightly out. The rotund mass of Pimenta waddled towards me with affection: "Long live my friend Zé Fernandes!"

"Ah, my fine Pimenta!"

I introduced the lord of Tormes. "Isn't Silverio here?" I asked Pimenta.

"No. It's almost two months since he left for Castelo de Vide, to visit his mother who was wounded by the toss of a bull."

I stole an anxious look at Jacinto: "Well now! And Melchior the head-farm-hand? . . . Isn't he here with the horses to take us up to the farm?"

117

The station-master arched his maize-coloured eyebrows.
"No! Neither Melchior, nor horses . . . It's an age since I've seen Melchior."

The porter rang a bell for the train to leave. Then, turning round and finding neither servants nor luggage on the platform, my Prince and I uttered the same agonized cry . . . "What of Cricket? What about the luggage?" We ran along the side of the train, which was already moving out, yelling "Cricket! Cricket! Anatole! Cricket!"

In the hope that he or Anatole had fatally overslept themselves, we leaped on to the steps of the carriages thrusting our faces into various compartments and calling their names, startling the passengers within, with the cry "Cricket, are you there, Cricket?" Then from a third-class carriage in which a guitar was tinkling a jesting voice yelled "Anyone seen a cricket? Here are some gentlemen looking for a cricket." Not a sign of Anatole or Cricket!

The bell tinkled once more.

"Oh Pimenta, my dear friend," I cried. "Don't let the train go out! Our baggage will be lost."

In the deepest distress I pushed the enormous station-master towards the luggage-van to try to unearth our twenty-three trunks. We only saw barrels, willow baskets, cans of milk, and one trunk, tied up with rope. Jacinto lividly bit his lip. Pimenta, gazing wide-eyed, entreated us:

"But, my dear fellows, I can't delay the train any longer."

The bell rang again. And with lovely white smoke curling to the sky, the train disappeared behind the high crags. There we remained completely frustrated and lost in the mountains without the manager, the steward, the horses and our luggage. I had my overcoat with the *Jornal* inside it. Jacinto had a walking-stick. These comprised our portable goods. Pimenta stared at us pityingly with his tiny pouched eyes. I then recounted to him our frantic adventure in Medina in the rain; how Cricket must have missed the train, been stranded with our twenty-three boxes, and was probably on his way back to Madrid without leaving us a single clout.

"I haven't even got a handkerchief. This *Jornal do Commercio* is the nearest thing to white linen that I have left."

"What a terrible vexation!" muttered Pimenta, deeply distressed. "And now, what are you going to do?"

"Now," I exclaimed, "we'll have to climb to the farm on foot—unless we can arrange for a couple of donkeys round here."

Then the porter remembered that quite near, at the Farm of the Giesta (Broom-bush) which still belonged to the Tormes estate, the foreman had a fine mare and a jackass. The obliging fellow set off at a run to the Giesta—while Jacinto and I sank panting and exhausted on the station seat. The huge Pimenta with his hands in his pockets did nothing but gaze at us, and murmur, "How very vexing!"

The river in front of us descended somnolently in the heavy calm of May, embracing without a murmur a large island of rock which glittered in the sun. The mountain range rose beyond in gradual undulations with one deep fold in which a bright little village nestled. The immense space around was filled with an immense silence. In this solitude of mountain and crags, even the little sparrows flitting on the roof-top seemed to be much bigger than they were : and the massive rotundity of the station-master dominated the whole region.

"Everything is arranged, sir. The animals are on the way . . . The only thing lacking is a saddle for the donkey."

It was that excellent man, the porter, who had returned from the Giesta flourishing in his hands two odd spurs of different shape, but matching perfectly in rustiness. Soon appeared a dapple-grey mare, a donkey with a pack saddle, a boy and a spaniel—to take us to Tormes. We shook the sweaty hand of Pimenta. I yielded up the mare to the Lord of Tormes. We began to climb the rough road which had not been smoothed or tamed since the time it was trodden by the Jacintos of the fourteenth century. Soon after crossing a crazy timber bridge, over a rivulet purling on gravel, Jacinto with the eye of a master-farmer suddenly sharpened as though by hereditary instinct, noticed the robustness and the healthy growth of the olive trees. Very shortly our misfortunes were all forgotten in the beauty of those blessed mountains.

With what brilliance and masterly inspiration had the

divine Artist made the mountains! How lovingly he had cared for them! How richly he had endowed them in this, his well-beloved Portugal! Their grandeur was equalled by their grace. Down the profoundly hollowed valleys descended armies of trees so thickly foliaged and smoothly rounded, and of such a luscious green, that they seemed a carpet of moss whereon it would be delightful to fall and roll. From the slopes overhanging the rugged path, huge branches over-canopied us with tents of shade, from which the flocks of birds, as they scattered, shook down fragrance over us. From every clod, from every cranny, wild flowers blossomed. White crags, polished by wind and sun, strewed the hillsides with their solid nudity: others, covered with lichen and forests of wild flowers, jutted like the prows of galleys garlanded for some pagan feast day: and here and there, between those which towered at the summit, could be seen shepherd's huts, which seemed to be looking out through their black windows, from beneath the wisps of verdure which the wind had sown on their tiles. Everywhere was the whisper of water, creative, fertilizing water. Lively springs fled laughing over the pebbles, between the hoofs of the donkey and the mare. Headlong streams fell crashing from rock to rock: straight, shining threads, like silver wires, trembled and flashed as they hung from the sides of ravines: and many a fountain, placed by the side of a footpath, spouted the beneficent refreshment of man and beast. Sometimes a whole hilltop would be a cornland whereon an immense ancestral chestnut-tree would dominate the scene as if it were its lord and guardian. Under steep embankments were shining green orange-groves. Paths of flat, loose stone-slabs ran through rich meadows where sheep and cattle were frisking. The narrowest of them ran between steep walls, and disappeared into the fresh gloom of overhanging vines. Then we would climb up some little street through a village of ten or twelve huts, buried in the foliage of fig-trees, from whose roofs rose a white smoke, fragrant with pine. On the more distant ranges, above the blackness of the pines, shone little white hermitages. The pure fine air entered one's very soul and filled it with vigour and joy. A faint sound of cowbells faded through the gullies. Jacinto, in front on the dappled mare, murmured. "What beauty!"

And I behind him on the ass of Sancho Panza, murmured: "What beauty!"

Fresh green branches stroked our shoulders. Across the hedges weighted with berries, the brambles offered us green masses of fruit, since none were ripe yet. All the windows of an old house with a cross on its summit, flashed a hospitable greeting as we passed. A blackbird followed us, from oak to elm, for a long time, singing our praises. Thank you, brother blackbird. Thank you, bramble vines. Here we come! Here we come! And we shall always remain with you, hospitable sierra, sierra of contentment and peace, most blessed sierra of all the sierras in the world!

Thus wandering and full of wonder we came at last to the avenue of beeches which always enchanted me with its lordly solemnity. Giving the donkey a cut with his switch our boy, with the dog frisking at his heels, shouted: "Here we are, my masters!" And away at the end of the beech avenue appeared the gate of Tormes, with its coat of arms in granite, covered with the moss of ages, which rendered it more venerable still. The dogs were furiously barking already, within the gate. And when Jacinto on his sweating mare with me behind on the donkey of Sancho passed the manorial entrance, a fat man came down the worn stone steps from the lofty porch, with his head shaven like a priest, without a coat or a waistcoat, and began to call off the dogs who seemed to be especially infuriated with my Prince. It was Melchior, the head of the farm-hands. He had no sooner recognized me than his mouth opened in a toothless smile of the warmest hospitality. But no sooner had I revealed the identity of the gentleman with the golden moustache, who got down from the mare, rubbing his hindquarters, than the good Melchior recoiled in amazement and terror, as if from a phantom.

"Well now! . . . By the holy name of God . . . Well then . . ."

And between the snarling of the dogs, wildly waving his arms, he began a story which, in his turn, terrified Jacinto as if the whole dark wall of the mansion were about to topple on to his head. Melchior had not been expecting His Excellency (he said " Incellency ") . . . Senhor Silverio had been in Castelo de Vide since last March with his mother, who had received a horn wound in the groin from a bull. There must have been some mistake, letters had gone astray perhaps. Because Senhor Silverio hadn't counted on a visit from His Excellency till the following September at vintage time. In the house the reconstruction was going on little by little. The roof on the southern wing had not been tiled yet. Most of the windows had not been paned with glass yet. And there was not a single bed arranged in the whole house.

Jacinto crossed his arms in a furious rage which seemed to suffocate him.

" But the cases . . . the cases I had sent from Paris four months ago? "

Poor Melchior stared with his little eyes moistening with tears. The cases? None had arrived! None had appeared! And in his agitation he seemed to look for them under the arches of the courtyard and to feel for them in his pockets. Cases? No, he hadn't seen any cases.

" And what now, Zé Fernandes? "

I shrugged my shoulders. " Now, my son, the only thing to be done is for you to come with me to Guiães . . . But that means a good two hours more in the saddle. And we have no horses now. The best thing is to have a look round the house, eat the chicken which Melchior will roast on the spit for us, and, early tomorrow morning, before the heat sets in, trot away up there to my Aunt Vicência's."

Jacinto replied with furious determination : " Tomorrow I trot, but down there to the station . . . and then on to Lisbon ! "

He went up the worn steps of the mansion in a bitterly rancorous mood. Above, a verandah went along the front of the house under a porch of black beams, adorned within its granite pillars and piled with wooden boxes full of carnations. I picked a yellow one, and followed Jacinto into the noble rooms, which he contemplated with a horrified grumble of curses. They were enormous rooms each with the sonority of a cathedral chapter, their walls blackened by age, freez-

ingly cold, desolately bare, with here and there an osier basket
or a mattock surrounded by planks. The windows without
glass still had those solid shutters, with bolts and bars that,
when they are closed, spread pitch darkness. Under our footsteps now and then a rotten plank creaked and gave way.

"Why, it's completely uninhabitable," Jacinto roared. "It's
infamous! It's horrible."

But later, in other rooms, the floor-planks alternated with
new boards and repairs: and even in the ancient, dark oak
ceiling were new white planks. The walls repelled one with
the glaring crudity of their thick coats of brilliant whitewash: and the sun had difficulty in piercing the newly set
panes, so spattered were they with lime and marked with
putty by the fingers of the glaziers. We entered the last and
largest room of all, which was lit by six windows, and contained a wardrobe with a straw pallet in one corner. We
halted by this pallet where we deposited all that remained
of our twenty-three trunks—my coat, Jacinto's stick, and the
Jornal do Commercio which was our joint property. Through
the wide-open windows without panes, the great wind of the
sierra entered and circulated freely bringing the fresh scent
of gardens being watered. But what we saw from the edge
of the pallet was a forest of pines covering the crest of the
peak and descending the smooth slopes like an army on the
march with the leaders standing out, very straight, with black
plumes streaming in the wind: beyond the river, farther
away, the ranges were of a fine smooth violet colour: and
from the valleys beneath us, lost and melancholy, rose the
voice of a shepherd singing.

Jacinto went slowly to a stone window-seat: whereon he
seemed to collapse helplessly before this sudden disappearance
of Civilization. I felt the pallet which was as hard and cold
as granite in midwinter. Then thinking of the luxurious
cushions of down and springs which had been so prodigally
packed at Number 202, I also gave vent to my indignation.
"But those packing-cases. Good God! How could anyone
lose some thirty-odd packing-cases of such an enormous
size?"

"Scattered about, I suppose, here and there, or somewhere

in a shed . . . Perhaps in Medina, that unspeakable Medina!
. . . The indifference of the Railway Companies; the laziness
of that damned Silverio . . . The whole peninsula is an unspeakable barbarism."

I knelt on the opposite window-seat, looking out with eyes
consoled by Heaven and the mountains beneath it. "How
beautiful it is!"

And my Prince, after a very grave silence with his chin in
his hand answered : " It is beautiful . . . and what peace !"

Beneath that window a garden luxuriated with beans,
lettuces, cabbages and huge pumpkin leaves. A cement
threshing-floor, very old and rough, dominated the valley,
from which already the mist was rising from a hidden river
very far down. All the corner of the mansion on the side
where we were jutted out into a big orange-grove. And from
a rustic fountain, half-buried in trembling roses, spouted a
long and glittering streak of water.

"I am simply desperate for a drink of that water," said
Jacinto, quite seriously.

"I, too. . . . Let's go down into the farmyard."

We returned to the verandah. My Prince, somewhat more
resigned to the inclemency of his fate, picked a yellow carna-
tion. By another low door with very stiff hinges, we came
into a room, strewn with rubbish, roofless and over-arched
only with massive rafters, from which whirled a flight of
sparrows.

"Just look at this horror," Jacinto exclaimed shuddering.
We went down a gloomy castle-stairway, groping along a
huge corridor of rough slabs, encumbered with huge chests,
capable of storing the grain of a vast province. In this darkness, in a corner, on the black soil, flamed a red fire, licking
pots and pans of iron, and discharging through a barred opening in the wall, a torrent of smoke which flowed out into the
leaves of a lemon-grove. Round that enormous hearth where
the Jacintos of the Middle Ages had roasted their chunks of
beef and pig, but now neglected by the frugality of the farm-
hands, were blackened and rusted dusty piles of baskets and
heaps of old iron. Light entered through an open chestnut-
wood door, which showed a garden full of jonquils and

lombard cabbages. Around this fire an excited crowd of
women plucked fowls, stirred saucepans and chopped onions,
with heated, talkative fervour. They all fell silent when we
appeared—and in the midst of them with his blood flushing
red in his pale fat face of an Abbé, Melchior ran towards us,
swearing that " the little supper of your Incellencies will not
be delayed for longer than it takes to say the Creed."

" And what are we going to do in the way of beds,
Melchior ? "

The worthy man whispered a bashful excuse : " On straw
pallets on the floor."

" That will suffice," I said, to console him. " For one night
with clean sheets."

" I can answer for the sheets," said he. " But it is a great
pity. You have caught us without a single woollen coverlet,
or even a sirloin of beef . . . But I've suddenly thought . . .
your Incellencies could go and sleep at ' The Nest ', the house
of Silverio. He has iron bedsteads and washstands . . . It's
still a league away and the road is bad . . ."

Jacinto broke in good-humouredly. " No : everything will
be all right . . . I even prefer to sleep at Tormes, in my own
house in the mountains."

We went out into the open, a piece of garden cut off and
surrounded by big rocks covered with creepers, which bordered on the terraces of the mountain side where the rye was
beginning to grow golden. My Prince drank deeply the snowy,
clear water of the fountain with his lips to the spout. The
crisp thick lettuces made his mouth water : and he made
several jumps to try to catch the high branches of a luscious
cherry-tree which was covered with fruit. Then passing the
old wine-press with a flock of white pigeons on its roof, we
went down to a path cut in the side of the mountain. Walking pensively along, my Prince stared with wonder at the
maize-fields, at the ancient oaks planted by the earliest
Jacintos, and at the peasants' huts scattered over the summits
on the fringe of the pine-forests.

Once more we entered the lordly avenue of beeches and
entered the noble gateway amidst the barking of dogs, which
were now more docile, instinctively scenting their master.

125

Jacinto admitted there was a certain nobility in the front view of his old home. But he delighted in the long avenue of beeches which was so straight and massive, as if it had been designed for cavalcades of lords and ladies with waving plumes and pages. Afterwards, from the height of the verandah, noticing the new roof on the chapel, he even found a good word for that " lazybones " Silverio for having at least looked after the dwelling of the Good Lord.

" This verandah is also very agreeable," he said, sinking his face into the scented carnations. " It will require big armchairs and some wicker couches."

Inside the house, in " our room ", we both sat at the window-seats contemplating the mild crepuscular peace that slowly settled over hills and valleys. Very high up burned the tiny diamond of Venus, announcing the night and all its consolations. Jacinto had never considered for long that planet of amorous refulgence which still commemorates in our Catholic Heaven the incomparable Goddess of Love : nor had he ever, with attentive spirit, watched the majestic peace in which Nature turns to her sleep. The blackening of the mountains as they muffled themselves in shade : the trees falling still as if weary of whispering : the whiteness of the houses softly growing dim : the blanket of mist under which the cool valleys nestled and covered themselves : the solemn sound of a chapel bell rolling over the crags and ravines : the secret whispering of the watercourses to the grasses—were all initiations for Jacinto.

From this entrancement Melchior jolted us with the announcement that the supper was ready for " your Incellencies." It was in another room more abandoned and naked than the one we had just left. At the door my super-civilized Prince stopped dead as if frightened by the discomfort, the bareness, and the roughness of everything. On the table against the blackened wall, which was stained with the soot of oil-lamps, on a table cloth of sacking, two tallow candles in tin candlesticks illuminated huge dishes of yellow earthenware, flanked with tin spoons and iron forks. The glasses of great thickness still bore the red shade of all the wine which had passed in and out of them during many years of bumper-

126

vintages. The clay bowl which was heaped with black olives would have delighted Diogenes. Struck into the crust of an immense loaf gleamed a huge knife like a scythe blade. And from the ancestral chair reserved for my Prince, one of the last relics of the ancient Jacintos, stiffly backed with leather and with woodwork eaten away by borers, the horsehair fell out in handfuls from the tears and rents in the polished seat of it.

A formidable-looking maid with huge breasts that shook about in the folds of the crossed kerchief on her bosom, still sweating and red from the heat of the fire, entered crushing the floor-boards with a steaming earthenware soup tureen. Then Melchior, who entered carrying the pitcher of wine, hoped that our " Incellencies " would forgive him because there had not been time to let the soup get properly clear . . . Jacinto took the ancestral seat and for some moments (moments of terrible anxiety for the poor head-farm-hand) energetically rubbed the black fork and the tarnished spoon with the corner of the table cloth. Then, very suspiciously, he tasted the soup, which was of chicken, and smelt very good. He tasted it and then raised to me (his comrade in hardships) two eyes that shone with delighted surprise. He tasted a bigger spoonful and considered the result for a longer time. He smiled, and said, in amazement: " It's good!"

It was delicious. It contained liver and gizzard. Its perfume filled one with tenderness. Three times I attacked that soup with fervour.

"I am also having another," exclaimed Jacinto, with immense conviction. " I am still very hungry . . . Good God. It's years since I felt such hunger."

He greedily scraped the bottom of the soup tureen: and was already looking through the door for the bearer of such delicacies, that sturdy girl with the shaking breasts who at last appeared redder than before and placed on the table a dish heaped over with rice and broad beans. What a disappointment! Jacinto, in Paris, could never abide broad beans. Nevertheless, he tried a timid forkful and once again his eyes, which had momentarily darkened with pessimism, sought

127

mine, shining with pleasure. He took another large forkful with the deliberate slowness of a Friar who is enjoying himself at a feast. Then he shouted enthusiastically: " Couldn't be better. This sort of broad beans, yes! By all means. Oh what beans! What a treat!"

This blessed appetite of his led him on to praising the wholè sierra, the women downstairs who were stirring the pots, and the good Melchior who had presided over the soup . . .

" Melchior, my friend, you could not get such rice and beans in the whole of Paris."

The dear old man smiled, completely cheered up. Well, that's the food of the farm-hands here on this farm. Plateful after plateful till your Incellencies would burst out laughing. . . . But now he is here, Senhor Dom Jacinto will be able to grow strong and stout also.

The good old foreman sincerely believed that lost in faraway places such as Paris, the Lord of Tormes, far from the abundance of his land, really starved and got thin. Jacinto, in truth, seemed to be sating some ancient and atavistic memory of abundance, as he broke out into more lavish praises with every dish he tasted. Before the golden-crusted chicken which had been roasted on the spit, and the salad which had made his mouth water so in the garden, but was now tempered with oil of the mountain olives worthy of the palate of Plato, he cried: "This is divine!" But nothing pleased him so much as the wine of Tormes, falling from high up, out of the raised pitcher, and possessing more soul, and penetrating the soul more deeply, than many a poem or sacred book could so. Inspecting by the light of the tallow candles the thick glass which it fringed with rosy foam, he began to recite Virgil: " *Quo te carmina dicam, Rethica?* Who is worthy to sing your praises, beloved wine of these mountains? "

I, who did not want to be outshone in classical knowledge, also dusted up my Virgil in praise of the country life: " *Hanc olim veteres vitam coluere Sabini*; So lived the ancient Sabines. So lived Romulus and Remus . . . and so the valiant Etruria. By such means Rome became the marvel of the world."

Immovable, and tightly clutching the pitcher of wine,

128

Melchior gazed at us with infinite wonder and religious reverence.

We dined delightfully under the superintendence of Melchior, who, like some tutelary providence, even supplied us with tobacco afterwards. And as the night lengthened before us, we went to the paneless windows of the largest room to contemplate the sumptuous skies of the summer night. We philosophized that night with calm and lazy eloquence. In the City (Jacinto observed) one never noticed the stars since they were obscured by gas-flares and electric globes. For that reason (I continued) one never entered into communion with the Universe which is the unique glory and consolation of this life. But in the mountains, without six-storeyed buildings, without the pall of smoke that hides God, without the cases which, like leaden weights, drag one's soul down into the dust—a Jacinto, or a Zé Fernandes, can sit smoking at a window, and look at, and be looked at by, all the stars in heaven: and they, those others inquisitively, anxiously, with a light that beckons and calls to one, seem to be trying to reveal their secrets to us and, from those immense distances, trying to unravel our own.

"Jacinto," I asked. "What star is that that flames so brightly just by the edge of the roof?"

"I don't know, Zé Fernandes . . . and that other just at the crest of the pinewood?"

"I don't know."

We did not know: I—because of the thick crust of ignorance with which I issued from the womb of my spiritual mother Coimbra University: Jacinto—because in his library he possessed three hundred and eight treatises on Astronomy and knowledge when thus accumulated forms a mountain which cannot be transported, or chipped into samples. But what did it matter to us which one was Sirius and which Aldebaran any more than it mattered to the stars which of us was Jacinto and which Zé. They, so immense, we so tiny, are the work of the same Will. And all, whether one is Uranus or merely Zé Fernandes Lorena de Noronha e Sande, constitute different expressions of the same unique Being, and our diversity adds

129

up to the same compact Unity. Molecules of the same all, governed by the same law, rolling to the same end. From the star to the man, from the man to the clover-flower, from the clover-flower to the ocean—all form the same body through which circulates, like blood, the same God. Not a single tremor of life, however tiny, passes through a single fibre of that body, its repercussion is felt by all, even to the most humble, even to those that appear the most inert and insensible. When a sun, which it never saw and will never see, dies of exhaustion, that slim branch of a lemon-tree down there in the garden feels a secret shudder of death: and when I stamp my foot on the soil here in Tormes, the monstrous Saturn yonder feels a tremor which runs through the whole Universe. Jacinto dropped his hand on the window-sill, and I cried: "Believe it!—even the sun trembles."

And then (as I observed) we should take into consideration that on every one of those luminous grains of dust was a whole creation incessantly born, dying, and being reborn. At this very moment other Jacintos and other Zés are seated at the windows of other Tormeses contemplating the midnight sky and perhaps even that infinitesimal point of light which is our majestic earth as we see it. All of them will not necessarily be framed as fragilely or uncomfortably as ourselves, nor be so singularly burlesque and ugly as we are (if the Vatican Apollo and the Venus de Milo are not so, themselves). But whether horrifying of ineffably lovely: whether colossal with flesh as hard as granite, or light as gases and waving in the wind, all of them are thinking beings and conscious of life—because certainly every world possesses its Descartes, or else our Descartes has visited them all with his method, in his dark cape, with his elegant acuteness, formulating what is perhaps the only certainly which is really certain: *I think, therefore I exist.* Accordingly all we inhabitants of worlds who are sitting at our windows, away there in Saturn or on our little earthlet, are constantly perfecting an act which penetrates us and melts us in one: that is to feel in thought the common nucleus of our modalities, and so realize for one moment in our consciousness the Unity of the Universe!
—"Eh, Jacinto?"

My friend half-snored: "Perhaps . . . I'm dropping with sleep."

"So am I. 'We are going back a long way' as Pestaminha used to say at Coimbra. But nothing is more beautiful, nor more useless than a chat in the mountains when one is looking at the stars. Are you still set on going tomorrow?"

"Certainly, Zé Fernandes. With the certainty of Descartes, *I think, therefore I'm leaving!* What else can one do in this old ruin, without a bed, an armchair, or a book? Man does not live by rice and beans alone. But I'll stay in Lisbon to talk to the Administrator of my estates, Sesimbra. Also I hope these reconstructions will soon be finished, that the packing-cases turn up, and that I can come back here decently with my linen washed for the transference . . ."

"That's true, the bones . . ."

"Also there's Cricket . . . What a fat-head! . . . Where on earth can that poor lost soul be wandering about?"

Then slowly walking up and down the big room, where the tallow candle shone with the light of a cigarette in a desert, we speculated on the fate of Cricket. The worthy negro, excited by the cries of haste, must have jumped out, with the twenty-three boxes, on to the mud at Medina . . . or else dozing comfortably he might be rolling back with Anatole to Madrid. But whatever had happened, my Prince found it equally disastrous for his personal comfort.

"No, listen, Jacinto," I said. "If Cricket was stranded at Medina, he would spend the night at the Railway Inn catching bedbugs, and come on this morning to Tormes. When you go down to the station at four tomorrow, you'll find your man, on the very same train in which you are going on to Oporto and the Capital!"

Jacinto writhed his arms like somebody struggling in the meshes of a net.

"But what if he went on to Madrid from Medina?"

"Then some time this week, he'll turn up here at Tormes, where he'll receive the order to go to Lisbon and re-enter your service. There remains the interesting subject of my own luggage. If you meet Cricket at the station tomorrow, separate from your luggage my black box, my canvas bag,

131

and my hat-box. Cricket knows. And tell Pimenta to let me know at Guiães. If Cricket manages to reach Tormes itself with all that pile of luggage, he can leave my stuff with Melchior. I'll speak to Melchior tomorrow."

Jacinto furiously shook his collar: " But how can I leave for Lisbon with a shirt I've been wearing for two days running and which is giving me a ghastly itch already? And without a handkerchief? Not even a toothbrush? "

Fertile in ideas, I made a tutelary gesture with outstretched hands like a guardian angel: " All will come right, Jacinto, all will be well. I shall leave here early in the morning at six. I shall reach Guiães at ten, and before I have a bit of breakfast or a chat with Aunt Vicência, I'll send a boy with a sackful of white linen. My shirts and drawers may be too big for you, but a beggar like you cannot afford to be fastidious about elegance or the cut of his clothes. The boy, at a good trot, will get here in two hours. You'll have time to change before you leave for the station. I'll put in a toothbrush."

" Oh, Zé Fernandes, for God's sake put in a sponge, too, and a bottle of eau-de-Cologne."

" Lavender-water, if you like, made by my Aunt Vicência."

My Prince sighed deeply, very much impressed by his squalid misery, and this gift of linen.

" Well, let's go to bed. I'm exhausted what with so many emotions and so many stars."

Just then Melchior opened the heavy doors to tell us that our beds were ready. Following the farm-hand, who held a lamp over his head, what did we see, my Prince and I, who but a moment before had been proudly "brothering" the stars and the suns? In two tiny partitions which were separated by a low stone arch, lay two pallets of maize-husks on the floor itself. By the larger pillow, which belonged, of course, to the Lord of Tormes, was a candlestick on a bushel-measure turned bottom up: at the foot of the bed was a glazed earthenware bowl on a three-footed stool, by way of a wash-stand. For me, a highlander of those sierras, there was neither a bowl nor a bushel-can.

Slowly, with his foot, my civilized friend felt the pallet. Certainly it must have seemed of an intransigeant hardness, since he remained leaning over it and running his fingers over his face in dismay.

" But the worst of it isn't the pallet," he mumbled with a sigh. " It is that I have no nightshirt nor slippers. And I can't lie down in a starched shirt."

Through an inspiration of mine, he referred to Melchior : he came back with a pair of clogs for Jacinto's bare feet, and an enormous nightgown belonging to one of the farm women of coarse cloth, as rough as the hair shirt of a penitent, with flounces and embroidery more stiff and hard than woodwork-carving. To console my Prince I reminded him that neither Plato, when he wrote the *Banquet* nor Vasco da Gama, when he was rounding the Cape, were sleeping on the best beds at the time. Hard pallets make strong spirits, Jacinto ! It's only the rough serge tunic that ever gets into Paradise.

" Have you, by any chance, anything to read ? " my friend asked drily. " I can't go to sleep without reading."

I ? A book ? I had only that old copy of the *Jornal do Commercio* which had survived the dispersal of our property. I tore the copious sheaf down the middle and gave him half with fraternal impartiality. He took his half which comprised the advertisements. Anybody who did not see Jacinto then, squatting on the side of his pallet, beside the tallow candle, with his feet in wooden clogs, half-lost in the rough folds of a highland farm-woman's nightdress, and reading through a piece of an out-of-date Gazette, the arrivals and departures of the mailboats and liners—could never know what the absolute image of intense dejection looks like !

Already having retired into my spartan cubicle, I was unbottoning my waistcoat, full of delicious weariness, when Jacinto called out :

" Zé Fernandes !"

" What ? "

" Send me also a boot button-hook in the bag tomorrow."

Comfortably stretched on my stiff couch I was murmuring " God be praised !" as I always do before the advent of sleep, who is the cousin of Death. Then I took the half of the *Jornal do Commercio* which belonged to me.

" Zé Fernandes !"

133

" What's the matter? "

" You might also put into the bag some tooth-powder, a nail-file, and a novel."

My *Jornal* was already escaping from my sleepy hand when I heard through a yawn :

" Zé Fernandes !"

" Eh ? "

" Write to me to the Hotel Braganza in Lisbon. . . . At least the sheets are fresh and smell nice and wholesome."

9

EARLY next morning, soundlessly, so as not to to wake Jacinto who, with his hands crossed on his chest, slept beatifically on his couch of granite, I left for Guiães.

At the end of a week, returning one morning for lunch, I encountered my long-lost luggage in the passage; it had been brought by a farm-hand from the Giesta with the good wishes of Senhor Pimenta. My thoughts leaped towards my Prince, so I sent off the following cheerful telegram to him at the Hotel Braganza in Lisbon : " Are you still there? I see you have recovered Cricket and Civilization. Hurrah! A hearty embrace! I am all turned to asparagus! Reply when you return. Delightful weather. Twenty-three Centigrade in the shade. How are your bones feeling? " After that came the popular religious festival of Our Lady of Roqueirinha. During the new moon I had to attend a clearing of brushwood on my land at Corcas. My Aunt Vicência was suffering from an indigestion of her own black puddings. The stony silence of my Prince seemed ungrateful and unfriendly.

Then, one afternoon, when I was returning from the Farm of the Geranium Flower, my cousin Joaninha's place. I stopped at Manuel Rico's country store to taste a certain white wine which my spirit knows well—and craves for always.

At the smithy door opposite was Severo, the nephew of Melchior of Tormes, and the finest vet and farrier in the range. He was chopping up tobacco, straddled on a bench.

I ordered another pint of wine; Severo was patting the neck of my mare which he had once saved from a severe chill. I asked after Melchior, he told me he had supped with him the night before at Tormes, and had also seen *the Master.*

"Well, I never! . . . So Dom Jacinto is at Tormes?"

My amazement amused Severo. "So your Excellency did not know? Why, he has been at Tormes, he has, during the last five weeks! It seems he is staying on for the grape-harvest. Big things are happening there!"

Heavens above! The next day, a Sunday, after Mass I saddled up and set out at a trot for Tormes without being discouraged by the sweltering, heavy stillness of the day. To the barking of the sheep-dogs, Melchior's wife ran to greet me from the corral with an earthen pot at her hips.

"Senhor Dom Jacinto? . . . He's down there with Silverio and Melchior in the fields of the ash-wood."

"And Senhor Cricket, the coloured man?"

"I saw him a little while ago with the Frenchman, picking sweet lemons."

All the windows of the old mansion shone with new glass. In a corner of the courtyard I saw tubs of whitewash and buckets of paint. A stonemason's ladder was taking its Sabbath-day rest, leaning against the eaves. By the chapel wall, two cats slept on a mountain of straw that appeared to have been disembowelled from a considerable number of big packing-cases.

"Well," I thought, "here comes Civilization again!"

I stabled my horse and ran up the stair. On the verandah, under a pile of laths, a zinc bath blazed in a ray of sunlight. Inside the house, I found all the floors had been repaired and brushed smooth with hard brooms. The walls, thickly white-washed, froze one like those of a convent. A room to which I was led with true highland frankness by three wide open doors, was certainly Jacinto's. Clothes hung from wooden pegs. An iron bedstead with a fustian cover timidly shrunk its virginal rigidity into one corner between the wall and a wooden bench on which a brass candlestick stood on a copy of *Don Quixote*; on an imitation bamboo washstand, the jug and basin and a huge cake of soap could hardly find room for themselves; and a tiny shelf sufficed to hold the neat array of brush, comb, nail-scissors, shaving mirror of the kind you buy at fairs, and the little flask of lavender-water I had sent from Guiães. The three windows, without curtains, looked straight out into the beauty of the range, breathing a soft and delicate air which had been first perfumed by the resin of the pine-forests, and then by the roses of the garden. Opposite, across the passage, another bedroom duplicated the same frugal simplicity of the first. Obviously the foresight of my Prince had dedicated this room to his friend, Zé Fernandes. Hanging from the rack was an old silken dust-coat of mine.

But in the immense room where we had philosophized and star-gazed, Jacinto had arranged a sanctuary for study and repose—and here apparently had happened the " big things " referred to by Severo. Copious Madeira armchairs offered the comfort of cushions of printed cotton. On an enormous table of plain white wood, carpentered in Tormes, I admired a triple candlestick, a monkish inkpot, stuck with goose-quill pens, and a chapel-vase filled with carnations. Between two of the windows was an ancient chest of drawers with wrought-iron work which was soon to receive on its rose-coloured marble cover the sacred weight of the Christmas crib, the manger where the Kings, the shepherds with bright smiles, the lambs with shaggy wool, would press around the child, who from his grotto would open wide his arms, beneath an enormous royal crown of gold. A wooden bookstand occupied another space of the wall between two dark portraits in black frames. On one of its shelves were two guns : scattered on the other shelves like doctors on their benches in solemn council, were a few noble books, a Plutarch, a Virgil, an Odyssey, an Epictetus, and the Chronicles of Froissart. Beyond, in ornamental ranks, were wicker chairs, very new and brightly varnished. In a corner was a stack of cudgels and walking-sticks. Everything shone with cleanliness and order. The shutters of the windows were closed on one side to keep out the sun which was scorching the stone window-sills on the outside. From the floors, newly sprinkled with water, rose a pleasant coolness. The carnations blazed like fire. There was not a sound from the fields, nor in the house. Filled with the consoling peace of a rural convent, I ended by settling down in a wicker chair by the table, opening a volume of Virgil, and reading in a low voice these appropriate lines:

Fortunate Jacinthe! Hic inter arva nota
Et fontes sacros, frigus captabis opacum . . .

Fortunate Jacinto! How true! For now among fields which are your own, and waters which are sacred to you, you at last have found shade and peace.

I read other lines. Then with the fatigue of two hours of smart trotting in the heat, I irrevently nodded and dozed over the pages of the divine bucolic poet—when I was suddenly awakened by a friendly bellow. After freeing myself from his hearty embrace, I looked him over, and very emphatically decided that, as some exhausted plant which has pined away in darkness amongst carpets and curtains, when it is suddenly restored to the sunlight and the fresh air and lavishly watered, grows green once more, buds and blossoms and honours Nature—so it had happened with Jacinto. He stooped no longer as he walked. Over the listless pallor of super-civilization, the mountain air and the living of a more real life had spread the swarthy flush of renovated blood which had superbly made a man of him. From his eyes which had always seemed so crepuscular and lost to the world while he was in the City, there flashed the brilliance of noon, resolute and wide-sweeping, as if happy in being able to absorb the beauty of all things. Even his moustache had grown crisp. He no longer ran his fingers over his face, but struck his thigh triumphantly with his whole hand. It was a new Jacinto! And I was almost afraid, because it seemed I would have to learn and enter into new moods and new ideas in dealing with this new Prince.

"Well, Caramba! Jacinto! What now?"

He jovially shrugged his shoulders which seemed to have broadened. He strode regally up and down the repaired floor in his white, dust-covered shoes and recounted to me how, when he had awakened in Tormes, washed in a tub and

137

donned my clean linen, he suddenly felt cheered up and "disentangled", as he put it. He had a plate of eggs with farm-cured pork sausages which were sublime. He took a walk through the mountains with strange new feelings of liberty and peace. He sent to Oporto for an iron bedstead and some pegs and shelves, and there he was!

"For all the summer?"

"No. But perhaps a month. Maybe two. While there are farm sausages and water drunk from a tile or a cabbage leaf I shall manage divinely."

I sank into a wicker chair and watched my Prince with delight and with amazement. He was rolling in its winding-sheet of cigarette-paper a scroll of chopped, coarse tobacco which he took from a glazed bowl. He said, "I walk round the fields from the break of day. Today I caught four magnificent trout—down there, in the Naves, there is a brook that runs into the valley of the Seranda. We'll have those trout for supper."

But I was dying to hear the story of his resurrection.

"So you did not go to Lisbon at all . . . I telegraphed to you there."

"What telegram? What Lisbon? No! I was up yonder, in the shade of a great big tree, *sub tegmine* I don't know how it goes on, reading this adorable Virgil . . . and also arranging my mansion. How does it seem to you, Zé Fernandes? In three weeks it was all floored, glazed, whitewashed and filled with chairs and seating. Even I was painting, with an enormous brush. Have you seen the dining room?"

"No."

"Well come and admire beauty in simplicity. It's wonderful."

It was the same room wherein we had so highly praised the rice and beans, but very well scrubbed, brilliantly white-washed, and with a wainscot painted such a strident blue that I at once recognized in it the master hand of my Prince. On the bottoms of all the heavy earthenware plates there was designed a splendid chanticleer. It was the same cock and the same earthenware as that in which we served the beans to the ploughmen at Guiães.

But the dogs were barking in the courtyard; and Jacinto ran to the verandah with a curious new lightness in his stride which delighted me. Definitely, at last, he had broken through the mesh of the invisible net which had been strangling him before! At that moment Cricket appeared in a linen jacket, holding in each hand a bottle of white wine. But his venerable face no longer radiated such a serene and happy sheen of ebony as it had done in Paris. It seemed to me he had grown round-shouldered. When I asked him what he thought of the change, he stuck out a thick lip: "The master likes it, and I like it too . . . the air's very good, master Fernandes, very good indeed." Then in a very low voice, including all the earthenware of Barcelos in his sweeping gesture of desolation, along with the bone-handled knives and the pinewood shelves as of a Franciscan monastery, he complained:

"But there is great poverty here, Senhor Fernandes, terrible poverty."

Jacinto returned at that moment with a sheaf of newspapers tied up in a bundle.

"It was the postman," he said. "You see I haven't altogether broken with Civilization. We're still on speaking terms. Here's the Press—but not *Figaro* or the horrible *Deux Mondes*. These are Agricultural papers. To learn how to produce the laughing harvest, under what sign to marry the vine to the elm, and what care the busy bee requires . . . *Quid faciat laetas segetes* . . . But for the rest of this noble education the *Georgics* would suffice me, which you do not know."

"Here, hold on," I protested. "*Nos quoque gens sumus et nostrum Virgilium sabemus.*"

But my brand-new friend, leaning from the window, was clapping his hands like Cato the Elder, to summon his slaves. "Anna Vaqueira," he cried. "A clean glass of water please, from the old fountain."

Highly amused I interjected, "O Jacinto? What about bicarbonate mineral waters, phosphates, soda-waters and sterilization?"

He shrugged his shoulders with superb disdain and acclaimed the apparition of the big glass with its sides frosted with the snowy-coldness of the sparkling water which a pretty girl brought him on a plate. I admired the girl. What eyes, of such a liquid yet serious blackness! In her walk, in the slenderness of her waist what harmony, what grace of a Latin nymph!

"Jacinto," I said. "I too would like a glass of water. And if that girl's going to bring it every time I'll be needing something, off and on, every five minutes from now. Caramba! My son! Here is the living poetry of the mountains for you!"

My Prince smiled with sincerity, "No, don't let's delude ourselves nor fabricate Arcadias. She's a beautiful girl but stupid. There's no more poetry nor sensibility, nor even more beauty there than in a fine Frisian cow. She deserves her name of Anna Vaqueira (Anna the Cow-Girl). She works well, digests well, conceives well. That is what Nature made her like that for, so healthy and sturdy. And she serves her purpose. The husband doesn't seem too pleased with her because he thrashes her. He's a fine animal too. No, my son, the sierra is beautiful and I'm grateful to it. But here you get the female in all her animality and the male in all his egotism. ... However, they are real people, absolutely real! And that reality, Zé Fernandes, is a great consolation to me." Lazily enjoying the coolness, the silence, and the freedom of the vast house, we returned to the large room which Jacinto already called the library. Then suddenly, seeing a large packing-case with the lid half-opened, I was overcome with a devouring curiosity.

"And all those immense packing-cases we sent from 202, Jacinto, crammed to bursting with Civilization? Did you ever hear what happened to them?"

My Prince stopped short and smote his thigh gaily. "It was sublime!" he laughed. "You remember the little man with a wallet slung round his neck whose sagacity and geographical knowledge we so admired? ... You remember? I had no sooner said 'Tormes' when he said he knew it and scribbled a note saying no more was necessary. 'Oh! Tormes! Exactly! Perfectly! Very ancient, very curious place.' ... Well he sent the whole enormous pile of packing-cases to Alba-de-Tormes in Spain! It's all in Spain!"

I scratched my chin in consternation: " Well, now! . . . To think of it! . . . A man so expert and efficient as he was and who was such an ornament of Progress and Civilization! . . . Everything gone to Spain! . . . Have you sent for it? "

" No. I may do later on. For the moment I am just savouring the new joy of getting up first thing and brushing my hair with a single brush."

Full of memories, I considered my friend.

" You used to have about nine brushes."

" Nine. I had at least twenty. Perhaps thirty. And they were a worry to me. There never seemed to be enough of them . . . I never felt properly combed in Paris. The same with my sixty thousand books. There were so many of them I never had time to read one of them. It was the same with all my interests and occupations. I was so overloaded with them that I was of no use in any of them."

During the afternoon when the heat had passed over, we went for a ramble along the winding paths of that rich farm which undulated for six miles over valley and mountain. I had never seen Jacinto in natural surroundings since that day when he had suffered so atrociously in the sociable and well-policed woods of Montmorency. But now with what confident security and idyllic love did he move in those very surroundings of Nature from which, for so many years, he had been estranged by theory and habit. He no longer dreaded the dampness of the grass: nor did he resent the impertinent touch of branches: nor did the silence of the heights depress him by suggesting the dispeoplement of the Universe. It was with real delight and with a feeling of recovered stability that he buried his thick shoes in the soft earth as in his natural, paternal element: he left the easy beaten tracks to feel the caress of the leaves on his face as he passed through the thick brushwood: on the hillsides he would pause motionless and sign to me to do the same, so as to saturate himself with the silence and peace: and more than once I surprised him listening and smiling by a chattering stream as if listening to a confidence. Then he would philosophize endlessly with the enthusiasm of a convert, impatient to convert others.

" How fully one's intelligence is liberated here, isn't it? And, like everything around it, animated with a strong and profound life? Do you say now, Zé Fernandes, that there is no thought here? "

"I? I say nothing at all, Jacinto."

" Well that's a very rude and narrow way of casting reflections . . ."

" Well I never! Listen to him! Why, I . . ."

" No! You don't understand. Life is not solely limited to thinking, my dear doctor . . ."

" I am not one."

" Life is essentially Will and Movement: in that patch of earth planted with maize lies a whole world of impulses and forces which openly reveal themselves and attain their supreme expressions, which is Form. No! Your philosophy is still too gross and clumsy . . ."

" Heaven's above! I have not said . . ."

" And furthermore, my friend, what an inexhaustible, what a miraculous diversity of forms . . . And all beautiful!" He grabbed my poor arm, insisting that I should take note of what he said with reverence. In Nature, he asserted, I would never discover an ugly contour or one which was repeated twice. Never were two ivy leaves of the same green or the same shape. But in the City, on the contrary, each house is a servile copy of its neighbour; all faces repeat the same indifference or the same unrest: all ideas have the same value, are of the same stamp and the same shape—like books: and even those things that are the most personal and intimate, one's illusions, are all identical; everyone shares the same illusions and breathes them, and they all fade into the same fog. Sameness! The horror of cities!

" But take that big chestnut-tree. I've seen it, every morning for three weeks and every morning it seems a different tree! Shade, sun, wind, clouds, rain, incessantly give it a new and different expression which is always interesting. I could never get tired of its company."

" It's a pity it can't converse," I muttered.

My Prince recoiled from me with his eyes flaming like those of an Apostle. " How do you mean—' can't converse '? Why, it is a most sublime conversationalist; it's true it has no sayings nor does it formulate theories in words with a human mouth. Yet I never come near to it without an idea coming to me or a truth being revealed to me . . . Even today, when I was returning from catching those trout, it made me feel that all its vegetable life is exempt from the labour, the anxiety and the effort imposed by human life : it does not have to preoccupy itself with nourishment, clothing, or shelter; a beloved son of God, he feeds it without its having to bestir itself. It is that very security which gives it so much grace and majesty. Don't you find it so? "

I smiled and agreed. All he said was very specious and far-fetched. But what did the strained metaphors and immature metaphysics matter? Amidst all that ideological verbiage one truth shone forth visibly—the reconciliation of my Prince to life. His resurrection was certain after so many years lying in a soft grave, like a mummy wrapped round and round in the endless bandages of pessimism.

That afternoon Jacinto fairly exhausted me. With insatiable curiosity he searched every corner of the sierra. He climbed each summit at a run as if in the hope of discovering, at its top, the never-seen splendours of some as yet unpublished world. His chief worry was not to know the names of the trees, and even of the humblest plant sprouting from a crack in the terraces. He treated me as if I were a botanical dictionary—turning over my pages without ceremony.

" I have taken every sort of course and studied under the most illustrious professors in Europe; I have sixty thousand volumes, and yet I don't know if that fellow there is a plum tree or a cork-oak."

" It's a holm-oak, Jacinto," I told him.

The evening was already closing in when we slowly retraced our steps. The adorable peace of the heavens which was truly celestial in every sense and that of the fields where every leaf seemed to be lost in contemplative quietude in the softly fading light, giving a caress to everything, penetrated so deeply into Jacinto's being that I felt in the silence that we both fell into that he was sighing from sheer relief.

143

Then he said very gravely, "And you say there is no thought in Nature . . ."

"What? Again! What a bore you are! I never said . . ."

"But it is because thought is suppressed in Nature that suffering is spared to natural things. We wretches cannot suppress thought, but certainly we can discipline it and prevent it from perplexing itself, as it does in the city, by imagining joys which can never be realized and 'certainties' which can never be reached. What these hills and trees counsel our wakeful, agitated souls to do—is to live in a vague dream, to covet nothing, to rebel against nothing, to let the world roll on without expecting more from it than a rumour of harmony which lullabies them and helps them to go to sleep at last in the hand of God. How does it seem to you, Zé Fernandes?"

"Perhaps. But then it would be necessary to live in a monastery with the temperament of a Saint Bruno, or to have an income of a hundred and forty thousand a year and the cheek of certain fellows like yourself. Also it seems we've walked leagues. I'm fagged out and hungry."

"All the better for the trouts and the roast kid."

"Bravo! Who cooks for you?"

"A god-daughter of Melchior's. A sublime woman! Wait till you try her chicken broth! Her stewed giblets! She's hideous! Almost a dwarf . . . with squint eyes, one green, one black. But what taste. What genius!"

It was true! Horace would have dedicated an ode to that roast kid; and with Melchior's wine, the trout and the giblets to which the sublime dwarf with squint eyes devoted her supreme inspiration which was not of this earth, and with the mildness of that June night which through the windows wrapped us in its black velvet, I became so happy that I fell into the largest cane chair I could find, with the best cushions, and uttered a yell of sheer delight.

Then, as an afterthought, wiping the coffee from my moustache, I asked: "Jacinto, what about the time when we used to go about Paris with our pessimism, groaning that all was delusion and sorrow?"

My Prince, whom the kid had rendered more lively,

144

sprightly and cheerful than ever, paced the floor with heavy strides, rolling a cigarette : " Oh what an ingenious blockhead that Schopenhauer is! And I was a bigger blockhead who took it all in, and made myself miserable with such sincerity! And yet," he continued, stirring his cup, " Pessimism is a very comforting theory for those who suffer, for it dis-individual-izes suffering and widens it into a universal law, the law of life itself: accordingly it takes away from suffering the pungent character of a special injustice committed against the sufferer by a factious and hostile destiny! Our own mis-fortune embitters us worst when we contemplate or imagine the happiness of our neighbours—because we feel ourselves singled out and chosen for misery when we might have been born to happiness like him. Who would grumble about being lame—if all mankind were lame? How that man would howl and roar who found himself besieged with the snows, frost and rain of a personal winter limited to himself and specially organized in Heaven to plague him alone—while all the rest of humanity around him were moving about in the benevolent warmth of spring."

" Very true," I replied, " that poor fellow would have excellent reason to howl and roar."

" And furthermore," my friend went on, " pessimism is excellent for most people because it attenuates the unhappy crime of inertia. If the goal of life is a mountain of grief against which the soul must finally dash itself to bits, why make for the goal through all the obstacles and troubles of this world? Besides, all the lyrists and theorists of pessimism from Solomon to the malign Schopenhauer launch their canticle or their doctrine to disguise the humiliation of their own miseries, subordinating them all to a vast law of life, a cosmic law, and thus adorning with an almost divine halo (as being of divine origin) their own trivial miseries whether of temperament or fate. The worthy Schopenhauer formulates all his Schopenhauerism while he is a philosopher without a publisher and a professor without students: while he suffers horribly from terrors and manias: hides his money under the floor: keeps his accounts in Greek in perpetual lamentation and distrust: lives in cellars in a continual fear of fire: and travels with a tin mug in his pocket for fear of drinking out of one which some leper might have contaminated. Then Schopenhauer was a true Schopenhauerist! Yet hardly had he become celebrated when his miserable nerves grew calm: a cheerful peace surrounded him: and there was not in the whole of Frankfort a more jolly old bourgeois with such a beaming face or one who enjoyed more systematically the good things of life or of the intelligence ... As for the other, the Israelite, that very pedantic King of Jerusalem! When did he discover all that sublime rhetoric about the world being illusion and vanity? When he was seventy-five years old, when the power was slipping from his trembling hands and when his seraglio of three hundred concubines had become ridiculously superfluous. Only then do his pompous complaints burst out. Everything was vanity and affliction! There was nothing durable under the sun! Well, to admit the truth, my dear Solomon, everything passes away—especially the potency of making love to three hundred concubines. But if, to this old Asiatic sultan who was becoming besmeared with the ink of mere literature, some miracle had restored some of his virility, where then would one have been able to look for his *Ecclesiastes*? No! In that case there would have been a second triumphal edition of the *Song of Songs*! "

Thus my friend discoursed in the nocturnal silence of Tormes. I think he must have propounded even more witty, jovial and profound conclusions on this subject. But I was already dozing in the arms of *Optimism*. However, shortly after, I leaped up with staring eyeballs to the sound of a violent, long, healthy and hearty laugh. It was Jacinto in a chair reading *Don Quixote*. Oh! My fortunate Prince! He still preserved the acute power of finding theories in a sheaf of corn which was still unripe, and by some kindness on the part of God he had regained the divine gift of laughter from the jests of Sancho Panza.

Profiting by my company, Jacinto spent the next two weeks of rural leisure in making preparations for the long-discussed and long-meditated transference of his ancestors' remains—of their " respectable bones " as Silverio, the manager, called them as he breakfasted with us one Friday morning, wearing a frightful jacket of yellow corduroy with a blue silk lining. The ceremony would require the greatest simplicity seeing that these confused, uncertain remains were now almost impersonal; which we were going to deposit in the new chapel in the valley of the Carriça, a chapel which was still cold and empty, as yet without a soul of its own and lacking the warmth of God.

"Because your excellency must understand," explained Silverio, wiping his table-napkin over his wide, perspiring face with its huge, black beard like that of a Turk, "what with all this mix up. . . . Oh, I beg your pardon, your Excellency, I meant what with all this confusion that was brought about when everything collapsed, we no longer know to whom any of these bones belonged. Nor, to tell the truth, do we even know which of the honoured ancestors of your excellency were lying in the old chapel for so many centuries because the lettering on their tombs was so worn as to be indecipherable—noble gentlemen to whom the greatest honour is due, but who were already, if you will forgive the expression, very much demolished, even before the disaster, since when there's been a proper mix up. And this is what I decided would be best after thinking it over. I ordered as many lead coffins as there were skulls collected amongst the rubble and stones under the old chapel. There were seven and a half skulls. I mean to say seven big skulls and one very small one. We put each skull in its coffin. What does your excellency say to that? There was no other way. And here let Senhor Fernandes say if he does not think we have proceeded with efficiency. To each skull we added a reasonable proportion of bones, sharing them out as equally as possible. There was no other way. We did not find all the bones. Many shinbones were lacking. And it's very probable that the ribs of many of these noble gentlemen have been awarded to the skulls of other gentlemen. But who could know? Only God. We did what prudence and common-sense suggested. Afterwards, on the Judgment Day, each one of these noblemen will be presented with the correct assortment of bones belonging to him."

He uttered these macabre and terrible sentences with deep

147

respect, almost with majesty in his voice as he looked from one to the other of us with his tiny, sharp eyes sparkling like glass beads.

I heartily agreed with this picturesque person.

" Perfectly! You have arranged everything perfectly, my dear Silverio. They are all so vague and so anonymous all those ancestors. Only it's a pity that the bones of Grandfather Dom Galleon should be scattered."

" He wasn't buried here!" Jacinto broke in. " I came here especially for Grandfather Galleon's sake, but found out that he was never buried here in the Chaped of Carriça.— Fortunately!"

" No we never had his Excellency Dom Galleon here. It is more than a hundred years since any gentleman of the House was buried here, Senhor Fernandes."

" Where can he be, then? "

My Prince shrugged his shoulders. " Somewhere about in this Kingdom. In the church or the cemetery of one of the many parishes in which he owned land. The estate is so scattered."

" Well," I concluded, " since we are dealing with uncertain bones that have neither names nor dates we should have a very simple and sober ceremony."

" A quiet little ceremony. Very quiet," murmured Silverio giving a whistling hiss as he sipped his coffee.

It was a quiet ceremony of a rustic and pleasant simplicity —the burial of those high and mighty lords. Early one slightly misty morning the eight small coffins, covered with red velvet more suited to a holiday than a funeral and each one containing its little heap of bones, went out on the shoulders of the gravediggers of Tormes from the Church of Sao José, whose small bell was tolling—oh how lightly and finely!— like the trill of a sad little bird. Before, a stalwart lad in a surplice proudly and zealously carried an old silver cross above his head. With his neck covered with a huge blue-checked snuff-handkerchief the old, bent sacristan pensively and carefully carried the aspersorium of holy water : the good Abbot of Sao José with his fingers in his half-closed breviary, moved his lips in a low, slow prayer which seemed to make the mild air more tender still. Then behind the smallest coffin containing the child's skull followed Jacinto and myself, almost bursting in a black suit of Jacinto's pulled in haste from one of his bags from Paris that very morning, when I remembered that I had nothing but country-wear and that there would not be time to send to Guiães for a decent suit.

Behind walked Silverio very solemnly in a huge white shirtfront over which his beard trailed blacker than ever. In a frock coat, with his big lip drooping, and the rest of him drooping with the melancholy of the funeral and that with which the mountains filled him, walked Cricket, with his arm through an enormous wreath of roses and ivy. After them all came Melchior amidst a crowd of women who, with their heads sunk in the shade of black lace mantillas, unwinding long rosaries, mumbled *Ave Marias* between long sighs, which sounded as sorrowful as if the loss of these ancient Jacintos had stricken them with inconsolable grief. So, through the tilled fields crossed by irrigation sluices, slowly climbing up the bush-clad slopes, more rapidly sliding down the rocky ravines, the little procession continued with the cross held high in front, flashing its silver from time to time whenever a sunbeam broke through the dispersing mists. Low boughs of nettle-trees or willows gave a last caress to the velvet coverings of the coffins.

Sometimes a stream would follow us for a while, with a discreet shimmer through the grasses and with a low whisper as if it was also praying, but happily. In the shady farmyards, as we passed, the cocks on heaps of firewood sounded their festive clarions. Then when we reached the fountain of Lira, seeing that the journey was lengthening, and wishing to spare the old abbot, we cut across the fields of corn which was already high, almost ripe, and full of red poppies. The sun was shining by now: under the breath of a strong breeze which lifted the mist, the whole vaporous mass began to undulate like slow golden waves in which the coffins rocked softly; and like an enormous poppy the reddest of them all, blazed the cotton parasol which the sacristan opened to shade the Abbot.

149

Jacinto nudged me: "How fine we look! How much grace and beauty there can be in a mere burial of bones!"

In the new chapel which dominated the valley of the Carriça, and was very lonely and bare, in the middle of a rough churchyard, without even the ghost of a lawn, or the shade of a shrub, two boys held sheaves of tapers, which Silverio distributed with grave courtesy and solemnity. Inside the chapel their small flames hardly gave off any light from their sad yellowness, they were so dimmed by the flaring whitewash on the walls, and the cheerful brilliance which fell from the high windows. Going round the coffins, which were placed on benches, which were covered with thick velvet, the Abbot softly murmured prayers in Latin, while in the background the women, bowed under their black headgear, groaned forth *Amens*, or gave an occasional respectful sob of sympathy. Afterwards, lightly raising his hyssop, the good Abbot sprinkled a last purification on the uncertain bones of the uncertain Jacintos. We all defiled before my Prince, who stood shyly beside the threshold, with Silverio at his side, pressing his huge whiskers against his starched shirtfront, with his features drooping, and his eyes shut as though restraining tears.

In the churchyard outside my Prince lit with pleasure a cigarette which he had begged from Melchior.

"Well, Zé Fernandes, what did you think of our little ceremony?"

"Very rustic, very tender, very cheerful—a sheer delight!"

But the Abbot, who was taking off his vestments in the Sacristy, appeared in his big frock coat of black silk, with his old crumpled hat, which his servant had brought in a bag from the Presbytery. Jacinto immediately thanked him for his services, and for the hospitality he had accorded to the bones during the construction of the new Chapel. And the kind old man, so white-headed, with his almost childish, pink and white face and a flashing smile of his healthy teeth, praised Jacinto very highly for having come from so far away, on such a long journey, to fulfil the duty of a good grandson.

"They are very remote grandfathers, and now they are so mixed up!" said Jacinto with a smile.

" Well, it is all the more deserving of your Excellency to have come so far! It's quite common to respect the bones of a grandfather. But to respect those of great, great, great, great Grandfathers, to the fifth or seventh generation! That's truly laudable!"

"Above all when nothing is known of them, and they did nothing worth knowing about," laughed Jacinto.

" Oh! Who knows? Who knows? Perhaps they were excellent men. Anyway, whoever lives as long in this world as I have done, must come to the conclusion, as I have, that there is not a single thing or a single being that is useless. Why, only yesterday I read in an Oporto newspaper that it is the worms who manure and work the earth, even before the ploughman and the oxen arrive with the plough. Even worms are useful. Nothing is useless. I had a clump of thistles in a corner of my garden at home, which I could never get rid of. They always sprang up again. They seemed an affliction. Then I reflected, and now I feast on their buds stewed in syrup. The grandfathers of your Excellency used to go about here; they used to work here and they suffered here, too. That means they were useful. And the fact that we say a few Paternosters for them cannot do anything but good, both to them and to ourselves."

Thus mildly philosophizing we found ourselves in a chestnut-wood, where the ancient mare of the Abbot awaited him, because that holy man, after the rheumatism of last winter, was not able any longer to dare the rough tracks of the sierra on foot, as he had done before. So that he could mount in comfort, Jacinto held his stirrup with filial courtesy. And while the mare pushed its way up the ravine, almost hidden beneath the immense red parasol which sheltered the old man, we went home, heading in a straight line over the mountain of the Lombinha across the maize-fields, in great haste, because I was nearly bursting myself in Jacinto's black suit.

" Well, all those worthy gentlemen have found a good lodging, Zé Fernandes. All that remains is to pray a few Paternosters for them, as the Abbot recommended . . . But the only trouble is I can't remember ' Our Father, which art in Heaven ' . . ."

151

" Don't worry, Jacinto, I'll ask Aunt Vicência to do it for both of us. She's the one who always says mine for me."

During the weeks when I was idling in Tormes, I witnessed with affectionate interest, a whole revolution going on in Jacinto's relations with Nature. From the sentimental, Rousseau-ish stage of contemplation in which he found theories and sermons in the branches of cherry-trees, and systems in the foam of a mill-race, my Prince slowly passed into a desire for action—direct and material action, in which his hand, at last restored to a superior function, would actually turn up his native soil.

After so much mere *comment*, he was evidently set upon *creation*. One afternoon, towards nightfall, when we were sitting in the orchard, at the side of the pond, while Manuel, the gardener, was picking oranges on a ladder leaning against a tall orange-tree, Jacinto suddenly said, more to himself than to me, " It's a queer thing: I have never planted a tree !"

" Well, it's one of the three great acts, without having performed which you cannot claim to be a real man—according to some, I forget which, philosopher . . . *To plant a tree, to have a son, to write a book*. You'll have to hurry up if you want to be a real man. It may be you've never done a good turn to a tree, like you would to a fellow man."

" Oh yes ! In Paris, as a child, I used to water the lilacs. In summer that's a real good turn ! But I've never planted anything."

Now, as Manuel was coming down from the ladder, my Prince who (poor fellow!) never really believed in my agricultural knowledge, immediately consulted his authority :

" Manuel, listen here ! What is there that one can plant or sow at this season? "

With a basket of oranges on his arm, Manuel exclaimed laughing slowly, between respectfulness and amusement :

" Plant or sow, Master? Well now, it's rather the time for picking and reaping. Why they're just cleaning up the threshing-floor for the threshing, Master !"

" Yes : but I don't mean necessarily maize or corn. For

instance, there, in the orchard, along the wall, couldn't one plant a line of peach-trees? "

Manuel's laughter increased. " Yes, my senhor; yes, but that's for about All Saints or Christmas. Now it's only purslane, spinach, or beans, but in cool earth . . . "

My friend shook off the idea of such vulgar vegetables with a disdainful gesture.

" Well, good night, Manuel. Are those oranges from the tree that Mechior says bears such sweet and juicy ones? Then take them home for your children. Take plenty for the little ones."

No! The thing to do was to plant trees. From the trees which he had contemplated in the mountains, in their true majesty, in the beneficence of their shade, in the freshness of their lulling whispers and rustlings, in the health of the nests with which they were populated, had begun, perhaps slowly, his love of the earth. And now he dreamed of a Tormes entirely covered with trees, whose fruit, verdure, shade, rustling voices and sheltered nests—would all be the work of his paternal hands. In the grave silence of the dusk which was rapidly falling, he asked:

" What trees grow the quickest, Zé Fernandes? "

" The tree that grows the quickest is the Eucalyptus, the ridiculous and ugly Eucalyptus. In six years you could have the whole of Tormes hidden in Eucalyptus."

" Everything is so slow, Zé Fernandes."

His dream was apparently to plant a few fruit stones which would have grown enormous trunks and shot out shady branches before he returned to 202 for the winter in Paris.

" A chestnut-tree. Thirty years before it is even worth looking at? What a discouragement!" said Jacinto when I had explained. " That would be all right for God, who can afford to wait . . . *Patiens quia aeternus.* Thirty years for trees that would only serve to shadow my grave!"

" But even that is a gain. And after that, for your sons, Jacinto . . . "

" Sons: where am I going to get sons? "

" Why it's the same thing as chestnut-trees. Planting the seed and there's plenty of agreeable soil to plant it in round

153

these parts. In nine months the plant is made. And with that sort of plant, the smaller, the younger, and the tenderer it is the more it enchants you."

He murmured, crossing his hands on his knees, " Everything takes such a hell of a time!"

At the edge of the pond we remained silent in the mild coolness of nightfall, in the fragrance of the honeysuckle that clustered on the wall, watching the crescent moon as it rose over the roofs of Tormes.

Certainly this haste to turn himself from a dreamer into a *doer* determined and livened his interest in stock. Repeatedly in our walks across the farm he noted the solitude.

" We need animals here, Zé Fernandes."

I imagined he was longing for the elegance of deer and peacocks. But one Sunday skirting the large plain of the Ribeirinha, where water was always scarce, but scarcer than ever during this dry summer, he stopped to look at three sheep belonging to the peasant there which were cropping their scanty fare from a poor pasture.

And suddenly he said with regret: " Just so : here is the space for a beautiful grazing ground, an immense meadow, all green and covered with fat white sheep like great blobs of cotton-wool all over the lawns. Wouldn't that be beautiful— and easy too, Zé Fernandes? "

" Yes. Bring the water down to the plain. There's plenty up there in the sierra."

My Prince, linking this inspired idea with another vaster and more ambitious one, thought how much beauty it would give to Tormes to enrich those green meadows and thick pastures, with herds of cattle, fine, fat, shining English cattle. Eh? Would not that be truly beautiful? To shelter these valuable herds, he would construct perfect sheds and corrals with light and serviceable architecture of iron and glass, swept everywhere with fresh air and washed throughout with running water. Then, with all those cows and the milk streaming in torrents nothing would be more easy than to instal a cheese factory in the cool Dutch manner, all white and shining, with tiles and marbles to manufacture Camemberts or Bries . . . or Coulommiers . . . What convenience for the house! And what activity and employment for the whole sierra!

" Don't you think so, Zé Fernandes? "

" Certainly. You possess the four elements in abundance : earth, water, air and money. With those four elements in hand, it is easy to set any big enterprise afoot—let alone a mere cheese factory."

" Yes, that's so, isn't it? And it would even be a business proposition. For me, the moral pleasure of the work would be the profit : the useful employment of one's time. But a cheese factory would bring in money. One would make prodigious profits. Such an innovation would educate the palate of the people, encourage the installation of similar factories; and enrich the country with a flourishing new industry. Well when this industry is properly set up, how much do you think each cheese would cost me? "

I shut one eye to work it out. " Each cheese . . . let's see . . . one of those little cheeses, like a Camembert or a Rabaçal, would cost you, Jacinto, the cheese-maker, between two hundred and fifty or three hundred escudos apiece."

Jacinto recoiled in amused surprise. " How do you work it out to three hundred? "

" Well, let's say two hundred to make quite safe. With all these meadows to fertilize, the pipes and canals of water that would have to be laid on, the cost of the English cattle, the buildings of porcelain, marble and glass, with all the separators and cheese-making machines, your own extravagance and the bucolic wantonness of the peasants, each cheese would cost you, the producer, two hundred escudos or two thousand pennies. But certainly you'd be able to sell each cheese for a penny apiece in Oporto. Put down five-pence for the cost of the transport, the box, the wrapping and the commission. You would only lose on each cheese a matter of a hundred and ninety-eight escudos and fourpence."

My Prince was not discouraged. " Exactly! Then we would make one of those cheeses every week for you and me to eat on Sundays."

His new optimism filled him with such energy and he was so keen to breed stock that, dragging Silverio and Melchior

155

with him over hill and dale, he visited every inch of his farm to determine where the rich pastures were to grow and where the elegant sheds and corrals were to glitter in the sun of Tormes. With the splendid security of his hundred and nine thousand a year, there was no difficulty or objection that was laughingly raised by Melchior or mentioned in respectful horror by Silverio that he didn't sweep aside with easy grace as if it were the stalk of a wild rose lying across his path.

Now, those rocks yonder were an obstruction. Let them be dug out and removed. An importunate valley divided two fields. Have it filled in. Silverio sighed; sweat poured over his swarthy baldness almost in anguish. Poor Silverio! Roughly shaken out of the sweet leisure of his humdrum farm manage-ment, making calculations of expenses which appeared super-human to his highland thrift and forced to pant beneath the hottest suns of June in tireless attendance on his master, he caught in the mountains the dejection which Jacinto had left behind in Paris. It was he who ran nervous fingers through his great black beard. He was relieving his feelings to me one day in a corner of the verandah while Jacinto, in the library, was writing to his friend the Count Rylant, major-domo of the Royal Palace in Holland, asking for architectural designs for a perfect cheese-factory.

"Well, Senhor Fernandes, I am simply warning you that if all this grandioseness continues, tens of thousands of pounds will just be shovelled uselessly away, and buried in these mountains."

And when I alluded to Jacinto's wealth, to whom all these vast operations which were changing the ancient face of the sierra cost as little as to others the repair of a single terrace on the hillside—the good Silverio hung down his long arms along his thighs with an even more dejected air than before.

"But it's for that very reason, Senhor Fernandes. If Senhor Dom Jacinto didn't have such an endless store of money he would relent. As it is, it's *crash! crash!* straight ahead. If I enjoyed the income of his Excellency, it would lead me also into a kind of agriculture of caprices. But not here, Senhor Fernandes, in these mountains amongst these cliffs. Why, he possesses that lovely property of Montemor on the banks of the Mondego river where you could have gardens that would eclipse those of the Crystal Palace in Oporto. And what about Veleira? Does Senhor Fernandes not know Veleira, near Penafiel? Why that's a flat plain with fat earth all in one piece, a whole county with the house right in the middle with a high tower. That's where you have meadows fit for English cattle, that's the place for a cheese-factory, with wonderful vegetable gardens and thirty turkeys in the fowl-run."

"But what can you do about it, Silverio? Jacinto loves the sierra. And, after all, it is the original family manor dating from the fourteenth century!"

Poor Silverio in his desperation forgot the respect due to the secular nobility of the Jacinto family.

"Well. Well. Those ideas don't suit educated men like Senhor Fernandes in this century of Liberty ... What? Must we be referring back to feudal baronies, when everything is shaping everywhere for a modern Republic? Read the *Seculo*, Senhor Fernandes! Read the *Seculo* and you'll see. Also I'd like to see what Senhor Dom Jacinto would do here in winter, with the fog coming up from the river every morning, the cold piercing one's bones, winds that pull up great chestnut-trees by the roots and rains on rains that wash away the mountains in landslides and avalanches. Listen! Even for the sake of Senhor Dom Jacinto's health, which is delicate and accustomed to the City, it will be necessary for him to leave the sierra. It's in Montemor, in Montemor only that he will be well. That is the place for him. It's your duty as his best friend, and having so much influence over him, to insist and shout at him till you get him to go to Montemor."

But unhappily Jacinto threw out roots, strong roots, amorous roots which attached him to the wild sierra. It was as if he had been planted as a sapling in that ancient soil from which his race had sprung. And it was as if that ancient earth dissolved in him, flowed through him and penetrated him entirely so as to transform him into a rural, almost vegetable Jacinto, as much a part of the soil and a prisoner of the soil as the venerable tree that he so much loved.

But, above all, that which attached him to the mountains was having found there a thing which, in spite of his sociability, he had never been able to find in the City—namely to find days so full, so deliciously and actively occupied, with such enjoyable interests, that he rose to every new day, as to a feast or a triumph.

The first thing in the morning, as I was voluptuously stirring on my cushions of maize-husks, I would hear his heavy shoes in the passage and his happy voice singing out of tune more gaily than a blackbird. Then he would fling wide my door with a bang, with his low-brimmed hat on, and his cherry-stick in his hand, restraining his eagerness to be treading those well-known tracks up the mountain. His news was always the same but delivered with conscious pride: " I've slept wonderfully, Zé Fernandes. So well and so serenely that I'm beginning to think I'm a just man! It's a lovely day. When I opened the window at five I almost shouted for joy."

In his haste he refused to let me dawdle in the coolness of my bath. And if I paused to improve the hasty parting of my hair, this one-time possessor of thirty hairbrushes would protest at the effeminate waste of time which real men owed to the joys of the land. But when, after caressing the sheep-dogs in the courtyard, we came out of the avenue of plane-trees and, dividing whitely through the verdure, the winding paths of the farm opened before us, his haste abated and he entered into the precincts of Nature with the reverent, slow tread of someone entering a temple. He always maintained that it was contrary to the principles of Aesthetics, Philosophy and Religion to walk hurriedly through the fields. Besides, with that subtle bucolic sensibility which was developing in him and went on growing more and more refined, any fleeting or momentary beauty of the air or of the earth would suffice to enchant him for a considerable period. He could quite happily spend a whole morning walking silently through a pinewood from trunk to trunk, saturated in the silence, the coolness and the fragrance of resin, and pressing the carpet of dry pine-needles and cones with his feet. Any kind of water would retain his interest and move him tenderly to see the eagerness and generosity with which it ran singing towards the thirsty clods, gave itself up to them and was lost in them.

I still remember how he detained me for half a Sunday after Mass on a hilltop near an old ruined corral beneath a great tree—only because there was peace all round, a soft breeze, a sweet trill of birds in the branches, a whisper of water in the green reeds and over the hedge at our side the fresh fine perfume of hidden flowers.

When I, familiar from birth with the mountains, failed to abandon myself to the same ecstasies that filled his soul which was yet a novice to these things—my Prince would roar with the indignation of a poet who found a grocer yawning over Shakespeare. I laughed.

"My son," I would say, "I may not be more than a very small landed proprietor. But with me it's not a question of knowing that the land is *beautiful* or the soil is *good*. Listen to what the Bible says: *You will plough the soil in the sweat of your brow*. It does not say, *You will contemplate it in the heat of your imagination*."

"That may be," he exclaimed, "You are quoting from a book which was written for a people who always had their muddy eyes on lucre! Take note, my good man, of this bit of valley here, and try not to think of the thirty escudos income it brings in. You will see at once that it gives you more pleasure in your soul than thirty escudos would give you in your body. Only the soul really matters in life!"

Coming home to the mansion we found that the windows had already been half-closed and the floors were bespangled with beams of June sunlight which kept us sitting on in the library, idling, after lunch.

But really the gay energy of my friend never ceased or weakened under the heavy persuasion of the siesta hour. At that hour of the day, when even the noisiest sparrows slept and the sun itself seemed to pause for a nap, motionlessly pausing in its glitter of rays—Jacinto, with his spirit still wide awake and eager to enjoy everything now he had recovered the power of enjoyment—would be " taking his book " with delight. Because the ex-owner of sixty thousand books, since his resurrection, had now become a One-Book Man. That same Nature which had released him from the shroud of boredom with the cry of *Ambula* (" Walk ") now cried out to him *et lege* (" and read "). When after the conversation with Melchior's nephew, the farrier Severo, I had rushed to Tormes to find Jacinto, he was just finishing *Don Quixote* and I was in time to hear the last laughs with which he bade farewell to the profound sayings of the fat Sancho jogging on his donkey. But now my Prince was plunged in the *Odyssey*— and his whole being vibrated with the rapture and amazement of having met the wandering old man Homer " in the middle of the road of this life."

" Zé Fernandes, can you explain to me how it came to pass that I arrived at this age before I ever read Homer? "

" I suppose other more urgent reading interposed, such as *Figaro*, George Ohnet, etc."

" Have you read the *Iliad*? "

" I pride myself sincerely on never having read the *Iliad*."

" Do you know what Alcibiades did one afternoon in the Portico to a sophist who was priding himself that he had never read the *Iliad*? "

" No."

" He raised his fist and gave him a tremendous blow in the face."

" Well, you can restrain yourself, Alcibiades! I *have* read the *Odyssey*."

Yes but (according to him) I had surely read it carelessly without paying it full attention with my soul: and he insisted on initiating me and conducting me through the peerless work as my guide and tutor. I laughed. Laughing, and full of a heavy lunch, I ended by consenting to his instruction and stretching out full length on a cane settee. He, upright on a chair at the table, opened the book gravely and pontifically as though it were a missal and began in a slow emotional chant. That huge sea, which is the *Odyssey*, resplendent and resounding and always so blue, totally azure with its flocks of white gulls, rolling and softly creaming on the marble rocks of divine islands—exhaled its welcome health-giving saline fragrance in the calm of the June weather in which the mountains were dozing. After the stupendous trickeries of the subtle Ulysses and his superhuman perils, such sublime lamentations and such a longing for his lost home-land together with all that intrigue which enmeshed the old heroes while enjoying goddesses and eluding Destiny —all these things intensified their delicious savour out there at Tormes, where one's ingenuity and subtlety were not preoccupied by anything else, where life continued in the immutable security in which the sun is reborn each morning and the cornlands and maize-fields grow, sprout ears, and ripen . . . Rocked by the rhythmic, grave monotony of Jacinto's chanted verses, I would slightly close my eyes . . . Soon, a vast tumult which seemed to shake the earth and sky would arouse me. These were the roars of the Cyclops or the cries of Ulysses' companions robbing the cattle of Apollo. With staring eyeballs fixed on Jacinto, I would murmur encouragement. "Sublime!" And always, just at that moment, the ingenious Ulysses with his red Phrygian cap and an oar over his shoulder, astounded some charitable Prince with his eloquence, or demanded the presents due to a guest, or curried some favour from the gods. And still Tormes went on slumbering in the splendour of June. Again I closed my eyes under the ineffable caress of the wide-rolling diction of Homer . . . And half-sleeping, yet enchanted, I kept incessantly before my eyes in the divine Hellas between the deep blue sea and the deep blue sky, the white sail hesitating, veering, and seeking the cliffs of Ithaca.

After a siesta, my Prince always went out again into the fields. At this time of day, he was the most energetic and always eagerly referred to his " plans " and the vast developments of culture and luxury by which he intended to cover the whole sierra with rural magnificence. One of his plans was for an immense vegetable garden which would also be a flower-garden and contain all the classical and exotic vegetables in magnificent squares which would be bounded by hedges of roses, carnations, dahlias and lavender. The irrigation water would flow through gutters of enamelled earthenware. The lanes between would be shaded by dense vines of muscatel grapes climbing on pergolas of tiled stucco. My Prince designed the plan of this formidable garden on a vast piece of paper which Melchior and Silverio, whom he consulted about it, contemplated at great length—the former laughing and scratching his nape: and the latter, with his arms stiffly crossed and a tragic expression.

But this plan, or the plan of the cheese-factory, or that of the hen-house, or that of the dovecote which was to be so sumptuous and so thickly populated with pigeons that the whole sky of Tormes would turn white and tremble with their wings—none of these fabulous projects ever took a more definite form than we gave it in our enjoyable confabulations, or on the papers whereon Jacinto drew them, which kept on accumulating on the table in a heap between the brass ink-stand and the flower-vase.

No earth was so much as broken with a hoe, no stone was shifted with a crowbar, no wood was sawn with a saw, to begin the actual construction of any of these marvels. Against the revolving and slippery resistance of Melchior and against the respectful inertia of Silverio they were stranded like beautiful-looking galleys on the quicksands and the rocks.

One should not meddle with anything before the harvest and the grape-vintage, and Silverio and Melchior would add with a smile that promised great things, the old proverb " For good works, the month of January."

For the rest it more than satisfied my Prince, who was rather of an imaginative than an operative cast, to conceive these wonderful ideas and to point with his walking-stick to the privileged places in the mountains or valleys where he intended them to take shape. While he meditated these trans-formations of the soil very progressively and with admirable zeal, he was getting to know better and better the men whose life was to till that soil. When he first arrived at Tormes, Jacinto suffered from a strange timidity of the farm-hands, the daily workers, and of any boy who passed him driving a cow to the pastures. He never loitered to chat with them when, in some field which they were weeding, they stood up holding their caps in their hands with the respect of heredi-tary vassals. He was certainly restrained by his laziness: and there was also a certain *pudeur* or shyness, which he felt in trying to bridge the enormous distance which separated his complicated, super-civilized type from their rough and simple natures. But, above all, he was restrained by a fear of letting

162

them see how great was his ignorance about tilling the soil; he also feared to appear disdainful of occupations and interest which, to their humble natures, were supremely important, almost amounting to a religion. He remedied this reserve with the profusion of his smiles, and the blandness of his nod of recognition, raising his own hat when they raised theirs, with such courteous emphasis that I was almost afraid he would address them as " Your Excellencies ".

But now, after a few weeks in the mountains, knowing (though his knowledge was yet somewhat fragile) the seasons for sowings and harvests, and that fruit-trees are planted in winter, he began to take pleasure in stopping beside the workmen restfully contemplating their labour, and making vague, affable remarks.

" Well, how is it getting on? . . . So much the better . . . This bit of soil looks rich . . . That bank there needs building up."

He enjoyed making these remarks since he felt they helped him to penetrate more intimately into the mysteries of the earth and to consolidate his incarnation as " a man of the fields " who was no longer a mere shadow drifting about among realities. And now he never passed a lad driving a cow but he would detain him a moment with a question or two: " Where are you going? Whose cow is that? What's your name? " Then, pleased with himself, he would praise the easy vivacity of the boy or the sharpness of his eyes. Another thing that gave Jacinto great satisfaction was to know the names of all the fields, the sources of the streams and the boundaries of his farm : " You see that pinewood over there beyond the river . . . That is not on my land . . . It belongs to the Albuquerques."

With the perennial happiness of Jacinto, our nights on the sierra slipped swiftly and easily away. My Prince's soul was undergoing a process of simplification. Any little pleasure satisfied him entirely and filled him with peace and kindness. With real delight, after coffee, he would stretch out in a chair to savour the nocturnal tranquillity of the mountains under a silent sky full of stars.

The simple homely stories I told him about Guiães, the

163

Abbot, Aunt Vicência, and my relatives at the Ranch of the Geranium Flower, interested him so much that I began for his entertainment a complete chronicle of Guiães, with all its love affairs, feats of strength and all its quarrels and feuds about rights of way and water supply. Sometimes we had a game of backgammon on a fine board of dark wood with pieces of old ivory lent us by Silverio. But nothing pleased Jacinto more than to go to a little room which looked out on an orchard and there, leaning at the window, without a light, in the deepest peace to listen long and voluptuously to the nightingale singing in the orange-trees.

10

ON one of these mornings—the day before I returned to Guiães—the weather which had till then been one long, laughing glitter of sunlight in the sierra, clothed in azure and gold, making white dust on the roads and delighting all nature from the birds to the streams, suddenly in one of those changes to which the temperament of the weather (like that of man) is subject, became sad, sullen and wrapped itself in an ash-grey mantle with a heavy sorrow which contagiously spread itself all over the mountains. There was not a single bird to sing any more and the rivulets fled under their verdure with a sound of weeping.

When Jacinto entered my room that morning I couldn't resist the temptation of frightening him. "The south-west wind! Nothing but crows cawing through all the woods! We shall have plenty of water, Senhor Dom Jacinto! Rain for at least two weeks! And now we'll see who this fine lover of Nature is, with this steady rain, with the gale and with the whole sierra sliding and slithering off its base."

My Prince went to the window with his hands in his pockets.

"True! It's clouded over. I already told them to fish out a waterproof from my Paris luggage. It doesn't matter. The trees will get greener. And I should get to know Tormes in her winter clothing."

But as Melchior reassured him that the rain would only fall in the afternoon, Jacinto decided to go, before lunch, to a wood known as the "owlery" to decide the fate of some chestnut-trees which were very old, very picturesque, interesting in every way but so gnawed and worm-eaten that they threatened to collapse. Confiding in Melchior's foresight as a weather prophet, we left without Jacinto's having taken any precautions against rain. However, we hadn't got half-way when, after a shudder had run through the trees, a black cloud swelled over us and discharged a heavy, slanting rain lashed by the gale, which half-stunned us as we clutched our hats and revolved in the blast. Hearing ourselves called in a loud voice which was almost drowned by the wind, we saw Silverio in a field higher up at the side of a shed. Under a red umbrella he was beckoning to us to go up a track which made a short cut to where he stood. So we burst through with the rain streaming down our faces, skating in the mud and dizzily staggering around in the storm, which in a minute flooded the fields, filled the river-banks with torrents, undermined the earth of the terraces, made the forests groan with anguish and turned the range black, wildly desolate, hostile and uninhabitable.

When, at last, under the vast umbrella of Silverio who waited for us at the edge of the field, we had reached the shed, and in its unexpected shelter were dripping and panting to recover our breath, my Prince, wiping his face and neck, exclaimed weakly, "Hell! What ferocity!"

He seemed really terrified by that brusque and violent rage on the part of such a kind and hospitable sierra which for two whole months till that moment, had offered him nothing but kindness, shade, bland skies, quiet branches and the discreet and gentle murmur of water.

"Heavens above! Do storms like this often happen?"

Immediately Silverio took his chance to frighten Jacinto.

"This is only child's play. The summer's only having a bit of fun. Your Excellency should see what it's like in winter— if you are still here then. Why, at every gust, the mountains shake and tremble!"

He recounted how he, too, had been caught in the storm

on the way to the "owlery". Fortunately early in the morning when he felt the threat in the air and saw the leaves of the black poplars trembling, he had taken his umbrella and put on his rain-hat and his knee-boots.

"I was going to shelter in Esgueira's house, who is a farm-hand here. That house down there by the fig-tree. But his wife has been ill for some days . . . And as it might be something catching, smallpox or something like that, I thought to myself: 'Nothing doing. Those who take precautions die old.' I went into the shed here. And I had not been here for the time of saying one creed than I saw your Excellency . . . That is how it was . . . Now Senhor Dom Jacinto should go home and change because we are in for a day and a night of heavy rain."

Jacinto rested. I went on shaking myself and stamping my sopping feet which were beginning to chill me. And the good Silverio, passing a pensive hand over his black beard, reflected and began to revise his prognostics.

"Well, no, sir . . . It may settle now and stop raining . . . The wind has changed. That's why."

The shed which covered us was roofed over two walls which were joined at an angle and were made of loose stones, the debris of some dismantled cottage. At that time it only contained some wood, a heap of empty baskets and an old ox-cart on which my Prince sat rolling himself a comforting cigarette. The rain came down in copious long shining threads. We were all three silent in that inert, thoughtless contemplation in which a heavy rain always plunges eyes and souls together.

"Senhor Silverio," slowly muttered Jacinto, "what were you saying about smallpox?"

The manager turned him a surprised face. "I, your Excellency? . . . Ah yes! The wife of Esgueira! It well might be. Do not imagine, your Excellency, that we have no illnesses here. The air is good. I don't deny that! Healthy air, good water, but sometimes, if your Excellency will excuse my saying so, there are a lot of fever and agues around here."

"But haven't you a doctor, or a chemist?" asked Jacinto.

166

Silverio laughed in a very superior way as the inhabitant of civilized and well-provided regions.

"How could there not be a doctor, or a chemist? There's a chemist at Guiães, near the house of our friend. He is a clever fellow, that Firmino is he not, Senhor Fernandes? A capable man. Then there's Doctor Avelino four and a half miles from here . . . But these humble people are poor. They have enough to do for their bread, let alone medicines!"

Again silence fell inside the shed where the cold of the wet sierra began to penetrate. Beyond the river, the promising patch of brightness did not widen between the two thick curtains of dark grey cloud. All through the country, sloping down before us, ran continuous torrents of muddy water. I ended by sitting on the wood-pile feeling enervated by the hunger for food which that wild morning had sharpened within me. Jacinto, on the edge of the cart, with his feet dangling, stroked his damp moustache and began to feel his face, wherein I was terrified to behold a ghost of the the old expression he used to wear at 202.

Just then appeared from behind a wall, a feeble and very thin little boy with a tiny pinched face, very yellow under the dirt which plastered it, with two huge black eyes which stared at us in vague fright. Silverio knew him at once:

"How's your mother?" he asked. "Don't come too near. I hear well. How's your mother?"

I did not understand what the poor little lips murmured in reply. But Jacinto was interested and inquired: "What does he say? Let the boy come in! Who is his mother?"

Silverio respectfully informed him: "It's that woman I told you about, who is ill, the wife of Esgueira, from the house by the fig tree . . . She has another smaller than he. They don't lack for children."

"But this little fellow seems ill, too," exclaimed Jacinto. "Poor little chap, so yellow, too! Are you ill too?"

The boy was silent; he sucked his finger and looked about wonderingly. Silverio smiled kindly and said: "No! He's healthy enough. He's only so yellow and thin because you see . . . because . . . he gets nothing to eat. There's plenty of poverty. Badly fed . . . that's all. When there's a bite of bread it's for the whole family. It's hunger. It's hunger."

Jacinto leaped from the edge of the cart. "Hunger? Can he be hungry? Do people here suffer from hunger?"

His eyes shone with shocked emotion and they seemed to enquire now from Silverio, now from me, some confirmation of this unexpected misery. It was I who put him wise.

"Of course there's hunger, man! You imagine that Paradise was perpetuated here in the Sierra without labour or misery . . . In every part of the world there are poor people, even in Australia, in the gold-fields. Wherever there's work there's the proletariat, whether in Paris or on the banks of the Douro."

My Prince gave a gesture of suffering impatience: "I don't want to know what's on the banks of the Douro. I want to know if, here, at Tormes, on my property, on these fields which are my own, there are people who work for me, and yet go hungry . . . If there are other little children, like him, who are hungry? That's what I wish to know!"

Silverio smiled at such candid ignorance of life in the sierra.

"Well, sir, it is easy to see that a lot of farm-workers are very poor . . . Nearly all of them are. That Esgueira, with the vast number of children he has . . . it's a terrible misfortune. You ought to see inside their cabins. They are like cattle-stalls. That of Esgueira . . . down there . . . look at it."

"Let's go and see it," said Jacinto with determination. He went out of the shed without waiting for the rain to clear, though it was falling more lightly and sparsely. But immediately Silverio opened his arms before him as if saving him from a precipice.

"No! Your Excellency must not enter the house of Esgueira. Nobody knows what she's got. Prudence and chicken broth . . ."

Jacinto didn't waver in his patient politeness: "I am obliged for your care of me, Silverio: open your rain-cap, and on the march!"

The manager bowed his shoulders, and noisily opened his umbrella with which he sheltered Jacinto respectfully, as he made his way over the puddled fields. I followed, thinking of the sumptuous alms which God was about to send that poor household through the agency of a remote dweller in the cities. Behind us walked the child deep in wonder.

Like all the huts of the sierra, that of Esgueira was built of loose stones, without plaster, with black moss-grown tiles on the roof, with a loophole high in the wall, and with a rude door which served for light, air, to let out the smoke, and let in the people. All around it nature and labour had accumulated vines and creepers and wild flowers, with patches of vegetables, fragrant hedges, old seats eaten away with moss and lichen, flowerpots with parsley, little singing water-courses, and scattered shade and puddles, which idyllically suited for some eclogue this dwelling-place of hunger, sickness and grief.

Cautiously Silverio pushed the door open with the point of his umbrella.

" Hullo, Aunt Maria—how are you, old girl? " he cried.

In the open crack of the door appeared a very tall girl, dark and dirty, with sad sunken eyes, which showed serene surprise at our visit.

" How is your mother? " asked Silverio. " Open the door. These gentlemen have come . . ."

She opened the door slowly and murmured in a painful dragging tone, but without complaining and smiling a resigned smile : " What can you expect, poor thing? Pretty bad . . . pretty bad."

And from within, with a moan that rose as if from the floor between gaspings and pantings, the mother repeated her disconsolate lament : " Ay! I am here, and pretty bad : pretty bad!"

Silverio, without crossing the threshold, holding his umbrella half-open, like a couched lance, to ward off infection, said : " Maybe it's not anything, Aunt Mary. It may be only a chill. Only a chill."

Then over his shoulder he said to Jacinto :

" There, you see, your Excellency. A great deal of misery and poverty! Even the rain comes straight through the roof."

And on the piece of the floor of stamped earth which they could see, a wet stain glistened, which had dripped from a broken tile in the roof. The wall, covered with soot from the smoke of the hearth, was as black as the floor. The dirty twilight within seemed to be littered with rags, potsherds, and broken bits of things lying about in disorder: the only thing that took a recognizable shape was a chest of black wood, and above it, hanging from a nail, between a saw and a lamp, a big red petticoat.

Then Jacinto in embarrassment stammered abstractedly: "All right! All right."

Then he went over the fields back towards the shed as if he was fleeing for his life, while Silverio must have revealed to the girl the august presence of the "Master"; for we heard from behind the door the sick voice crying out of its sorrow: "May our good Lord give you good luck! May our Lord go with you!"

When Silverio, with the big strides of his big boots, caught up with Jacinto and myself, we were already in the middle of the field. Jacinto stopped, looked at me, twisting his moustache with trembling fingers and cried:

"It's horrible, Zé Fernandes. It's horrible!"

Beside us Silverio's voice thundered:

"What do you want here again, boy? Go back to your mother."

It was the broken-down, starved child who had attached himself to us in blind wonder at such unwonted people, and perhaps in the vague hope that as from Gods met by chance on a journey, some relief or profit might flow from us. And Jacinto, at whom he stared the most specially with his sad eyes, and whom his dumb humility and misery most horrified, could do nothing but smile stupidly and murmur his vague "All right! All right!" It was I who gave a penny to the boy to get rid of him. But as he, clinging tightly to it, began to follow us once more, as if in the wake of our glory, Silverio had to scare him off like a sparrow, by clapping his hands and shouting: "Go back home. Take it back to your mother. Run! Run!"

"And now for lunch," I cried looking at my watch. "The day is going to turn out fine again."

Over the river there shone a well-washed patch of clear

blue sky. The huge masses of dark clouds were slowly rolling away in the sweep of the wind which bore them away to some hidden corner of the heavens.

We returned home slowly by a steep path which Silverio showed us, where a slender rain-torrent was still leaping and tinkling. From every bough we touched, raindrops showered down. All the verdure of the country, having deeply drunk, shone refreshed.

Brusquely, as we emerged from the path into a wider road, Jacinto stopped, between a terrace and a row of vines, slowly pulling out his cigarette-case.

"Well, Silverio, I want no more of these horrible miseries on my farm," he said.

The manager shrugged slightly with a vague "Eh! eh!" half of obedience, half of doubt.

"Before anything else, order Doctor Avelino at once for that poor woman. And let the medicines he prescribes be fetched from Guiães. Tell the doctor to return tomorrow and every day till the woman recovers. And I want you to take her money for broths and diet. Would ten or fifteen escudos be enough?"

The manager could not restrain a respectful laugh. Fifteen escudos? A few pennies would suffice. It was not a good thing to accustom them to such largesse. They would all begin wanting the same and demanding it too.

"Well, all of them are going to get it," said Jacinto simply.

"You have only to command," said Silverio. He shrugged his shoulders, halting in the middle of the road, as if dazed by such extravagance.

I had to hurry him impatiently. "We are still walking around and talking. It's midday and I am as hungry as a wolf: come on!"

We walked on with Silverio in the middle, pensively, with his brows furrowed under the wide brim of his hat, his huge beard hiding his chest, and the exorbitant roll of his huge scarlet umbrella under his arm.

Jacinto, nervously pulling his moustache, cautiously formulated a few more beneficent ideas, though somewhat cowed by his indomitable fear of Silverio.

"The houses too . . . That house is a hovel. We must house these poor people better . . . I suppose those of the other farm-hands are equally bad . . . A reform is necessary. We must have new houses for every tenant on the estate."

"Every tenant?" stuttered Silverio, and then fell silent.

"Every tenant," mumbled Jacinto somewhat startled at his own emphasis. "Well, I mean to say . . . How many are there?"

Silverio made an enormous gesture. "There are twenty-something. Twenty-three, if I remember rightly. No! No! Twenty-seven."

Then Jacinto fell silent too, as if suddenly realizing the vastness of the undertaking. But he wanted to know how much each house would cost. "I mean a simple house but clean and comfortable, like Melchior's sister's house."

Silverio halted again. A house like that of Ermelinda? Does your Excellency really want to know? And he threw the figure as if it were an enormous boulder from very high up, to squash Jacinto altogether.

"Two hundred escudos, and that's the very least!"

I laughed at the tragic menace of the excellent fellow. And Jacinto very blandly said to conciliate Silverio:

"Well, my friend, let's say six contos of *reis* . . . or rather ten contos because I wish to give them all linen and furniture."

Then Silverio gave a yell of terror: "But then, your Excellency, that will be a revolution!"

As we could not help laughing at his eyes which were staring in horror, and his huge arms opened behind him, as if he saw the world collapsing, he continued:

"Ah! Your Excellencies are pleased to laugh, are you? Houses for everybody, with furniture and crockery! At ten contos of reis! Ten thousand escudos! Well, I'll laugh too . . . Ha! Ha! Ha! It's a good joke!"

And then he said in deeply measured tones as if declining all responsibility:

"Well, in the end it's your Excellency who commands."

"Well, the order has been given, Silverio. Also I want to know the rents paid by these people, and to see the existing contracts so that they can be improved. There's plenty to improve. Come and lunch with us now, and we'll discuss it."

Silverio was so saturated with horror that this last sally about "improving the rents" made absolutely no further impression on him. He thanked Jacinto heartily for his invitation, but asked permission to make a detour to the wine-press to see the carpenters who were mending the lock of the river. It would only be for an instant, after which he would be at his Excellency's orders. He went off, leaping a low gate. We went on with steps which were lightened by the lateness of our lunch, by the clearing of the weather, and by that act of mercy which had been done to the poverty of the sierra.

"You did not lose your day today, Jacinto," I said with a tenderness I could not disguise as I patted his shoulder.

"What misery, Zé Fernandes. I had never even dreamed of such a thing. To think that there are houses in view of my own, where the children are hungry. It's too horrible."

We were now entering the avenue. A ray of sunshine streaming between two cotton-pods of cloud, struck a corner of the mansion with a glitter of pure gold. The bugles of the cocks sounded clear and high. And a soft wind which had just arisen stirred the new-washed leaves with a gentle tremor.

"Do you know what I was thinking, Jacinto? That the legend of Saint Ambrose has happened to you . . . No, it wasn't Saint Ambrose . . . I can't remember which saint. Maybe he wasn't a saint either, but just an ordinary sinner who fell in love with a woman with his whole soul, just through seeing her at a distance in the street. Sometime after that he was following her when she entered a church and there suddenly lifting her veil, she opened her blouse and showed him her breast disfigured with a terrible wound. You also fell in love with the sierra without knowing it, except in its beauty of summer. But today the sierra (crash!) has shown you its huge ulcer . . . It may be your preparation for becoming Saint Jacinto."

He halted pensively with his fingers in the hollows of his waistcoat.

" It is true. I saw the scar. But thanks be to God it is not one of those which I cannot cure."

I did not discourage my Prince and we both climbed happily up the steps of the old mansion.

11

ON the day which followed these great charities of Jacinto's, I left for Guiães. And from then onwards I so often trotted those three leagues between our avenue and the ancient avenue of Jacinto, that my mare, if ever she had to deviate from the well-known road leading to the familiar stable where she had struck up a friendship with Melchior's pony, would whinny with sheer yearning to be back on the road once more. Even Aunt Vicência was getting a bit jealous of Tormes, to which I was constantly going, and of that rejuvenated Prince whose public benefices and agricultural ideas I was always talking about.

One day, as my Aunt was knitting away, she suddenly said to me, as her needles clicked louder, and with a gleam of kindly irony: " Look, here! You can be proud of yourself: you have raised my curiosity so much that I want to know that Jacinto of yours . . . You must bring him over here." I laughed, " Calm yourself, Aunt Vicência, I shall bring him over to dinner on my birthday. Let us give a party and have a dance in the courtyard; and ask all the neighbouring gentry. Who knows, perhaps we might even find a wife for Jacinto."

I had in fact already invited Jacinto to this birthday party. It was only right that the Master of Tormes should meet all these representative families of the sierra . . . Above all, as I had laughingly said to him, it would be a good thing if he met a few of those fine strapping girls from the surrounding properties; for Tormes enjoyed an almost monastic solitude; and a man living in such solitude and without any feminine company soon grows as rough as the bark of a tree. " And all this Tormes business, Jacinto, this reconciliation of yours with Nature and your renunciation of all the falsities of

174

civilization, is all very pretty—but, damn it all, one must have some women about!"

He agreed, laughing languidly, as he lay back in his garden chair.

"You are quite right; Woman, with a capital W, is indeed missing here. But, you know, I can't help thinking that those ladies from round about must be awfully like vegetables. Healthy, nutritious, and excellent as daily food—but still vegetables. The women who are compared by poets to flowers, are those that grace courts or live in the great capitals —those are the ones, my dear fellow, that, ever since Hesiod and Horace, have inspired the poets . . . and evidently there is neither scent, charm, elegance, nor refinement, to be found in a carrot or a cabbage . . . No, those good ladies from these mountains can hardly be very interesting!"

"Now, let me see . . . Your nearest neighbour is the daughter of Dom Teotónio: well, yes, with all due respect to the distinguished family of Barbedos she is, I am afraid, a scarecrow. Then there is the sister of the Albergarias, they own the Loja property—well, she wouldn't even tempt poor Saint Anthony himself, and less if she stripped because she is an absolute asparagus. I am afraid she *does* look like a vegetable and at that not a very appetising one."

"You have said it—asparagus."

"There is also Dona Beatrice Veloso . . . That girl is pretty, but, my dear fellow, she is terrifically high-brow! She talks like a heroine out of one of Camillo's novels. By the way, I don't believe you have read anything of Camillo's . . . And then she speaks in a tone of voice that beggars description, just as though she were declaiming from the stage of the Dona Maria in one of their romantic plays. But you have never been inside the Dona Maria, have you? Anyhow she is a bore and asks the most dreadful questions . . . 'Aren't you deeply moved by Lamartine, your Excellency?' She actually asked me that, the goose!"

"What did you say?"

"I just stared at her with wide open eyes; 'Oh! Lamartine!' But, poor thing, she is a nice girl. Now, a little further afield we have the Rojões, they are the daughters of João

175

Rojão, lovely creatures, very lively, very gay, they are like a breath of fresh air and besides, they are simple, straight-forward girls . . . Aunt Vicência adores them. Then, we have the wife of Dr. Alípio, she is a beauty—a splendid creature! But then after all she *is* the wife of Dr. Alípio and you have renounced the pleasures of civilization . . . and anyhow she is a good woman completely taken up by her two babies who look like two little Murillo angels. And who else is there? I want once and for all to finish this list of possibles. Well, we still have Melo Rebelo, very engaging and with lovely hair, she embroiders to perfection and makes the most delicious sweets worthy of a nun of the good old days. There was also a very pretty girl called Julia Lobo but she died. I can think of no more. But yes, I can! I have left out the Flower of the Sierra, my cousin Joaninha from the Farm of the Geranium Flower. She is a beauty if ever there was one."

"But what about yourself, cousin Zé, how have you resisted her?"

"Oh, we are just like brother and sister, we were brought up together and nothing is more destroying of romance than that. Her mother was Aunt Vicência's only sister, and she died very young. So Joaninha was brought up here in our house at Guiães almost from the cradle. Her father, Uncle Adrião, is a very decent chap, rather learned, an antiquarian and a bit of a magpie. He collects all sorts of strange things, bells, spurs, seals, buckles; he has the most curious lot of things. It is a long time now since he has been wanting to come to Tormes to call on you . . . but the poor man has bladder trouble—he can't ride—and the road between here and the farm of the Geranium Flower is impassable for a carriage."

Jacinto stretched himself: "It is obvious I shall have to go and call on your uncle and on Aunt Vicência—besides, I want to know my neighbours. But not now, later when things have quieted down. Now I am completely taken up with my people."

Indeed Jacinto had become like some founder of a kingdom and a great builder. All over his properties, repairs were going on to the tenants' houses; some were being repaired, others, that were too old, were being pulled down to be rebuilt larger and more comfortable. One constantly saw carts laden with stone and wood creaking along the country lanes.

In Peter's tavern, at the entrance of the parish, there was an unusual coming and going of masons and carpenters, who had been engaged for the building, and Peter, standing behind the counter, with his sleeves turned up, was constantly filling the glasses from a huge pitcher.

Jacinto, who had acquired two horses, went the rounds early every morning to see how the work was getting on. It was with a feeling of anxiety that I sensed that, once again, Jacinto was a prey to his old passion for accumulating sensations.

His original plan of reconstruction was constantly being enlarged and improved. It was decided to put in glass in the windows which, according to the custom of the mountains, should only have had shutters, although the foreman, with great honesty, warned him that, after a month, no room in the house would have a single pane of glass left in it. He wanted to hide the old beams by plastering the ceilings, and I could see that he was resigning himself, in fact bracing himself with Common Sense, not to place an electric bell in each room. I did not even turn a hair when he declared to me one morning that country people were dirty because they had no proper place to wash in and he was seriously thinking of putting a bath in each house. At that moment we were riding at random down a steep and rocky lane; a light breeze rustled through the trees and a little brook bounded gaily over the stones. No, I did not turn a hair but it really did seem to me that the stones, the rivulet, the branches and the wind were all laughing at Jacinto. Over and above these luxuries—which João with his eyes starting out of his head called " those grandeurs "—Jacinto was thinking up others, but these were to be of the spirit. He had already ordered from his architect in Paris a plan for a school which he intended to build in a certain field called Carriça, near the chapel which sheltered " the ancestral remains." Little by little he also meant to build up a library in which there would be picture-books to amuse those men who would never be able to learn to read.

I shrugged my shoulders thinking; "there goes a terrible accumulation of Ideas, there go Books invading the sierra." On the other hand, some of Jacinto's ideas were to the point —and I myself got enthusiastic, and made Aunt Vicência so also, with his plan for a crèche; there she hoped to spend some very happy mornings watching the little ones crawling and stumbling after a ball. Our chemist at Guiães was already engaged to establish a small branch of his shop at Tormes to be run by a godson of my Aunt Vicência who had published an article, on the popular holidays of the Douro, in the "Almanac of Remembrances", and he had already offered a retaining fee of 600 escudos to the doctor at Tormes.

"The only thing missing is a theatre," I said laughing.

"A theatre, no. But I am thinking of having a large room, with a magic lantern in it, so as to show these poor people some pictures of great cities, life in Africa, and a little bit of History."

I also took pride in this innovation, and, when I told my uncle Adrião about it, this old gentleman in spite of his rheumatism gave himself a terrific slap on the thigh. "Yes sir! A splendid idea. Like that, with pictures, one could teach these poor people some Bible History, Roman History and even some Portuguese History!" And turning towards my cousin Joaninha, uncle Adrião added that Jacinto was a kind-hearted man.

And all along the sierra the popularity of Jacinto grew. In that "God bless you, sir!" with which the women addressed him as they passed and turned to follow him with their eyes, there was an almost reverent feeling, a sincere desire that God should indeed protect and bless him all his days. The children, to whom he gave pennies, scented his arrival from afar, and surrounded on all sides with their dark dirty little faces and large staring eyes which, if they *did* still show amazement, had at least long ceased to show any fear. One afternoon, Jacinto's horse stumbled and fell on some stones that were blocking the road near the avenue. The very next day, a group of men, appalled at the risk their good master had run, turned up, entirely of their own free will, and levelled that dangerous bit of road. That appellation of "the good master" had now spread all over the sierra. The most aged members of the parish never met him without exclaiming, some with gravity, and others with great toothless smiles; " this is our benefactor ". Sometimes, an old woman would come running out from the back of her yard, or, on seeing him in the road, would stand at the door of her hovel yelling, as she waved her thin arms; "Ah! May God abundantly bless you, may He abundantly bless you."

On Sundays, Father José Maria (a good friend of mine and a good sportsman) came from Sandofim, on his roan mare, to celebrate Mass at the chapel. Jacinto heard Mass from his tribune, just like the Jacintos of other times, so that the simple country folk should not think him a stranger to his God. Nearly always after these occasions he received presents which the daughters of the farm-hands and the little children brought him; they would come blushing to the verandah bearing sweet basil or a bunch of carnations and sometimes even a large duck. Then cakes and meringues from Guiães would be handed round to the girls and the children—and in the courtyard pitchers of white wine would be brought out to the men. Silverio maintained with growing respect that the Senhor Dom Jacinto would soon have more votes in the elections than Dr. Alípio. I was impressed myself when Melchior told me that João Torrado, an eccentric old man, with a long beard, who came from our part of the world, a herbalist, vaguely a veterinarian and a fortune-teller—and who lived in a mysterious cave high up in the mountains— was assuring everybody that the " good master " was Dom Sebastião himself, who had at last returned.

12

so September came round and with it my birthday which that year fell on a Sunday. I had spent all that week in Guiães, busy with the vintage; and very early on that all-important Sunday morning, I went and leaned over the balcony of my lamented Uncle Afonso's room and watched the road along which Jacinto, who at last was coming to visit the home of his Zé Fernandes, was to appear. Ever since early morning Aunt Vicência had been very busy, coming and going between the kitchen and the pantry because, as she wanted to introduce the inhabitants of the sierra to my Prince, she had invited to dinner some of the members of the neighbouring families who had carriages or carts and who would therefore be able to return home late along the rough country roads. There was to be a dance in the courtyard which had been decorated with Chinese lanterns for the occasion. But presently, round about ten o'clock, I was exasperated on receiving a letter from Joaninha—brought over by a servant from the farm of the Geranium Flower. She wrote, that she was very sad to be unable to go but that Papa had had a boil, since the day before, and that she did not like to leave him. I ran full of indignation to the kitchen where Aunt Vicência was presiding over a violent beating of yokes of eggs in an enormous tureen.

" Joaninha is not coming! Always the same. She says her Father has a boil . . . Uncle Adrião always chooses these occasions to have a boil or a pain." The kind round, red face of my aunt filled with sympathy. " Poor man, it must be placed in such a way that he can't sit down properly. Poor man, listen, if you are writing tell her to make a poultice with rosemary leaves. That was *the* only thing that ever did your uncle any good."

I merely called out to the servant who was watering his donkey in the yard : " Tell the Senhora Dona Joaninha that we are very sorry; I may come round tomorrow morning."

I turned again impatiently towards the window because the clock in the passage had already struck half-past ten and Jacinto would be arriving late. But, no sooner had I reached the balcony, than Jacinto appeared at last, on horseback, wearing a large straw hat, and followed by Cricket, also wearing a straw hat and shading himself under an enormous green parasol. His legs straggled over the pack saddle of Melchior's old mare. Behind them walked a boy, balancing a suit-case on his head. I was overjoyed to see Jacinto trotting at last towards my village home on my thirty-sixth birthday and I thought of that other birthday, his, in Paris at Number 202 when, surrounded by all the splendours of civilization, we had sadly drunk " Ad Manes "—to our dead.

" *Salve!* " I shouted from the balcony. " *Salve, domine* Jacinto!" And the better to welcome him, I warbled a lively tune.

" But it is beautiful here," he called out from the yard, " and your mansion looks awfully grand. How do I get in? " But I was already flying to the courtyard where Jacinto, as he dismounted, described the torments suffered by his poor Cricket who had never ridden before and who had not ceased lamenting the dangers of that adventure. The good negro was breathless, shining with sweat, his face livid under his glossy black skin. He exclaimed, as he pointed with a trembling hand, at the poor mare which was loose, and which with its pensive expression and heavy legs seemed cut out of rock; " If you had only seen, Massa Fernandes, a wild beast that would not come along quietly. First to the left, then to the right, jog here, jog there, and all just to shake me up, yes it was." He could not resist it and with the sharp end of his parasol, he gave the mare's saddle a revengeful dig.

Jacinto, as he walked up the light staircase and into the cheerful passage, which had a pretty rose-covered window at one end, sang the praises of our house which, he said, was a nice change from the sturdy walls and great feudal doors of Tormes. Once in his room, he expressed his gratitude to Aunt Vicência for the maternal kindness which had prompted her to fill two China vases with flowers and place them on the chest of drawers, and cover the bed with one of our richest Indian counterpanes, a yellow one, covered in great golden birds. I was touched and smiled. We then gave each other a good hug in honour of my birthday.

" Thirty-eight aren't you, Zé Fernandes? "

" Thirty-six, you brute."

And Jacinto opening his suit-case, a sombre affair worthy of a philosopher, gave us " the noble gifts, our due " as the wily Ulysses says in the *Odyssey*. There was a tie-pin with a sapphire and a cigarette-case worked in dull iron hoops and adorned with branches of apple-blossom in delicate enamel, also a paper knife of old Chinese workmanship. I protested against such generosity. "They are all taken from the Paris trunks, I had them opened last night. I took the liberty of bringing Aunt Vicência this keepsake. It is not of any value, but it *did* belong to the Princesse de Lamballe."

It was a little holy-water stoup worked in silver, very ornate and even gallant.

" Aunt Vicência has not the vaguest idea who the Princesse de Lamballe is, but she will be delighted; anyhow this will be your guarantee for she suspects you lack religion; as you come from Paris—that land of unbelievers. But now wash your hands and let us have our meal."

Aunt Vicência was at first surprised and then delighted by my companion whom she had really thought of as a Prince : arrogant and difficult. And when he gave her the holy-water stoup, asking her to remember him in her prayers, my kind aunt blushed as red as the roses on the table, for she had never before been offered a present in such a very charming way. But what really won her heart was Jacinto's tremendous appetite and the enthusiasm with which he helped himself to large quantities of tasty country stew, mountains of rice and beef with fried onions. He said that never in his life had he tasted such cooking; she beamed.

" It does one good to see you eat, yes it does! Now please do just have another of those stuffed potatoes."

"Certainly—even two! My capacity for eating at a meal like this is Gargantuan."

" Don't quote Rabelais," I interrupted delighted, " my aunt does not read such profane books. But come, try some of this white wine; it is our own vintage, and let us thank God for the juice of the grape."

The meal went off gaily and we chatted long and intimately. We talked about Jacinto's plans for Tormes, his nursery school—this idea of an infant school filled my aunt with delight—of the chances of a good vintage, of my cousin Joaninha whose father was ill, and of the frightful state of the roads. But the high spot of the occasion was reached when coffee was served after lunch and the man servant placed a little plate, with cinnamon bread on it, beside

Jacinto. He had the rather strange custom of always eating some after lunch.

My dear aunt had not forgotten this little habit of his, and there he was eating it away. She wanted him to feel at home, just as though he were at Tormes and that cinnamon bread was the symbol by which she showed that she had adopted Jacinto as her nephew.

Soon she left us to go to the kitchen where she had to supervise the preparations for the banquet, and we went off to the garden to smoke our cigarettes near the fountain under the shade of the cedar-tree. Afterwards, with that inexorable selfishness of the landowner, I showed Jacinto over all my property. I was pitiless and didn't excuse him from visiting a single flower-bed, furrow, tree or vine, and it was only when he grew really pale, looked exhausted and could only say in a stupefied way " very pretty, lovely place," that I turned back towards the house. But I still could not resist taking him the longest way home so as to show him the wine-press, and asparagus-bed and the place where stood the ruins of a Roman camp. When, after walking across the garden, we entered the cool room, I drove him, like a martyr, into the library of my uncle Afonso. I wanted to show him some of my rare books; the history of Dom João I by Fernão Lopes, a first edition of the Emperor Clarimundo, the *Henriad* signed by Voltaire, charters of King Dom Manuel and other rarities. As he closed the last volume with a sigh of relief, I dragged him off to the cellar to admire my wonderful wine-barrel which had, carved on its head, the complicated coat of arms of the Sandes. It was four o'clock; by now my Prince had a haggard livid aspect. I fixed him with a glassy look and, with an expression which I myself knew to be ferocious, declared that we should now go and see the granary. But, at last, he was forced to give in and whispered humbly in an almost childish murmur: " What wouldn't I give to sit down a little." Finally, I showed him pity and gave up my prey—I allowed him to drag himself behind me to his room where he frantically drew off his boots and flung himself on a sofa while he muttered " lovely farm ".

I generously left him to his sleep, and went down to see if

Gertrude had put out the lace towels in the room where the visitors, on their arrival, would go to wash their hands and brush away all traces of the dusty road from their clothes. Just then a calash drove into the courtyard; it was Dom Teotónio in his travelling chaise drawn by his two grey mares. I peeped out of the window and discovered with joy that he was alone, was wearing a white tie under his dust-coat, and, above all, that he was there without his hideous daughter. I sprinted to my aunt's room where, with the help of Catarina she was clasping on her magnificent topaz bracelets.

" Aunt Vicência, Dom Teotónio has just arrived and thank heavens without his daughter. Hurry up! The others will be arriving soon. Manuel has got to be beautifully groomed and with his collar good and stiff. I wonder how the party will go!"

13

ALAS, my birthday party was not a success.

When Jacinto walked into the drawing room, where all the other guests were now assembled, he looked very smart indeed thanks to the Paris trunks he had opened the day before. He was wearing a white rose in the buttonhole of his black jacket, a white waistcoat and an enormous cravat in white silk the folds of which were held together by a black pearl. All the men, Dom Teotónio, Ricardo Veloso, Dr. Alípio, fat Melo Rebelo from Sandofim and the Albergarias brothers, from Loja, were all of them standing in a closed circle, in one corner of the room. The ladies of the party were sitting grouped round Aunt Vicência's sofa. There were Beatrice Veloso, with her dishevelled mass of curly hair dressed in white muslin that accentuated her thin and airy aspect; the two Rojões, with their Aunt Adelaide Rojão, both as pink as a couple of berries and dressed in white; and the pretty wife of Dr. Alípio looking like a rustic Venus in a heavy, black dress. As Jacinto entered the room an embarrassed silence fell on everybody. You would have thought he was a real royal Prince from one of those northern countries where princes are so magnificent and distantly cold that they freeze one. All eyes were fixed upon my unfortunate Jacinto as though he were an Indian tiger about to emerge from the fringe of the jungle. It was in vain that Jacinto, in the hurried and confused introductions that followed, showed himself to be perfectly simple and quiet.

The gentlemen clearly reserved their judgment and watched him as he made his way towards the ladies who all of them took shelter round my Aunt like a flock of sheep round the shepherd when it fears the wolf. By now I was a bit disturbed and decided to throw Dom Teotónio into the fray; he was the most decorative of all the gentlemen.

" Dom Teotónio has been most kind in coming, Jacinto. It is seldom that we can get him to leave his delightful house at Abrujeira."

Dom Teotónio smiled as he stroked his thick, white military moustache.

" You have arrived straight from Vienna, Your Excellency? "

" No, I came straight from Paris with my friend Zé Fernandes."

Dom Teotónio insisted: " But you have certainly often been to Vienna."

Jacinto, surprised, smiled: " Vienna, why? No, it is at least fifteen years since I have been to Vienna."

The fidalgo murmured slowly, " Ah." His eyes lowered as though deep in thought, his hands tucked back under the flap of his long blue coat.

I then decided to try Dr. Alípio: " Our Doctor, my dear fellow, is the most influential man about here."

The Doctor bent his handsome head with its admirably groomed glossy black hair. At that moment my Aunt Vicência rose from her sofa and called Jacinto because fat Manuel had just announced dinner. This he had done in dumb show, merely indicating by a gesture the dining room by a stiff inclination of his whole body.

On the table were trifles and large dishes filled with egg sweets and in the crystal decanters the light played on the rich colours of the old port and madeira. Jacinto sat between

185

my aunt and her god-daughter Luisinha who ever since *I*
could remember, had had the habit of placing herself at table
close under the protection of her kind god-mother. The
chicken broth was eaten in a long and heavy silence which I
was so anxious to break that I exclaimed at random, quite
forgetting that I was in my own house: " What delicious
soup!"

" Divine," Jacinto echoed.

But as all the guests were obviously surprised by my
exclamation and Jacinto's exaggerated admiration the silence
which up to now had only been due to the formality of the
occasion, became charged with embarrassment. Happily,
Aunt Vicência smiling kindly had again noticed that Jacinto
seemed to like Portuguese food; and I, with the purpose of
enlivening the conversation, did not even give Jacinto a
chance to agree with her but interrupted:

" What do you mean, ' like ', why he simply adores it of
course! Think of his being so long in Paris deprived of all
our choice Lusitanian dishes."

Fortunately I suddenly remembered the rice sweet which
the cook of Number 202 had prepared for Jacinto's birthday
party. I told the story lengthily and exaggeratedly, assuring
them that the rice had contained *foie gras* and that on the
top of a decorated pyramid, and above the bust of Chambord,
had floated the tricolour flag. But that Parisian pudding did
not interest any of them and when I turned alternatively from
one to the other of my guests, exclaiming:

" Wonderful, wasn't it? "

I only received a few strained, polite smiles.

Dom Teotónio observed mysteriously that the cook must
certainly have known for whom he was cooking. And the
beautiful wife of Dr. Alípio dared to murmur blushing:

" It must have been a pretty dish and perhaps not so bad."

In my anxiety to get some animation into the dinner party,
to get some conversation going, I attacked with violent gaiety
the Senhora Dona Luisa for defending the profanation of our
national delicacy, but oh dear, poor me! I had so frightened
this handsome woman by my noisy talk that she blushed
deeply and lapsed into silence looking even more beautiful.

Another silence descended on the table like a cloud, when my aunt, providentially, excused herself to Jacinto for having no fish. But what was to be done about it, it was impossible to get any in the sierra even if you were prepared to pay for its weight in gold; unless of course you bought salted whiting or cod. That reminded my excellent friend Rojão that the Senhor Dom Jacinto had a long stretch of the River Douro with the right to fish chad. Jacinto said he had never thought of the possibility of there being chad in those waters. Dr. Alípio turning to him said that this did not surprise him as those fisheries had been sold twenty years ago to Cunha, the rich chap from Brazil, when the Senhor Dom Jacinto was still a boy. But according to Dom Teotónio those fisheries were not worth two thousand reis; why there were not any chad! Thanks to the fisheries of the Douro the men, but without raising their voices, took up other rural subjects of conversation and the ladies, relieved from the formal silence which had been hanging over them since the beginning of the meal, made the best of the occasion and chatted to each other in low whispers. Afraid that this cheerless wave of whisperings was come to stay, I was determined—in the hope of cheering things up—to interrupt Jacinto and remind him of the ludicrous adventure of the Dalmatian fish stranded in the lift.

"That was one of the funniest things that happened to us in Paris. Jacinto gave a magnificent dinner because the Grand Duc Casimiro, you know the brother of the Emperor—had sent him a present of some very rare fish."

All eyes were turned on Jacinto who was helping himself to green peas. Melo Rebelo nearly choked as he drank in his anxiety to discover some reflection of the Grand-Ducal grandeur in Jacinto's face. I described in detail how the fish got stuck in the lift, how the Grand Duc tried to fish it up with a hook made from a hairpin belonging to the Princesse de Caraman and best of all, how the Duc de Marizac nearly fell into the shaft of the lift. But not a smile did I raise and they only listened out of politeness. It was in vain that I tossed together Princes and Princesses involved in burlesque situations. None of my guests knew how a lift worked or

187

could imagine a fish stranded in a dark lift-shaft, and when I came to the Princess's hairpin the Albergarias looked down their noses. My story didn't have a chance, my audience received it with a chilling reserve which was not helped by the innocent exclamation of my Aunt:

" My dear, what nonsense you talk."

Jacinto hurriedly started a long conversation with Luisinha Rojão, who was now laughing away, very ready to chat and looking very pretty. This lightened the atmosphere and after the roast, when champagne was served, things became a little livelier and everybody, forgetting Jacinto for a time, made discreet conversation. But again the conversation grew gloomy and low-toned and this time I finally gave up any idea of cheering up the dinner. I plunged into talk with the beautiful wife of Dr. Alípio and discussed with her the marriage of Dona Amélia Noronha with a land steward; this was at the time the chief subject of conversation in Guiães. I was defending Dona Amélia's right to marry whom she wished when again a silence fell—this time it was Jacinto who came to the rescue, bowing and holding up his glass he said:

" Your health, my dear old man. Many happy returns of the day and many of them in company with your distinguished Aunt whose health I also drink."

All glasses were raised in a friendly manner. I beckoned to Manuel to fill the glasses again.

" Gentlemen," I said rising, " I want to ask you to drink to the health of my old friend Jacinto who honours this house with his presence for the first time; I may add who honours his own country with his presence for the first time! May he stay among us, here, in these mountains, for many a happy year. Your health, my dear fellow."

Again a murmur arose through the room but it was formal and lacked enthusiasm. Our speeches had certainly not fired their imaginations. Aunt Vicência jangled her half-empty glass against Jacinto's who in his turn touched his neighbour's Luisinha Rojão, who was beaming and looked pinker than a peony. Then followed a whole series of healths drunk with half-empty glasses; neither Uncle Adrião nor the parish priest, who were both suffering from boils, was forgotten. At last my aunt gave one of those meaning looks round the table which starts off a general scraping of chairs—when Dom Teotónio—lifting his glass of port with one hand, while leaning on the table with his other and half-rising, called out to Jacinto in a respectful almost cavernous voice:

"This one is absolutely private just between you and me . . . I drink to him who is absent" and he emptied his glass slowly and reverently. Jacinto amazed and without understanding, drank. The chairs were pushed back and I gave my arm to Aunt Albergaria. I myself only understood the mystery once I was in the drawing room. Dr. Alípio with his coffee cup in his hand and smoking a cigar said to me, with one of his shrewd looks which had gained him his nickname "Dr. Sharp":

"I hope that at least here, in Guiães, we won't have the gallows raised." And with the same shrewd look indicated Dom Teotónio who had dragged Jacinto behind the curtains of the window and was talking to him with an air of profound mystery. Great Heavens! Of course, it was *Miguelism*. Dom Teotónio obviously thought of Jacinto as a hereditary, inflexible Miguelist and saw, in his unexpected arrival at Tormes, a political mission; the beginning of an energetic propaganda and who knows but perhaps the first step towards a restoration. And I sensed that in the reserve those gentlemen had shown Jacinto, lay the suspicions of the Liberal, the fear that in the next elections, the wealth of this young man, coupled to his being a novelty, would carry great weight, and they felt a rising irritation against the reactionary ideas of this rich man who represented a civilization so superior to their own. I nearly upset my coffee at my delighted surprise at their folly. I detained Melo Rebelo who was putting back his empty cup on the tray and, with a slight smile, fixed my eyes on "Dr. Sharp":

"Now tell me frankly did all these people imagine that Jacinto has come home to work for the Miguelist cause?"

With a very serious air Melo Rebelo approached his great moustaches to my ear:

"People are even saying that the Prince Dom Miguel is with him in Tormes."

As I looked at him wide-eyed, this sharp Dr. Alípio agreed,
" Yes, that's what's said—disguised as a servant."

" As a servant? By jove, it was Baptista!"

Just then Ricardo Veloso came up to me puffing at his
cigarette, which he wanted to light from my cigar, and Rebelo
immediately asked him to confirm his statement:

" Isn't it true that there is a rumour that the son of Dom
Miguel is in hiding at Tormes? "

" Yes, disguised as a footman." He lit his cigarette, blew
away the smoke, and raising his meditative eyebrows continued: " Yes that is how it is, although frankly to me it
seems just a bit of swank but mind you I wouldn't mind
seeing him. They say that he is a handsome, well-built man.
But anyhow, my Uncle João Vaz Rebelo was hacked to pieces
in the gaol of Almeida—and it will be a bad business for all
if that starts up again. Now your friend . . . " He held his
peace.

Jacinto who had managed to escape from old Dom
Teotónio was walking towards me, a smile of amused amazement playing round his lips.

" Extraordinary," he burst out, " I see that here in the
mountains they still cling to the good old times and its
ideas."

" It depends what your Excellency means by ' good ideas ',"
retorted Melo Rebelo unable to contain himself.

I was now angry; it was too bad that this fantastic invention which was enclosing my poor friend in a wall of hostility,
should spoil what should have been an agreeable evening.

" Do you play Ombre? " I asked Jacinto in a tone of suppressed irritation, " No, you don't. Well then let me get two
tables going; Dom Teotónio will certainly want to play
cards."

I carried off Jacinto towards the ladies who again nestled
round Aunt Vicência who had established herself in her usual
corner on the sofa. They all stopped talking and seemed to
shrink back fearfully on seeing Jacinto as though they were
doves and he a vulture. I left this dangerous man assuring
the wife of Dr. Alípio—she was a little withdrawn from the
flock of timid birds—that it had given him great pleasure

meeting all his neighbours. She opened and shut her fan nervously and smiled. Jacinto decided that he had never admired in Paris a redder mouth or more brilliant teeth. But, after I had organized a table for Ombre, I had to sit down and play myself, to take the place of Manuel Albergaria who was a dyspeptic and said that he felt sick and wanted to take a turn on the verandah to breath some fresh air. All the men complained of the heat and I had the windows that gave on to the mimosas in the courtyard opened. Veloso as he shuffled the cards puffed as though he were oppressed:

" How sultry it is, we shall yet have a thunderstorm."

Dr. Alípio ran to the window to have a look at the sky which had grown dark and heavy. He was worried as they had an hour's drive ahead of them and one of his mares was nervous.

" I am afraid you are right, it is going to rain."

The branches of the mimosas rustled shivering and the curtains were blown about by wild gusts of wind. The ladies shared in the general uneasiness, for Aunt Albergaria now turned up and warned Jorge.

It would be prudent to leave, the night was threatening and Dr. Alípio, drawing out his watch, suggested that at the end of the hand they should all get ready to go. At that moment Albergaria came in from the verandah feeling quite recovered thanks to some gin. He took up his cards again and announced that there was going to be a terrific thunderstorm.

Returning to the drawing room I found Jacinto gaily installed among the ladies who, now that they were more used to him, were listening delighted to his description of his arrival at Tormes; without trunks or servants, in fact so unprovided even with necessaries that he had had to sleep in the nightshirt of the foreman's wife. But my poor birthday party was ending in chaos. Aunt Albergaria walked from one window to another watching uneasily the dark sultry sky and frightened at the thought of the drive back to Roqueirinha. The pretty wife of Dr. Alípio, as she slowly pulled on her gloves, asked if the game would soon be over. My Aunt hurried up the tea which Manuel, followed by Gertrude

carrying a tray full of cakes, was already serving to the ladies.
Jacinto was handing round the cups and joking:

"What! You are all in such a hurry and so frightened
because of a tiny little thunderstorm?"

They, grown familiar and feeling an increasing liking for
him, laughed back:

"Ah, it's all right for you to talk. You are going to remain
safe under a roof."

"We should like to hear what you would say if you were
going back to Tormes on such a night."

Both tables finished their games of cards and the players,
going to the windows, called out their orders into the black
courtyard where their carriages were ready waiting for them.

"Put up the hood of the victoria, Diogo."

"Light the lamps in the courtyard, the carriage lanterns are
not sufficient."

Quiteria, the maid, arrived at the door, her arms laden with
shawls and lace veils. As one of Albergaria's sisters had to sit
on the front seat of the victoria, I ran to get her my rain-
coat in case it rained. Dom Teotónio was the only person not
in a hurry for he was only separated by two kilometres of
good road from his house. So again he laid hold of Jacinto
and took him off to the most solitary corner of the room in
deep conversation, the gravity and importance of which was
conveyed by the stiff solemn gestures of his raised finger.
But Aunt Albergaria called out that it was already raining;
then there was a flurry of skirts and hurried kisses to Aunt
Vicência while the men in the hall hastily put on their over-
coats.

Jacinto and I went down into the courtyard to accompany
this hurried departure and one by one the old carriage of
Dr. Alípio, the Albergarias' victoria and the huge old-
fashioned chaise of the Velosos rolled out of the courtyard,
into the night, accompanied by our sincere wishes for a good
journey. At last Dom Teotónio drew on his black gloves and
getting into his calash said to Jacinto:

"Well, my dear cousin, God willing, some good will come
of our having met."

As he went up the stairs, Jacinto exploded: "But this

Teotónio is the strangest man. Do you know what I dis-
covered at last; he takes me for a Miguelist and thinks I have
come to Tormes to prepare the restoration of Dom Miguel."
" What did you say to him? "
" I was so appalled that I did not even disillusion him."
" And what is more, my poor friend, they all believe it.
They don't trust you, and they are afraid of seeing another
rising here at Guiães. There is a rumour that you have got
Prince Dom Miguel disguised as a footman at Tormes and
do you know who your Prince is? Baptista."
" Well if that isn't fantastic," murmured Jacinto, his eyes
wide open.
Aunt Vicência was waiting for us; she was sitting in the
drawing room feeling rather sad, the many lamps still shining
brightly in the peaceful silence of the solitary evening.
" Did you ever see such bad luck? They wouldn't even
stay to try a little of my jelly or drink a glass of port."
" I'm afraid, aunt, it was not a very lively party." I couldn't
hide my disappointment: " All these women make one dumb
and, on top of it, the men looking suspicious."
" Quite the contrary," protested Jacinto gaily, " I
thoroughly enjoyed myself. They are excellent people; very
unpretentious and the girls are charming. So fresh and gay.
I'm going to make good friends here, when they are certain
that I'm not a Miguelist."
We then told my aunt the extraordinary tale of Dom
Miguel hidden at Tormes. She laughed heartily. What an
idea, what an awful idea!
" But you aren't a Miguelist, are you? "
" No, Madam, I'm a Socialist."
I came to the rescue explaining to Aunt Vicência that
Socialist just meant being kind to the poor. Seen in that light
my aunt agreed that was the only thing to be.
" My dear Afonso, God rest him, was a Liberal, so was my
Father, he was even on friendly terms with the Duke of
Terceira."
Just then a violent thunderclap rolled like cannon through
the night and rain fell in torrents beating against the panes
and on to the stones of the verandah.

"Saint Barbara!" cried out my Aunt, "those poor people, I *am* worried about them, and think of the Rojões in their victoria."

And she ran to her room anxious to light the two candles in her oratory, before putting away the silver and reciting the rosary with Gertrude.

14

ON the next day, after breakfast, Jacinto and I decided to ride over to the Farm of the Geranium Flower to ask after my Uncle Adrião and his boil. I was frankly curious, and even anxious, to see what impression my pretty cousin Joaninha, the pride of our house, would make on my friend. Already on that morning, as we were walking round the garden choosing a beautiful tea-rose for Jacinto's buttonhole, Aunt Vicência had sung the praises of her beloved niece describing affectionately her beauty, charm, kindness and sweet temper. So much so that I had protested.

"Look here, aunt, those praises should be given only to the Blessed Virgin, you are committing the sin of idolatry and Jacinto, after all that, is going to meet a creature who is but a human being and he is going to be terribly disappointed."

And now, as we trotted along the good road that led to Sandofim, I remembered that morning at Number 202 when Jacinto, seeing her photograph in my bedroom had said that she looked like a healthy peasant. But that was an old photograph and belonged to the time when in fact she was just a handsome, robust flower of the mountains. But now she was close on twenty-five, she had become a sensitive, thinking girl and had developed a personality which had refined, softened and spiritualized her rustic beauty.

It was a beautiful morning; the thunderstorm of the night before had cleared the air and the countryside, washed by the rain, looked green, cool and luminous. On mornings such as these, Euripides or Sophocles has said, it is sweet to feel one's body in motion while one's spirit, free from bustle or care, roams lazily in thought. The road had no shade but the rays of the sun shone gently. The valley through which we rode reminded Jacinto of an eighteenth-century landscape of the French school. The gently-rolling hill, the peaceful flowing river and the little farms, harboured in the tender green, gave one a feeling of plenty and content. Our horses travelled at a slow pace, enjoying also the peace of that September morning. I am unable to remember the names of the wild flowers that, hidden from view, filled the country road with their scent that autumn day.

"What a lovely day," murmured Jacinto, "this road to the Geranium Flower is the road to Heaven. Oh, Zé Fernandes, what is this delicious smell?"

"I don't know," I said smiling thoughtfully, "perhaps it is a scent from Heaven. Look," I continued, as I reined in my horse, and pointed with my riding whip towards the valley, "over there, where you see that row of elm trees and a stream, is Uncle Adrião's property. He has an excellent orchard where grow the best peaches in Portugal. I must ask Joaninha to send you some, and the jam she makes with those peaches, my friend, is just not of this world. I am also going to ask her to send you some."

"That will be exploiting your cousin rather too much," he laughed.

And I, Heaven knows why, reminded Jacinto of those lines taken from a ballad and written in Coimbra by my poor friend Procopio:

"Send her a servant, beloved—
Good fortune befall you, my dear!
Let a ring be my present, dear lady
And with it a rose from my heart."

"Zé Fernandes," laughed Jacinto gaily, "that would be too much for just half a dozen peaches and a bottle of jam."

As we were laughing in this manner we reached, at the bend of the road, the long wall of the farm of the Velosos and then the chapel of Saint Joseph of Sandofim. Immediately I made for Torto's pub because of his white wine; whenever I go that way my soul yearns after it. Jacinto scolded me indignantly.

"Good Heavens! Are you going to drink white wine at this hour, after your breakfast?"

"It is an old habit of mine, I always drink a glass here, at Torto's."

We stopped and I shouted to Manuel who appeared, his great stomach heaving and rolling on his twisted legs, carrying a green pitcher and a glass.

"Two glasses, Torto; this gentlemen also wants a drink."

After a faint protest, Jacinto accepted, looked at the transparent golden wine, tasted it and emptying the glass with delight, smacked his lips appreciatively.

"Delicious; I must have some of this wine at Tormes. It is perfect."

"Hm! It is cool, light, aromatic and makes one pleased with life. Fill our glasses again, my friend. This gentleman, Torto, is the owner of Tormes; the Senhor Dom Jacinto."

And then from behind the threshold of the tavern a great solemn, deep voice called out:

"God bless the Father of the poor." And a strange old man, with long white hair and a beard that almost hid his brick-red face from view, and a tin box on a strap over his shoulder, fixed Jacinto with two sparkling black eyes. It was "Uncle" João Torrado, the prophet of the sierra. I gave him my hand which he shook without taking his eyes off Jacinto. I ordered another glass of wine and then presented Jacinto, who blushed from embarrassment.

"Well, here you have the master of Tormes, who is doing so much good around here."

The old man briskly drew out his dirty, hairy arm which protruded from a short sleeve.

"Your hand, sir."

And when Jacinto gave it to him, after quickly pulling off his glove, João Torrado held it long in his, gently and pensively shaking it up and down.

"Royal hand," he murmured, "giver's hand, hand that is sent from above, hand now seldom seen."

Then he took the glass that was offered him by Torto, drank very slowly, wiped his mouth with his hand, gave a jerk to the leather belt that held in place his tin box and striking the ground with his stick continued:

"May our Blessed Lord Jesus Christ be praised, who brought me here that I might see this man with my own eyes."

"But Uncle João," I said confidentially, as I bent down towards him; "tell me this: is it true that you are saying to people round here that King Dom Sebastião has returned?"

The picturesque old man placed his two hands on his stick and leaning his face, covered by his flowing beard, on his hands muttered, without looking at us, as though following the thread of his own thoughts:

"Maybe he will, maybe he will not. One does not know who comes or goes. Bodies are visible enough but not the souls that inhabit them, and there are bodies of the present day possessed by souls of other times. The body is but a casket containing a soul; that soul is the man . . . At the fair of Roqueirinha, among those shoving, pushing cowmen, who knows how many kings one may not accidentally meet. A vile body may harbour a great lord."

As he ended in a whisper, I caught the eye of Jacinto so that we might enjoy together the strange manner of the seer.

"But really, Uncle João," I insisted, "can you conscientiously say that King Dom Sebastião did not die in battle?"

The old man, wrinkling his face with an air of distrust, looked up at me, "That all happened a long time ago; and these subjects of conversation are out of place here. The wine was very good and your Excellency is in a hurry. The flower from the Farm of the Geranium has her father ill. It does one good to see a person living for others. A brilliant star is shining over Tormes and you must be on your way for it is a lovely day." He made a gesture with his thin hand for us to continue our journey and we were already riding past the old stone cross when we heard again his solemn, ardent cry:

"Blessed be the Father of the poor."

He was standing straight in the middle of the road and holding up his stick as though directing the cheers of a people.

197

Jacinto was amazed that there should still exist in the kingdom a Sebastianist.

"But we all are, Jacinto, here in Portugal. Whether in the mountains or in the city each one awaits *his* Dom Sebastião; why even the Misericordia lottery is a sort of Sebastianism. And every morning, even if it is not cloudy, I look to see if mine has at last arrived or better, not a Dom Sebastião but a Dona Sebastiana . . . And what about you, you lucky man? "

"You mean am I waiting for a Dona Sebastiana? I am too old, Zé Fernandes. I am the last of the Jacintos, I am in fact Jacinto full stop. What is that house over there with the two towers? "

"The Geranium Flower."

"It is three o'clock," said Jacinto looking at his watch. "We have been an hour and a half on the road but it was a nice ride and most instructive. What a charming place this is."

On a low hill dominating the landscape, and separated from the road by a grove of trees which was surrounded by a wall, stood the house of the Geranium Flower. The long front was flanked by two square towers and the windows of the house were framed by glazed tiles. The great iron gates, with stone benches on either side, stood at the farthest end of a great courtyard in which grew a large chestnut-tree spreading a cool, green shade. A little boy was waiting sitting on the bare roots of the tree and holding a donkey by the halter.

"Is Manuel da Porta anywhere around here? "

"He has gone up the avenue."

"Good. Open the gates for us."

We rode down a short avenue of old trees towards another courtyard in which stood a shed, a cottage for the servants covered with ivy, and a dog kennel out of which jumped the mastiff Triton, barking and dragging his heavy chain. The dog as soon as he recognized me quietened down. Manuel da Porta arrived to hold our horses, running from the fountain where he was filling a big bucket.

"How is my Uncle Adrião? " Manuel, who was deaf as a doorpost, smiled delighted.

" And how is your Excellency? Well? The Senhora Dona Joaninha was only just now in the orchard with Josefa's baby."

We walked up the sandy lane bordered by lavender and high bushes while I explained to Jacinto that the little Josefinho was my cousin's god-son and her latest passion.

" This Joaninha of mine although she is unmarried, has quantities of children in her parish and she does not only give them clothes and presents but she also helps their mothers. She often washes and dresses them and treats their coughs. Whenever I see her she has some child in her arms and at present most of her time is taken up with Josefinho.

But when we arrived at the orchard along the edge of which ran the cart road leading to the water tank, it was in vain that I looked everywhere; thrusting myself into the bushes and finally even shouting :

" Ho, Joaninha!"

" Perhaps she is farther down, by the water tank."

We continued our search; on either side of the road were thick trees, their great branches crossing overhead and giving a deep shade. A cool pellucid stream of water ran along an irrigation channel. The last wild roses of the summer were growing in profusion among the old trunks of the trees and in the distance we could see a field carpeted yellow and white with marguerites and marigolds.

The round tank, which had been emptied for cleaning, was now being filled again from a spout; the water was still very shallow and the red fish were quivering as they swam, joyful at having again found their little ocean. On one of the stone benches that surrounded the tank, lay a basket full of dahlias. A boy who was standing on a ladder, pruning a camellia tree, told us that he had seen the Senhora Dona Joaninha walk down to the vine arbour.

We then made for the vine arbour which was still heavy with black grapes. In the distance two women were washing clothes under the shade of a walnut-tree; I yelled out to them :

" There, you! Have you seen the Senhora Dona Joana? "

One of the women screamed back but her voice was lost in the vastness of that quiet country air.

199

"Well, let us go up to the house. We cannot go on following her tracks all the afternoon."

"A very nice property." Jacinto murmured, delighted.

"Yes it is, and well looked after. Uncle Adrião has an excellent bailiff—oh he is not your Melchior of course—look and learn, farmer; just see that onion seed."

We passed through the kitchen garden, but a kitchen garden where grew many flowers; the beds were hedged with lavender and the stone pillars round which wound thick coils of honeysuckle screened off the sun and shaded the paths. We passed by the chapel, round the porch twined a pale yellow rose-tree with one solitary rose left blooming on it and nearby grew a vanilla bush from which Jacinto plucked a sprig to smell.

At last we reached the house and the terrace with its stone balustrade covered with yellow jasmin. The glass door was open. We mounted the stone steps that led to the outer hall; the whole house seemed to lie in a deep and silent sleep. The high old ceiling was panelled and round the walls stood great wooden benches on which we could just see, in faded old paint, the complicated arms of the Cerqueiras. I opened a door giving on to a sitting room, the balcony windows were wide open and a birdcage hung in each.

"How curious," exclaimed Jacinto, "that looks like my Christmas crib and the chairs are also the same as mine."

It was true. Standing on an old chest of drawers was a crib the exact replica of the one Jacinto had in his library and the leather chairs were the same as those he had discovered in his cellar with the coat of arms of some cardinal embossed on them.

"Good Heavens; isn't there any servant about?"

I clapped my hands loudly but the gentle silence which seemed to penetrate from the quiet countryside, remained unbroken and was hardly even disturbed by the hopping of the canaries in their cage.

"But this is the palace of the sleeping beauty," Jacinto exclaimed under his breath, almost indignant. "Why not give a yell."

"Hell! I'll try the other room."

200

But at that moment, in the door, which was suddenly opened, appeared my cousin Joaninha. Her cheeks, from walking about in the sunny garden were suffused with a delicate pink, and her pale dress, slightly opened at the neck, showed up the splendid whiteness of her skin against the pale gold of her curly hair—and the smile of pleasure which lit up her face enhanced the beauty of her large, soft, dark eyes. A fat healthy baby, barely covered by its little shirt, nestled in her arms.

And that was how Jacinto, on that September afternoon at the Farm of the Geranium Flower, saw for the first time the young girl who became his wife in the following May when the great rose-tree, that covered the porch of the chapel, was covered in roses.

15

AND now five years have passed over Tormes and the sierra, it is the vintage time and the roses are all in bloom. My Prince is now no longer the last of the Jacintos—Jacinto, full stop—for in the old house which was falling into decay two lively children run; Terezinha my fat and rosy god-daughter and my good friend Jacintinho. Now that my friend was the father of a family he had greatly changed, but so much moral worth was perhaps a trifle boring and in spite of myself I missed that other Jacinto so picturesque with his constant philosophical yearnings and tormented by insatiable chimeras. He had become an excellent farmer and when we walked round his property together I almost lamented the disappearance of that other Jacinto who plucked a theory from every branch and cutting the air with his riding crop, tried to invent a mould made of the rarest crystal and porcelain to hold cheeses which would have cost their weight in gold.

Paternity had also awakened in him a sense of responsibility. He kept an account book, not a very large one it is true, but in which he scrawled in pencil his expenses and his receipts which looked like two disciplined armies ready to attack each other. He visited his properties in Montemor in

Beira. He kept these houses well-furnished so that his children later on, when they should be older, might find themselves in ready-made nests. I definitely realized that Jacinto was a changed man and that a perfect balance had established itself at last in his soul, when, just as he was getting over his first ardent simplicity campaign, he once more opened the doors of Tormes to civilization. Two months before Teresinha's birth a long line of carts, which had been requisitioned in the village, and heaped with large boxes, trundled up the road towards the house. These were the famous boxes which had been stranded all this time in Alba-de-Tormes and which were arriving to invade the country with the luxuries of town. I thought to myself: that looks bad, my poor friend is suffering a relapse. But I was wrong, for to my surprise nearly all the contents of those boxes were put up in the large attics where they were abandoned to the dust. The old house benefited only by the addition of a few carpets for the floor, curtains for the draughty windows and some deep comfortable armchairs and a sofa, in which Jacinto could lie back and rest. I put this moderation down to Joaninha who loved Tormes bare and simple, but she swore it was Jacinto who had decided it so. Three weeks later I trembled: a foreman arrived from Lisbon with workmen and more boxes to install a telephone.

" A telephone here in Tormes, Jacinto? "

He explained humbly: " Only to my father-in-law's house, you must understand . . ."

It was sensible and kind. However, the telephone, silently and subtly stretched out another long wire, this time to Valverde. Jacinto spreading out his hands, said with a gesture of supplication:

" It is to the doctor's, you understand . . ."

It was prudent. But one morning I woke up in Guiães to hear my aunt's voice raised in fury. A mysterious man had arrived accompanied by other men to install in our house the new invention. I calmed Aunt Vicência, swearing to her that the apparatus made no noise, did not bring diseases, nor even thunderclaps. But I hurried to Tormes. Jacinto smiled, shrugging his shoulders:

"Well, what do you expect? In Guiães you have the chemist, the butcher, and there is *you*."

It was fraternal. But still, I thought; we are done for, in another month we shall have poor Joaninha dressing by machine. But no—Progress, which on Jacinto's command had installed the latest marvel and certainly thought that he had conquered another kingdom to disfigure, was silently deprived of office and disillusioned, and we did not see in our beloved mountains his rigid shadow the colour of rust and iron. Then I did understand that in Jacinto's soul an equilibrium was at last established and with it, the kingdom of happiness. Jacinto had so long been a Prince deprived of his princedom.

One evening I met my old friend Cricket in the orchard; he had become reconciled to the sierra since it had given him children to whom to give piggy-back rides. I pointed out to the kindly negro, who was reading the *Figaro* and was wearing imposing round glasses:

"Well, Cricket, we can really say at last that the Senhor Dom Jacinto has become as steady as a rock."

Cricket pulled his glasses up on his forehead and lifted the five fingers of his right hand with a rounded gesture, as though imitating the petals of a tulip:

"His Excellency has blossomed."

Good old Cricket, always so right in his judgments, and so wise. Yes, that withered shoot from the city, transplanted to the mountains, had taken root and absorbed the rich earth of its ancestral home, growing in strength, its roots sunk deep into the earth, the trunk thickened and its branches burst into flower; strong, serene, prosperous and noble; it lavished fruit and gave shade and, living securely under this shade, a hundred cottagers blessed it.

16

JACINTO often spoke, during those years, of returning for two or three months to Number 202 to show Joaninha Paris. I was to have been their faithful companion and kept a record of the astonishment of my country cousin when faced by the great city. Then we thought it prudent to wait for Jacintinho to be two years old; we should travel more comfortably and he would by then be able to point things out with his fat baby finger. But when, in October, he had his birthday, my cousin felt very lazy and almost frightened by the idea of the railway journey, the noise of a great city, and by Number 202 and its luxury. " We are so comfortable here, the weather is so fine," she would murmur, with her dazzling smile, throwing her arms round the sturdy neck of her husband. Jacinto gave up the idea quite happily. " Let us go in April, when the chestnut-trees in the Champs-Elysées are in flower."

But April found Joaninha tired, though happy, and lying on the sofa in a loose dress with her face slightly freckled. So for a whole year once again our gay adventure was put off. In March it rained and the crops looked promising. A certain widow, Anna Vaqueira, who was healthy, well-made, and had filled all the corners of my heart, left with her brother for Brazil where he had a business. During the winter I felt that my bones were getting rusty and that in a little corner of my soul a spot of mould was growing. Then my mare died. I decided to leave for Paris.

Once in Hendaye, as soon as my feet trod the gentle earth of France, my thoughts—like doves winging to their dovecot —flew to Number 202. Possibly this was because of a huge poster showing a naked woman, with flowers in her hair and all twisted, holding in one hand a bubbling bottle and brandishing in the other a model of a corkscrew. And then, wonder of wonders, whom should I see in the quiet sunny station of St. Jean-de-Luz, but a slim, elegant young man who, after jumping into my compartment and finding himself face to face with me, called out—" Why, Fernandes!"

It was the Duc de Marizac. I already felt I was at Number 202. How grateful I was to him for having recognized me! and I shook him warmly by the hand. As he threw the overcoat and a bunch of newspapers, which his servant gave him, on to a corner seat, Marizac continued to exclaim " and Jacinto? "

I then gave him all the news; I told him about Tormes, and life in the mountains; about Jacinto's sudden passion for country life and his great love for my cousin and the two children to whom he gave piggy-back rides.

" What a dirty dog! " said Marizac, staring at me. " And he is probably very happy."

" Terrifically, madly, there are not adverbs enough . . ."

" Indecently," murmured Marizac very seriously. " What a dirty dog."

It was then my turn to ask questions; I wanted to know all about our group of Number 202. He shrugged his shoulders as he lit a cigarette.

" Oh, they are all alright."

" Madame Oriol? "

" She is still going strong."

" And how are the Trèves and Ephraim? "

" Oh, they are all three just the same." He continued with a languid gesture. " Nothing ever changes in Paris; it all goes on just the same. The women have their faces rather more powdered, a little more sagging and yellow; the men are a bit more dyspeptic than they were and so it just continues; we had anarchists. The Princesse de Caraman decamped with an acrobat from the Cirque d'Hiver—and that is about all!"

" And Dornan? "

" He is still about. I have not met him since the last time at Number 202. But I sometimes see his name in *The Boulevard*. His poetry is great; full of the most refined, subtle obscenities."

" What about the Psychologist? What was his name? "

" Oh, he is still kicking, and still runs after women at three francs fifty an hour. Duchesses in chemises, naked souls, all that sort of stuff sells well."

I was just going to enquire about de Todelle and the Grand Duc when the train steamed into Biarritz station and the exquisite Marizac, rapidly seizing his things after giving my hand a friendly squeeze, jumped down on to the platform, while his servant held the door open for him. " Goodbye," he called out, " come to see me in Rue Camberie."

Once I was alone in the empty carriage I yawned. I was overwhelmed by a strange feeling of monotony; I already felt besieged by people I had seen too much of, all telling, with weary smiles, the same old stories and repeating the same eternal chatter. On either side of the line lay the great monotonous plain; the reseda, which grew there in profusion, lent a dull ashy hue to the countryside which was cut up and cultivated into small strips. Not one splash of colour, not the smallest variation in the surface of the soil came to spoil the ordered and discreet mediocrity of that landscape. Pale poplars were planted in thin, tidy rows along the clear and straight canals. The houses, all of the same greyish colour, hardly stood out against the general faded green, as though they had bashfully sunk from view ashamed of their very dullness. A colourless sun hung in the smooth, cloudless sky which looked like a vast watery looking-glass from which all brilliancy had been washed away. I fell into a gentle insipid sleep.

I arrived in Paris on a beautiful May morning; the air was cool and soft and, though I was very tired, it was with a feeling of distaste that I entered a sombre four-poster bed in the Grand Hotel, all enclosed in thick velvet, and bearing cords and tassels like a gala platform. In that feathered hollow, I dreamed that in Tormes they had built an Eiffel Tower and that the most respectable ladies from the mountains, that Tia Albergaria herself, were all dancing round it quite naked and waving in the air enormous corkscrews. It took me a little time to come round after my nightmare; I then had a bath and unpacked. So it was nearly two o'clock before I was ready to walk out of the great doors of the Hotel and step onto the Boulevard after an absence of five years. And immediately I felt that during all those years I had remained standing at the door of the Grand Hotel; so familiar was the deafening roar of the city, the thin trees, the large signboards. The women looked the same, with their yellow dyed hair, and great feathered hats, and the men strutted proudly in their top-coats decorated with the rosette of the Légion d'Honneur; small boys, in low husky whispers, offered one the same packs of obscene cards and matchboxes. " Good God! but I have been here in Paris for years!" I bought a newspaper, *La Voix de Paris*, in a kiosk. I wanted to read the news of the great town during my lunch. The counter of the kiosk was almost buried under illustrated magazines and papers—and in every one of them was to be seen a repetition of the same women in different stages of undress, in some showing the thin ribs of a ravenous cat, in others turning towards the reader two large buttocks. I murmured to myself again, " Good God!" In the Café de la Paix a livid servant with a little powder still clinging to his face, advised me, as it was so late, to eat a fried sole and a cutlet.

" And what wine, Monsieur le Comte? "

" Chablis, Monsieur le Duc."

He smiled at my absurd joke and I, pleased with myself, opened my paper. On the first page, surrounded by a sea of complicated prose that reminded me of brilliant false jewellery, I caught sight of a naked princess, who was weeping, and a captain of dragoons.

I skipped the other items which were full of titbits about cocottes with sonorous names. On another page, eloquent writers boosted up digestive wines and tonics. Then came the usual crimes—no, there was indeed nothing new. I put aside *La Voix de Paris* and started a good old fight with the sole which had been fried against its will. The miserable thing absolutely refused to let me unglue even a fibre from its spine. It dried itself up into a brown impenetrable leather in which my knife bent back impotent and trembling. I called to the livid waiter. He arrived armed with a sharper knife and, digging his buckled shoes into the floor, pulled violently on the fish and two tiny strips of meat, like sticks, came away and I swallowed them in a mouthful. In another forkful I was rid of the cutlet. I paid fifteen francs for this meal with a gold louis; there were two false francs in the change which the waiter politely handed me. And then on this delicious May afternoon, I went on to the terrace of the café to drink a cup of coffee the colour of coconut and tasting of bean-husk.

As I smoked my cigar, I watched the Boulevard; at that hour it was at the height of its confusion and shrill sociability: a dense torrent of buses, old coaches, smart carriages drawn by magnificent pairs of horses, rolled quickly along, while a dark mass of humanity threaded its way between wheels and horses. The continuous rough motion of the crowd soon stupefied me after my five years of quiet life in the country.

I tried, rather childishly, to fix some object which was standing still; some bus or hansom cab which had suddenly stopped short on its poor old jade nearly falling down. But almost at once somebody would scramble into the cab and engulf himself in it, or a dark group of people would climb into the bus : and rapidly the resounding roll of traffic started up again. Certainly the tall buildings, mountains of stone and concrete, stood still, and kept back and disciplined that breathless crowd. But from the street to the roofs, on every balcony, and all over the walls as far as eye could reach signboards upon signboards reared their ugly heads—and it also exhausted me to feel the existence of all that work going on behind the scenes, and the hungry fever after riches which was panting behind those decent silent exteriors. And so while I smoked my cigar I was strangely filled with the memory of those feelings Jacinto had experienced long ago, when first living on his property, and which had so amused me. Sitting there at the door of the café between the bustle and the indifference of the great city I felt with a vague sadness, as he had in the country, my fragility and solitude. I was indeed lost in a world which was unfriendly. Who knew me? Who cared about Zé Fernandes? If I had been hungry and confessed it no one would have given me a crust of bread and however tragically my face might have shown my anguish, nobody would have stopped in their hurry to console me. And of what use, either, would the better qualities of my soul have been to me? Had I been a saint, that crowd would have remained indifferent to my sanctity; and if, there in the Boulevard, I had opened my arms and cried out, "My dear friends, you are my brothers," those men would have turned on me more ferociously than the wolf had turned on Saint Francis of Assisi, and laughing would have passed on their way. Only two impulses seemed to live in that multitude, the love of pleasure and the love of gain.

My soul, isolated in the middle of those two impulses and influenced by daily contact with them would soon shrink and grow a thick crust of egoism. And of that human being which I had brought from the mountains there would soon only remain that crust and, beneath it, the two appetites of the city: to fill one's purse with money and to gratify every bodily desire. Little by little, I felt towards Paris the very same exaggerated feelings that Jacinto had indulged in towards nature. A deadly boredom trickled towards me from the Boulevard, extracted from its millions of microbes. I expected a trickster to emerge from every door and rob me, every face I caught sight of looking out of the cabs I suspected belonged to a gangster. All the women reminded me of sepulchres, they were putrid inside.

How dreadfully melancholy it all seemed, with something of the sordid glamour of the circus; the affected gestures, the rounded bosoms and the tall feathers in the hats of the ladies, their false and painted expressions, and then the old men, round-shouldered, looking at indecent pictures in the shop-windows. Yes, all this may have been very childish, almost funny, but it was what I felt in the Boulevard. I needed to plunge myself into the sierra so that its pure air should unloose the gross crust of the city and that I might once again become human, in fact—Zé Fernandico.

To dissipate that nightmare of solitude, I paid for the coffee and left slowly to visit Number 202. As I was passing in front of the bus stop at the Madeleine, I suddenly wondered; what could have become of Madame Colombe? But horror; as I thought of her, I was seized with a short but brutal desire for that thin and filthy hag. It was the cesspool in which I used to poison myself and which was overwhelming me once again. Later, as I crossed the Rue Royale, to get to the Place de la Concorde, I ran into a large, powerful man who put out his arm and called out in a commanding voice: "Eh, Fernandes!"

It was the Grand Duc wearing a pale coat and a Tyrolese honey-coloured hat. I gave the Prince a grateful, respectful handshake because he had recognized me.

"Is Jacinto with you?"

I told him all about Tormes, the mountains and how contact with nature had rejuvenated our friend. I told him about my charming cousin and her magnificent children. The Grand Duc shrugged his shoulders, genuinely upset, "Oh, dear! oh, dear! married in the country and father of a family; he is done for! Just imagine, such a useful chap and such good company. That pink dinner party he gave was marvellous—there has not been anything like it since in Paris. And Madame Oriol, I saw her a few days ago, in the Palais de Glace, she is not bad-looking still not quite my taste; too sweet and milky, vanilla and cream for me. But, Jacinto! Who would have thought it!"

"Is your Highness remaining much longer in Paris?" The great man bent his head down and said frowning and confidential: "No, Paris is unbearable. Completely spoilt. One cannot even eat here decently any longer. At present everybody goes to Ernest's in the Place Guillon, you know, it is the Ernest who was the maitre d'hotel at the Maire, have you ever had a meal there? Well it is awful, but it is the whole rage. I have just come from there; I had a *salade Chambord*, tasted like straw. He has not the vaguest idea how to made a salad. Paris is a thing of the past. Theatres are bosh. Women; not a fresh one among them. There is nothing to be seen, though in one of the smaller theatres of Montmarte at the Roulotte there is a revue called: "Step up, Ladies!" Amusing, lots of naked flesh. Célestine sings a nice little tune, half-sentimental, half-dirty, called: *Love in a W.C.* It's funny and cheeky. Where are you staying?"

"At the Grand Hotel, sir."

"What a barn. And what news of your King?"

"His Majesty is very well, thank you."

"I'm glad. Well, Fernandes, I really was delighted to see you. But I cannot get over your news of Jacinto. Go and see that Revue, Célestine has a fine pair of legs and *Love in a W.C.* is terribly funny."

A vigorous handshake and His Highness climbed heavily into his victoria, he gave me a parting wink which captivated me; an excellent man, this Grand Duc! Feeling almost reconciled to Paris, I crossed the Champs-Elysées. All down this wide and noble avenue, with its chestnut-trees in bloom, cyclists pedalled madly along. I stopped to look at this hideous novelty; the thin legs, astride the spine-like wheels, moved up and down in violent agitation, fat old men with red necks rode heavily, lank rogues with thin shins whizzed past. And the women, over-painted, wearing short boleros and bagging trousers whirled away even faster, enjoying the rather ambiguous pleasure of newly-acquired speed astride their iron perches. And every moment other horrible machines passed; victorias and four-wheeled carriages driven by steam made up of a hideous mass of boilers, long tubes, pipes and chimneys spouting the stench of oil as they rattled along. I continued on my way to Number 202, wondering what on earth a Greek of the time of Phidias would say were he to see the grace and charm of our new methods of travelling.

Old Vian, the porter of Number 202, showed a touching joy as soon as he recognized me. He wanted to know all about Jacinto's marriage and all about his children. He seemed especially glad that I should arrive just as everything had been spring-cleaned. As I wandered about the beloved house I felt my solitude more keenly. There was not a trace in the whole house of its old air that could have made me live again even for a few seconds the old companionship with my Prince. Huge dust sheets hid the tapestry in the anteroom and covered the chairs and walls. In the library, the ebony shelves—on which were ranged the thirty thousand beautifully-bound books in neat array, like doctors at a council—were also separated from the world by long strips of stuff. From Jacinto's desk, in his study, had disappeared all that untidy heap of little contraptions whose existence I had almost forgotten. And only complicated pieces of machinery standing on their different pedestals, which had been recently dusted, shone brightly. The gears, tubes, wheels, all stood in that cold inert immobility of objects no longer used, waiting to take their place in some museum where they would show to future ages the decaying mechanism of a past epoch. I tried to use the telephone, it would not work, the electric switch refused to light a single lamp; all the universal forces had abandoned Number 202 like discharged servants. As I walked through the different rooms, I had the impression I was wandering through a museum of antiquities; and that later other men, possessed of a purer and more exact understanding of life and happiness, would also wander through long rooms filled with the instruments of a Super Civilization; and that like me they would shrug their shoulders in front of the great Illusion which had ended, for ever useless, stowed away as historical sweepings beneath dust sheets.

When I left Number 202, I took a cab to the Bois de Boulogne. I had only been driving for a few minutes along the Avenue des Acacias, in a decorous silence which was only broken by the sound of the breaks and the crunching of the wheels on the gravel, when I began to recognize the same old faces adorned by the same old smile, and covered by the same powder. The heavy drooping lids and greedy eyes gave to all these faces a waxen immobility.

The writer of *The Cuirass* drove past in his victoria and fixed me with his smoked monocle; he remained indifferent to my presence. The black tresses which covered Madame Verghane's ears seemed blacker than ever in the midst of all the white she wore; hat, feathers, flowers, veils, and the bodice out of which her immense bosom undulated like a wave. In the walk under the acacias, lolling on two chairs, the editor of *The Boulevard* sucked the remains of his cigar; and in a big landau Madame de Trèves continued with the same eternal smile of five years before with just two looser wrinkles on either side of her dry mouth.

I jogged off yawning to the Grand Hotel just as Jacinto had done in former times. I finished my day in Paris at the Théâtre des Varietées quite stupefied by a fashionable play which was much applauded. It sparkled with pure Parisian wit; the plot centred round a Bed where alternately wallowed ladies in nightdresses, men in drawers, a colonel with a poultice of linseed oil on his behind, cooks in embroidered silk stockings and more people still, all of them noisy and skipping about like animals on heat. I drank a sad cup of tea at Julien's surrounded by the sordid love-making of tarts hurriedly making the most of a quick job. Two of these women were obviously Oriental; from their bronzed oily skins, slanting eyes, and black frizzy hair emanated a feline charm. I asked the waiter, a hideous being, fat and flabby like a discoloured eunuch, who they were?

"Women from Madagascar," explained the monster in a soft nasal voice. "They were imported when the French occupied the island."

From then on I dragged through Paris days of utter boredom. I saw again in the shop-windows the very same expensive objects of which I already had a surfeit five years before, there was not even an amusing novelty or clever invention to be seen. In the bookshops I could not discover a single book worth reading; I turned the pages of hundreds of yellowbacks but on every page my eye happened to fall on, always the same tedious theme of the Bedroom cropped up, and with it a foetid smell of flesh and face powder, and all this written in flowery style that reminded me of lace on underclothes. For dinner, at whatever restaurant I might find myself, I ate the same sauce, hiding and disguising the meat and chicken and tasting of hair-grease, which I had already had with my lunch in another restaurant, with my fish and vegetables. I paid an enormous price for our astringent country wine of Torres, but ennobled by being Château this or Château that and with its bottle covered in fancy dust. And every night, at the theatre, I met the everlasting Bed, which was presented as the centre and goal of life, attracting, more strongly than the dung-hill does the gad-fly, a swarm of erotic stupefied humanity buzzing with a senile hum.

The sordidity of the Plain sent me seeking a breezier wit in the hill of Montmartre; there among elegant ladies, duchesses and generals and all the cream of the city, I received from the stage torrents of obscenities which were heard with convulsions of joy by the hairy-eared bankers and which caused the elegant stuffed bodices of the ladies to pitch and plunge with joy. I would retire at night feeling a little nauseated from so many bedroom scenes and with slight indigestion from the hair-grease sauce I had eaten at dinner, and, above all, displeased with myself because I had failed to enjoy myself. I could not understand the city, and I wandered through it with the absurd austerity of a Censor or a Cato. "But am I incapable of enjoying myself in this charming

213

town, am I getting mouldy from old age? " I wondered sadly.

I passed the bridge that separates in Paris the Temporal from the Spiritual world. I plunged into the Latin Quarter, I conjured up in front of certain cafés the memory of my Nini; and as before I lazily mounted the steps of the Sorbonne. In one of the amphitheatres, where you heard a heavy hum of voices, a thin man, with a large white head sculptured to hold the highest and noblest thoughts, was lecturing on the Institutions of the Middle Ages. Not long after I had entered his clear and elegant speech was drowned by yells, roars and stampings. It was a bestial, tumultuous hooting which escaped from the young men heaped on the benches and who represented the thinking youth, the young life and the spring of the country. Yes, the spring, of which I had once been a faded flower. The Professor paused, he looked coldly round him and fingered his notes. Once the animal-like grunting of the angry students had subsided, he continued with unabated serenity. All his ideas were cold but substantial and expressed with force and accuracy. But again he was immediately interrupted by a wild and furious burst of whistling and booing—some students neighed like horses, others crowed like cocks and their hands waved about in an impotent effort to strangle Ideas. An old man sitting beside me with a bad cold and all wrapped up, was looking on the scene with a melancholy air.

"What is the matter with them? " I asked the old man. "Are they fed up with the lecturer, or is it politics? "

"No," said the man shaking his head and sneezing, "it's always like this now. They don't want ideas, I think they want songs. It is a general love of filth and scoffing."

I was suddenly seized with such indignation that I called out at the top of my voice:

"Shut up, you brutes."

And, behold, an abortion of a boy, yellow, greasy, with long hair and wearing huge shiny glasses stands up haughtily, fixed me with his eyes and bellowed:

"You dirty Moor!"

I lifted my heavy mountaineer's fist and the wretched fool, his face covered in blood and his hair all over the place,

214

collapsed like a heap of soft rags, howling dismally, while the hurricane of booing, crowing, neighing and whistling enveloped the Professor who, with his arms crossed, was serenely waiting for silence.

From that moment, I decided to leave this exhausted town; and the only happy and enjoyable day I spent in it was the last, buying magnificent presents for my nephew and niece at Tormes. They were large complicated objects; steel boats, a lion in real lion skin which roared most fearfully, and dolls dressed by Laferrière with gramophones in their tummies.

Finally one afternoon, after saying goodbye from my window to the City, I left: " Well goodbye and until never again. You will not catch me again slopping about in your vice and mud or in the rottenness of your vanity. What is good about you, your intelligence and elegant clarity, I shall receive all that at home by the post. Goodbye!"

On the following Sunday afternoon as I leaned out of the window of the train, which was slowly wending its way beside the peaceful river, in a silence made up of sun and blue sky, I at last caught sight of the family from Tormes, as they stood waiting for me on the platform of that quiet country station. My god-daughter Teresinha, looking very healthy, was staring hard at the train with her magnificent eyes and beside her stood Jacintinho grasping in his hand a white flag. The emotion with which I kissed and hugged my dear ones would have been perfectly suitable had I just returned home alive from some distant war in Tartary. In my joy at finding myself again among my mountains, I even kissed the guard Pimentia who was ready to burst from fat and was hurrying up and calling out to the porter to be careful with my trunks.

Jacinto who was looking very smart in his mountain hat and jacket, hugged me again:

" And how was Paris? "

" Damnable," I answered as I picked up Jacintinho. " And what are you doing, young man, with that flag? "

" It's the flag of the castle," he answered, while a look of intense seriousness crept into his charming eyes.

His mother laughed. Ever since he had known that Tio Zé

215

was coming home the child had been carrying this banner about which Cricket had made for him. It had not left him even while he was eating and he had brought it down with him to the station.

" Well done, my pretty cousin, you are looking charming. I come from seeing nothing but sallow Paris skins—and you look wonderful—and how are Uncle Adrião and Aunt Vicência? "

" All are very well," said Jacinto gaily. " The sierra prospers, thank God, and now let us get home; you are staying at Tormes to-night. We want to hear all about Civilization."

In the small square behind the station, beneath the eucalyptus trees, which I saw again with pleasure, three horses were waiting and two beautiful white donkeys, one with a chair for Teresinha, the other with a basket, in which to put the heroic Jacintinho, and both donkeys were attended by a groom. I was helping my Cousin Joaninha to mount when the porter arrived with a packet of newspapers I had forgotten in the carriage. It was a whole heap of papers I had bought as I left Orléans, full of ladies in different stages of undress, dirty stories, Parisian jokes and eroticism.

" Throw all that stuff away," said Jacinto with a great laugh recognizing them.

And I threw all this refuse of a putrid Civilization on to a rubbish-heap which stood in a corner. I mounted my horse but before taking the road to the hills I turned round to call out goodbye to Pimenta whom I had almost forgotten. The good creature was bending over the rubbish heap and picking out lovingly, one by one, all those beautiful pictures which told of the pleasures and seduction of Paris.

We started to climb the steep track in single file. The summer light softened as it sank into evening. A gentle breeze wafted towards us the scent of wild flowers. The branches of the trees moved their living glossy leaves with a hint of friendly greeting. All the birds sang in a transport of joy and praise. The little streams, rippling gloriously, gave out a sparkling brilliance as they hurried on their way. In the distance the window-panes of friendly houses glittered with a golden radiance. The mountain gave itself to us in its eternal and true beauty. And ever, as we rode, in the front, floated the white flag of Jacintinho which he held firmly as he sat on his donkey. It was the flag of the castle, he had assured us.

And indeed it did seem to me, as we made our way along the lanes and through the quiet cultivated countryside, that my Prince, sunburned by the noonday heats and the wind of the mountains, and that sweet and loving mother, my Cousin Joaninha, with her two first-born, and I—were at last all treading an everlasting, solid earth. And now, with our souls at peace with God, we could serenely and securely climb towards the Castle of Great Happiness.